## A MYSTERIOUS STRANGER

Eric took Bethany's shoulders and pressed her against the stone wall. She stared at him, astonished. He had always treated her with gentleness.

Lightning seared her when his gaze explored her face with tender yearning. When his hands caressed her shoulders, outlining their curves with warmth, she started to pull away. But Eric's hands tightened.

"No!"

"No?" he repeated, arching his eyebrows.

"I promised Father to—"

"To recall how you should behave, and you have been behaving quite well, as a daughter should." He gave her a wry grin. "*I* promised not to attempt to kiss you."

"But—"

He swept her up against him. "So I shall not attempt it. I shall do it."

Books by Jo Ann Ferguson

HER ONLY HERO
MISTLETOE KITTENS
AN OFFER OF MARRIAGE
LORD RADCLIFFE'S SEASON
NO PRICE TOO HIGH
THE JEWEL PALACE
O'NEAL'S DAUGHTER
THE CONVENIENT ARRANGEMENT
JUST HER TYPE
DESTINY'S KISS
RAVEN QUEST
A MODEL MARRIAGE
RHYME AND REASON
SPELLBOUND HEARTS
THE COUNTERFEIT COUNT
A WINTER KISS
A PHANTOM AFFAIR
MISS CHARITY'S KISS
VALENTINE LOVE
THE WOLFE WAGER
AN UNDOMESTICATED WIFE
A MOTHER'S JOY
THE SMITHFIELD BARGAIN
THE FORTUNE HUNTER

And writing as Rebecca North

A JUNE BETROTHAL

Published by Zebra Books

# AN UNEXPECTED HUSBAND

*Jo Ann Ferguson*

Zebra Books
Kensington Publishing Corp.
http://www.zebrabooks.com

ZEBRA BOOKS are published by

Kensington Publishing Corp.
850 Third Avenue
New York, NY 10022



First Printing: February, 2000
10 9 8 7 6 5 4 3 2 1

Printed in the United States of America

*For Marianne—*
*the "perfect" daughter—one who reads Regencies.*
*Enjoy!*

# One

How could her brother be so stupid?

Bethany Whitcombe pushed aside the ferns beneath the trees, too upset to notice the flowers that were growing in their shade. So often, she had come to this wood to enjoy nature's beauty and the quiet of a lazy summer afternoon. Today she found no comfort.

How could there be any solace when her younger brother Jay had told her only this morning, vowing her to secrecy, that he intended to join the army and go to fight the French on the other side of the Channel? She had agreed to say nothing of what he told her before she had realized the magnitude of this secret. A Whitcombe held such a vow sacred, but how could she remain silent? Jay's seventeenth birthday was coming at the end of the summer, and she longed for him to reach his eighteenth.

She dropped down to sit on a mossy rock. Mayhap she could go to their older brother Titus, but he was seldom at Whitcombe Hall now, preferring to spend his days and his evenings paying court on Miss Deborah Gillette. It would be an excellent match, the heir to their father's title wedding the daughter of a neighboring squire. Father had expressed his curiosity about why no announcement had been made, but Titus refused to be hurried. In choosing a bride, he would make the decision as deliberate and well-thought out as he did with all he decided.

If only Jay had inherited his older brother's good sense, instead of being as quick to jump to conclusions and to action as Bethany was. But even she was not so precipitate as to speak of leaving their home in Kent and buying a commission in order to fight the Frogs.

And he had said not a word to Nana. Mayhap because he knew what their grandmother would say. Had Jay never heeded a single word that Nana had spoken when she had told stories of Grandfather's trials during the American colonies' battle for independence? Grandfather had not returned from the war, leaving his wife a widow who had to oversee his estate alone, and leaving a young son who never had a chance to know his father.

No, Jay could hear nothing but the sounds of the drums and trumpets in the triumphal march that would come when the war reached its end. He spoke of the brave deeds of Sir Walter Raleigh and Nelson, choosing not to remember how both of those men had paid for their bravery with their lives.

She looked down at the bouquet of flowers that she had picked in a meadow closer to Whitcombe Hall. Shivering, she tossed them at the trees. She did not want to think how soon she could be gathering flowers to put on Jay's grave next to Mama's in the churchyard in Fair Cove, the village by the shore.

Bethany hurried through the wood. She was spending too much time alone with her thoughts. Going back to Whitcombe Hall and sitting Jay down for a reasonable talk would be the best thing to do. If he would not heed her, mayhap he would heed Nana when she returned tomorrow from visiting her cousin in Canterbury.

A rattle intruded on the afternoon, overwhelming the buzzing of bees and twittering of the birds overhead. Pushing through the last trees, Bethany smiled in spite of herself.

*A peddler's wagon!*

Any time a peddler came to Whitcombe Hall was a cause for celebration. The estate was set almost a mile back from the sea and nearly as far from the road that the mail coach and most of the travelers to Dover chose. Seldom did anyone come to this manor house on a hill overlooking the village of Fair Cove.

"Good day, miss!" called the man who was walking beside the brightly painted wagon. He bent to put a rock beneath the wheel beside him, so the wagon would not roll away. Its brake must be broken, for the road here was not steep. "You are a most pleasant sight on a fine day. Can I show you something that might interest you?"

His voice, as rich as chocolate melting in the sun, oozed over her. Her eyes widened. This was no weatherbeaten vagabond. Although his golden hair needed cutting, for it drifted over his shoulders, too long for anyone who sought entrance into the Polite World, he stood unbent by his rough life. His simple shirt, worn without a cravat beneath a dark green waistcoat, was as threadbare as his brown breeches and stockings that bore scars from his life on the road. His black shoes were scuffed and tarnished from mud and water.

She noted all that in the time it took to take a single breath, even though she could not draw one in as the peddler's cool, blue gaze held her. No, his gaze was not the cool color of the sea, but as heated as the summer sky. Standing as she was on a hummock by the edge of the hedgerow, her eyes were even with his.

When he bowed, his gaze still did not release hers. A hint of laughter wove through his voice as he asked, "Can I show you *something else* that might interest you?"

She gasped and looked back at the wagon. Fire climbed her cheeks, and she hoped the lace along the brim of her second-best bonnet hid her face, which must be as crimson as the paint on the wagon wheels. She was acting like a hoyden to stare at this peddler so boldly.

"Miss?"

"No, no thank you," she hurried to respond.

"Do you mean to say I have nothing here that might intrigue you?"

Bethany met his gaze squarely. He was enjoying this far too much. As the daughter of Lord Whitcombe, a well-respected baron, she had shown a decided want of manners in appraising this peddler as if he were no different from the items on his wagon, but that did not excuse him from being rude.

"No," she said.

"Nothing at all?" He smiled, not at all chastised by her cool answer. "How can you know that, miss, when you have given my wares no more than a cursory glance? It would be my pleasure to show you whatever you like."

She never had met a man who was so presumptuous, but she could not accuse him of being ill mannered when nothing he had said was outwardly wrong. 'Twas more the way he spoke, that twinkle in his eye, the way his lip curled into a smile that said even more than his words. Yet, his gaze did not slither along her as Dunley Morelock's did each time they met. A shudder coursed up her back. She did not want to think of that arrogant fool now.

"You are wasting your time in trying to sell me something today," she said as she stepped down onto the road. "I have no— Oh! *Mon Dieu!*" She gasped again when she realized the drop was greater than she had guessed, for she had not thought this peddler was so tall.

He put his hands out when she wobbled, but he drew them back as she steadied herself. "Take care, miss."

"I . . ." All words sifted away as her gaze rose over the stern line of his chin and past his tilted lips and his straight nose. He was tall! Even taller than Father, even taller than Sir Asa Morelock, mayhap even as tall as Sir Asa's son Dunley.

*No!* She refused to think of Dunley and his equally obnoxious father. The sole good thing about her distress with Jay's plans was that concern for her brother had driven from her head all thoughts of Sir Asa's intention of making a match for her and his son. Sir Asa had called only last week to present his arguments again of how such a marriage would benefit both families, but Father had said nothing to her, so she knew he had not made a decision yet. In that, he was like Titus, pondering every option before choosing one.

"Miss?"

Bethany looked at the peddler, who was smiling. He must think she had taken a knock in the cradle, for she had not said a single sensible word in his hearing. Suddenly all pleasure at seeing the peddler's cart vanished. She wanted to be alone to figure out a way to halt Jay from being a fool and to halt Father from listening to Sir Asa.

"Sir," she said quietly, "I have no interest in purchasing anything today."

"As you wish, but will you allow me to practice on you?"

"Practice? What?"

"I guess I would say my French."

"French?" she asked, wide-eyed, looking at the

shore from which the land of their enemies was not so distant.

"I believe I heard you speak French only moments ago."

"I know it, sir, for I have been taught several languages by my tutors, but it is not wise to use such language freely when our shores could be invaded at any hour."

He smiled. "On the contrary, think of how expedient it will be to confront your enemies with oaths in their own language."

Bethany gave him her coldest smile so he would not guess how close he was to the truth. She and her brothers had the habit of using French to say what would not be appropriate in English. However, she had no intention of standing on the strand and snarling curses at French soldiers.

"I bid you good day, sir," she said.

"Without letting me practice with you?"

"I said I do not wish to speak French."

He bowed, then looked at Whitcombe Hall, perched on its hill as it had been since its first walls had been raised centuries ago. "Miss, then let me practice something else with you. I have only recently arrived in this shire. Traveling about England, I have learned that what pleases the folks of one parish brings no pleasure to those in the next. Will you be so kind as to tell me which items that I have among my marvelous merchandise might convince your neighbors to part with a few farthings?"

Bethany was amazed when she smiled. "With such a patter, I believe you need little practice in luring customers to your cart."

"But you see right through me. Could it be that you're wiser than most, Miss . . . ?"

"Bethany Whitcombe." She stepped closer to look

into the wagon. What harm would it do to look? She might see something that would take her mind from her troubles.

"Whitcombe? Like yon hall?"

She nodded. "Lord Whitcombe is my father."

"And he lets you wander the countryside without a chaperon?"

Why did he have to sound like the Morelocks now? She was quite safe here where she was within earshot of the men working in the fields on the far side of the hedgerow across the road. And she had heard enough to know the danger came after dark when the smugglers were abroad. Only a chucklehead would go out then.

Instead of answering, Bethany looked into the wagon. Her eyes widened. What a myriad collection! And she could see no order to it, for light green fabric was draped across a box of dishes, and buttons were scattered about on the bed of the wagon as if they had no value.

"You are staring long at my wares," the peddler said, and she heard satisfaction in his voice. No doubt, he was anticipating the chance to make a sale. "Do you see something that intrigues you, Miss Whitcombe?"

She stiffened, her hands gripping the edge of the wagon, as his words brushed her nape. He stood too close. When he reached past her and lifted the material from the dish box, she edged away. He faced her, and she hoped her smile was properly polite.

"What do you think of this?" he asked. He dropped the fabric into her hands. "It is something that might appeal to the daughter of Lord Whitcombe."

Bethany swallowed the scold she had been about to fire at him as she touched the silk. Her mother's oldest dresses were made of silk, and, as a child, Bethany had enjoyed wrapping the cool slipperiness around her like a cloak. With the war and the French blockade, silk was as impossible to obtain as peace.

"Where did you get this?" she asked.

"I traded for it at a country house farther inland."

"But it's never been used."

He smiled. "Probably why it cost me so dear. There is not much. The length of silk would probably be enough only for the ruching on a lady's sleeves." He ran a single fingertip along the silk, outlining her hand with his much broader finger. "You seem to find it pleasing, Miss Whitcombe. Would you be interested in purchasing it?"

"No." She did not hesitate.

"No?"

"No." She smiled as she handed the silk back to him. "You will have to find another to buy it, sir."

"My name is Eric Pennington." His laugh took on a conspiratorial tone. "If you do not wish to buy the silk, mayhap you could give me the name of another in your household who would."

"Neither Father nor my brothers would have a use for it. If—" She bit back the rest, for his eyes twinkled again. And, once again, she met his gaze without flinching. He need not act as if she were revealing some deep secret. Anyone in Fair Cove would be quite willing to tell him who lived in Whitcombe Hall.

Bethany expected him to retort, but he only placed the silk in her hands again. When she started to give it back to him, he put his hand atop it. The cloth warmed with his touch. She should have pulled away, but then the silk would have fallen in the dust. She could not let that happen. At least, that was what she told herself as she savored the surprising pleasure of that warmth.

"You must keep this," he said.

"I cannot. Father would not allow me to take it."

"Because it's a gift from a stranger?"

"Yes," she replied, but that was mostly a lie. Father would have nothing in Whitcombe Hall that might have been brought over to England by the smugglers who plied the Channel, flouting the Regent's laws. No silk, no brandy, no lace.

"That is too bad." He sighed and leaned his elbow on the top of the wagon. "I had hoped you might consider such a bit of fabric as fair trade for a night's shelter and food for me and my horse." He patted the brown haunches of his horse. "We have traveled many miles today."

Bethany hesitated. How easy it would be to tell him it was a trade! He would not be the first to sleep in the stables. Father always welcomed visitors, whether of quality or not, to Whitcombe Hall. He would be especially interested now in what news Mr. Pennington might have. Father waited anxiously for any tidings that might signal an end to the war. She fingered the silk. She could not deny that she would like to keep this wondrous cloth.

With regret, she pressed it back into Mr. Pennington's hands. "I cannot take something of such value in return for shelter. You are welcome to find a place to sleep in the stables. Cook will give you something to eat."

"You are very generous, Miss Whitcombe, but I would rather pay for my food." He tossed the silk into the wagon as if it had no more value than an old piece of wool. "Is there nothing in here that you might be interested in trading for?"

"I told you. You are welcome to stay without—"

"Humor me, Miss Whitcombe. A man, even though he might be only a peddler, has his pride and wishes to pay his own way through life." He smiled.

Bethany could not keep from smiling in return. Eric

Pennington was unlike any peddler she had met before. Although he was as eager to sell as any others who had called at the kitchen door of Whitcombe Hall, he spoke like an educated man. She glanced at the wagon and saw no books within it, so he must have obtained his knowledge simply by honing his wit in whetted conversation with his customers.

"Mayhap you would see something here you would like." He opened a box in the middle of the wagon bed.

She looked at the dishes and combs and dismissed them. They had more of both than they needed in Whitcombe Hall. She was about to tell him that he would have to accept their hospitality when something glittered near the front of the wagon. Standing on tiptoe, she reached out to touch it.

"What have you found, Miss Whitcombe?"

"This." Lifting a small pistol out of a walnut case, she cradled it in her hand and smiled. It was engraved on the butt and the barrel with curlicues as fancy as a fine lady's hair at an assembly. Noting how well-balanced the weight was in her hand, she gripped it. Jay's hands were not much bigger than hers, so he should find this perfect.

Mr. Pennington took the pistol from her and set it back into the case by the seat. "No, Miss Whitcombe, I will not trade you that."

"Of course not." Again her face was hot. Did he think she intended to charge him so highly for the hospitality that was given freely at Whitcombe Hall? Although she guessed the silk was as valuable as the pistol, she could not impose on his generosity. "If you will tell me its price, I would be glad to listen."

"No."

"No?" Her eyes grew wide as his narrowed to cobalt slits.

"This is a gentleman's pistol, Miss Whitcombe. It isn't meet that a lady should bargain for it."

"But it would be the perfect thing for Jay, my younger brother—"

"I will gladly negotiate with him."

She clenched her hands at her sides. This man was as impossible as Dunley!

"You cannot bargain with Jay," she argued. "If we were to buy this from you, it would be as a present for his birthday."

"Be that as it may, I will not bargain with you, Miss Whitcombe." He closed the case and shoved it beneath the front seat of the cart. "Is there something else that I might interest you in buying?"

"I am interested in the pistol."

He smiled and shook his head. "And I told you that I will not bargain with a lady for a gentleman's pistol. You should not be handling such things."

"Handling a pistol?" She laughed, vexed at his condescending tone. "Mr. Pennington, I shall have you know that I have been riding to the hunt with my family since I first was able to keep my seat."

"Miss Whitcombe, I shall have you know that the traditions of your family in this regard matter not a rap to me." He kicked the rock away from the wheel and grasped the reins, so the horse would keep the wagon from rolling away. "As it seems we are at an impasse here, I think it would be wise to put an end to this conversation. I trust I might still seek shelter at Whitcombe Hall tonight."

"Of course, but—"

He put his hand on the side of the seat to climb back aboard. "Thank you, Miss Whitcombe. Please step back so that the dust from my wheels does not cake your pretty pink gown."

She knew she should let him go without speaking

another word. She should, but she gazed at the pistol. If Jay insisted on buying that commission and setting out to fight the French, she wanted him to have the best weapons possible. That might be the only way she could help bring him back to Whitcombe Hall alive.

"Mr. Pennington?"

He set one foot up on the board to climb into his wagon. "Is there something else you would be interested in, Miss Whitcombe?"

"I'm only interested in the pistol."

"Which I will not sell you."

"Will you sell it to my father?"

He turned to face her, still holding the reins loosely. "Do you think he would be interested in buying it?"

She almost said yes, but halted herself. Mr. Pennington's whole demeanor had changed with his question. Even though he still smiled, she noted a tension that had not been in him before. He was balanced on the balls of his feet, his hands hung close to his waist as if he intended to pull something out from under his waistcoat—another weapon?—and the twinkle was gone from eyes which were now storm-dark.

"Father would have to speak for himself on this." Her voice shook, and she wished she could take back her words. Too late, for Mr. Pennington's gaze drilled her, as if he intended to cut a hole right through her.

She took a single step back, then another. The branches of the hedgerow brushed her bonnet, halting her. She stared at Mr. Pennington. Moments ago, he had been jesting with her, but now . . . She shook off the fearsome thoughts. She was not caught between his gaze and the hedgerow; she was letting her own dismay betray her. In her memory, how many dozens of peddlers had called at Whitcombe Hall? Most of them had been eccentric. Eric Pennington was just odder than most.

When he held out his hand, she stared at it. What could he want?

"Miss Whitcombe?" he asked.

"What?"

His smile returned along with that capricious twinkle. He was amused again, and she had no doubt that she was what he found so amusing. And why not? She was backed up against the hedgerow like a vixen seeking to avoid the hunt when he had done nothing but give her an avaricious glance at the idea of making a profit off the sale of the pistol to Father.

"I would offer you a ride back to Whitcombe Hall," he said, "if you wish."

"That is kind of you." There. Her voice had not trembled so much on those trite words.

"But?"

"Pardon me?"

"I heard a 'but' in your answer, Miss Whitcombe. It would be kind of me to offer you a ride, but . . . ?"

"You are mistaken, Mr. Pennington. I would be grateful for a ride home."

"Then allow me." He held out his hand again.

She watched as her own fingers settled on a palm that was rough from long days of holding the reins and riding through all sorts of weather. He folded his fingers over hers, but said nothing as he assisted her up to the low seat at the front of his cart. Waiting for her to settle herself, he swung up easily to sit beside her. His legs seemed too long for the short space, and she shifted to give him more room.

"Now," he said with a laugh, "you can see why I often choose to walk instead of ride. It is cramped here, and what is not broken on this wagon threatens to fall apart at any moment."

"You should get another cart."

"I may when I can." He slapped the reins on the

back of the horse and smiled at her again. "A wheelwright charges dear for his services. I prefer to spend my profits on bread and meat, and oats for my horse."

"Turn left here." Giving directions saved her from having to respond to his comments. He spoke so well that she forgot the chasm between her life and his. While she worried about an unwanted betrothal and her brother's misbegotten plans to join the army, Eric Pennington must concern himself with selling enough of his wares so he would not starve.

"Ah, I can see the road ahead clearly now," he said.

She looked at the gray block that was Whitcombe Hall. Not an elegant house or a grand one, it called to mind its early days as a fortress built to weather the storms off the Channel and repulse anyone who dared try to wrest it from the Whitcombe family. She could imagine living nowhere else.

Her gaze flickered toward the Morelock house which was to the north and closer to the water. It hunkered there like a malevolent shadow, reminding her of the good sense of a match between her and Dunley, for the two families' lands shared a common border for more than a mile. Once the Morelocks had been vassals of Lord Whitcombe, but in recent centuries, they had gained a prestige and wealth of their own, a fact Sir Asa bragged about on every occasion. Morelock Park was far more exquisitely decorated than Whitcombe Hall and more expansive and up-to-date.

Yet, the idea of living there as Dunley's wife and Sir Asa's daughter-in-law horrified her. She must be certain that Father never gave Sir Asa's request serious consideration. Tonight, she would speak to him on that very subject, although he must be aware of her opinion on the matter, for she had avoided Sir Asa each time he had called.

"You are a most peculiar woman, Miss Whitcombe."

Bethany looked at Mr. Pennington and was captured anew by his scintillating eyes. Lowering her gaze to the hands clasped in her lap, she asked, "How so?"

"You have expressed no curiosity about why I would not sell you the pistol."

"You made it clear that there was no use in asking."

"As I said, you are a most peculiar woman." He chuckled.

*And you are a most peculiar peddler.* She did not speak that thought aloud, for she suspected the light in his eyes would vanish again and she would be facing that uncompromising glare once more.

She did not need more to trouble her now. She had too many problems already.

# Two

Eric Pennington hid his smile as he was led to the room on the first floor of Whitcombe Hall where Lord Whitcombe would receive him. It had been more than a year since he had been within the walls of a country home in this part of England, but little had changed. Dark wood and bare stone were only partially hidden behind tapestries that were almost as old as the house. Yet, in the comfortable room he entered, the walls were painted a delicate green, and plaster moldings brought to mind the newer houses that had sprung up like spring flowers around Bath and Brighton.

Lord Whitcombe motioned for him to approach the low desk at which he was working. Eric kept his surprise concealed, for Miss Bethany Whitcombe did not resemble her lanky, bone-thin father. She was petite and had enticing curves in all the places that drew a man's eyes and brought him a smile. What remained of Lord Whitcombe's hair was a tired gray, but his daughter's softly curling locks were a vibrant ebony. Only their warm brown eyes were similar.

However, neither Miss Whitcombe nor the baron must guess the truth of why Eric had been reluctant to sell her the pistol. 'Twas not solely selling the pistol that concerned him. He would have been equally stubborn, no matter what Miss Whitcombe had selected. It was his good fortune that she had chosen something that gave him an easy excuse to resist making a bargain with her, although he should have been more cautious and made sure that the pistol box was well secured out of sight before he called to her. *Dash it!* Why did she have to select the pistol out of all the items in his cart? However, he should consider its loss a small price for what he might receive in return.

As well, it gave him *entrée* into the house. Being offered a night in the stables and a plate in the kitchen would not suffice tonight. He had wanted this chance to meet Lord Whitcombe, not simply enjoy his hospitality. He had heard so much about the baron and his holdings here, and he was delighted to have an opportunity to meet the man and judge for himself if Lord Whitcombe was as honest and defiant of the French and their uneasy allies, the smugglers, as was whispered throughout the shire.

He could not recall the last time he had met a man who was unfailing in his loyalty and put country above the profit that he could easily have garnered from becoming a collaborator with the English owls who plied the Channel with their cargoes of brandy and silk. Eric had to own to being curious as to why this baron resisted that temptation. He was as curious about Lord Whitcombe as Miss Whitcombe was about him. He would have to guard himself closely around her, for she had already proven that she possessed an insightful nature that could doom everything he had planned.

"Good evening, my lord," Eric said, bowing his head.

"My daughter tells me that you are seeking shelter within our walls tonight." Whitcombe's voice was hearty and welcoming. The sign of an honest man or of one who was well practiced in his lies.

"Yes."

"Have you traveled far?"

Eric smiled. He understood this question was aimed less at having sympathy for his worn boots and the feet within them than in gauging what he might have heard and from where. Everyone on England's shores waited to see if Napoleon would toss his soldiers forth upon the next wave. He did not let his smile falter as he thought of how wise the folks in this shire were to be so worried. It was strange, in his opinion, that their anxiety had not been translated into greater vigilance, but he should be grateful that his work was no more difficult than necessary.

"I was in Dover not more than a week ago," he replied.

He had his host's complete attention now. As the tall baron came to his feet, Lord Whitcombe asked, "Any news of an invasion?"

"Only such rumors as you might hear repeated at any crossroads."

"Good." Whitcombe smiled and gestured for Eric to be seated. "I understand your name is Pennington."

"Eric Pennington, my lord."

"And Bethany tells me as well," he said, his smile broadening at the mention of his daughter's name, "that you have in your cart a pistol of rare quality that she believes would make the perfect gift for my younger son."

"So she tells me, my lord."

"And she tells me as well that you are not eager to part with it." Lord Whitcombe chuckled as he poured a glass of wine. "I should warn you I am as reluctant to assist my son in outfitting himself for the commission he has been seeking, although he thinks me unaware of his plans."

Eric hid his surprise when the baron handed him

the glass. He took an appreciative sip and smiled. It must have been aging in the manor's cellars since before the war. Such a choice vintage was not part of a peddler's life, so he could appreciate it all the more as it washed the road's dust from his throat. "You are very generous, my lord."

"I have learned from experience that the best negotiations are those done with at least an appearance of camaraderie." Whitcombe filled his own glass and sat again. "I would like to see this pistol that my daughter has praised, Pennington."

Eric reached under his waistcoat and drew out the weapon. Holding it for a moment across his palms, he berated himself for being so careless. He had not thought the price of his new life would be this remnant from his past. Silently, he set the pistol in front of the baron.

Lord Whitcombe arched gray brows and smiled. "I should have known that it would be something above the ordinary. Bethany is not given to exaggerating." He ran a finger along the etching on the barrel. "This is well made and not new." Squinting, he peered at the butt. "There appears to be some sort of crest here."

"The gentleman who sold it to me was not pleased to part with it," Eric hurried to say, being certain his smile would seem the insipid one of a peddler trying to please a potential customer. "However, his creditors had lost what patience they had with him, and I was able to give him enough guineas to soothe them."

"If you are weaving me a tale in hopes of increasing the price of this pistol, you need not. Give me the truth, man, so we might begin this bargaining in honesty."

Eric kept his flinch from showing. Brown eyes were not the only thing father and daughter had in common. They were too dashed insightful, seeing aspects of him that no one else did. His story about the pistol was an out-and-outer, but he had been certain Lord Whitcombe would accept it as the truth.

Mayhap he had been want-witted to come here. He hoped he would not come to regret this visit.

"And don't forget to remind Cook that Mr. Pennington will be coming to the kitchen."

When Bethany heard a muffled chuckle, she looked up from the list in her lap and saw that Mrs. Linders's face was contorted as the slender housekeeper tried not to laugh out loud. She tried to recall what she had said that was so amusing.

"That is, I believe, the fourth time you have mentioned the peddler," Mrs. Linders said, smiling. "He must have unsettled you greatly."

"He did. He showed a want of manners."

"Then why did you bring him to see your father?"

Bethany looked back at the list of tasks for the morrow, wishing she had waited to speak with Mrs. Linders until the morning. But, to delay the meeting they had each day at this hour would have created even more questions from the housekeeper, who treated Bethany as if she still were a child. She could not chide Mrs. Linders for caring so much, for, if the truth were to be told, the housekeeper treated Father with the same gentle concern. Not sure how old the housekeeper was, Bethany had been certain as a child that Mrs. Linders had been here since they had placed the foundation of the hall. She did know that Mrs. Linders had helped raise Father after his father's death in America.

"Father has been looking for a gift for Jay," Bethany answered, knowing that if she were not honest, Mrs. Linders would pose more questions. "The peddler had among his wares something I thought might be appropriate."

"And he is a man of rare handsomeness."

"Mrs. Linders!"

The housekeeper did not restrain her laugh now. "Miss Bethany, I am not so old as you believe, for I still enjoy the sight of a good-looking man. You are much younger, so I can only assume you do as well." She smiled. " 'Tis not only the gentlemen who enjoy admiring the differences God created between men and women."

"I realize that. However—" Bethany glanced toward the door as enthusiastic shouts rang out along the hall.

" 'Tis the lads. They were looking for you earlier." Mrs. Linders rose.

"I will give the rest to Cook after supper."

"Of course." Mrs. Linders smiled a greeting as she passed the two young men coming to a stop in the doorway. "You know his lordship likes the house quiet in the hour after tea, lads."

Bethany chuckled when Jay rolled his eyes as he always did when admonished by Mrs. Linders. Coming to her feet, she gave her younger brother a kiss on the cheek, surprised as always when she realized how much taller he had grown in just the past year. She held out a hand to Titus and smiled. The two brothers resembled their mutual sire closely, although Titus had a tendency to extra weight while Jay still was stretching out to his final height.

Titus adjusted his spectacles on his nose as he gave her a kiss on the cheek. "Sister dear, you look quite aglow this evening. Can it be that you expect a call from an ardent suitor?"

"That's not funny," Jay retorted with a frown, before she could respond. "If I were head of this household, I would declare that no mention might be made of any Morelock within these walls."

"Dunley Morelock would be an excellent match for Bethany. He is—"

"A want-witted beef-head."

Bethany put a hand on Jay's arm. "Enough, both of you. We are *en famille* tonight, so let us talk of matters that matter to all of us, not just to one."

"Your marriage matters to all of us," Titus said as he sat and folded his hands together on the knees of his green breeches. "We wish to see you well settled."

"That is Father's concern, not yours." She smiled at him. "Your concern is Father's interest in all the calls you have made recently on Miss Gillette."

"I go to speak to her brother Francis as well."

Jay sat on the arm of the settee and crowed, "Getting her brother on your side so he will agree to her marrying you? A brilliant plan, old chap!"

"Listen to him." Titus shook his head and pushed his dark hair off the gold rims of his glasses. "Barely out of his infancy, and he tries to sound like a swell upon the Season."

"I show more sense than you," Jay retorted stoutly, "because I will not be swayed by Dunley Morelock to persuade Bethany to accept his proposal."

"You haven't, Titus!" she gasped.

Titus's face flushed, but he mumbled, "It does make sense. The Morelocks could provide well for you, and you would be close to Whitcombe Hall instead of halfway across the shire as you would have been if Father had accepted Mr. Langler's offer to marry you."

"Mr. Langler offered for me?"

"You didn't know?"

She shook her head. To own the truth, she barely recalled anything about the shy man who had asked her to dance twice at a gathering almost a year ago.

'Twas not his offer that disturbed her or that Father had turned it down. 'Twas the fact that Father had not mentioned anything of it to her. She had believed he was being honest with her, but now . . . She was no longer sure.

"I'm glad Father was sensible about that," Jay announced, setting himself on his feet. "Louis Langler has never said anything worth listening to. Mayhap that is why he always holds his jaw. If you had married him, Bethany, you would have had to do all the talking, and you are no prattle-box."

"Have there been any others?" she asked Titus as Jay continued to play the magpie.

"Yes," he said reluctantly, "but you would have agreed with Father's decision each time."

Slowly she came to her feet. Why had she never guessed? She had seen the callers come and go. She had noted how Father seemed unlike his customarily jovial self after certain conversations. She appreciated his task of finding her a good man to marry, but she had not guessed that he had not made her privy to all discussions of her future.

"Bethany?"

She turned, not realizing she had been walking toward the door until Jay called after her. Facing him, she asked, "What is it?"

"I wanted you to know—"

"Say nothing!" hissed Titus.

Jay raised his chin and glowered at his older brother. "I shall say what I wish. Bethany deserves to know that Father told Sir Asa he would give him a decision before the fortnight is out."

"You ask to be treated like an adult," Titus said, "but you can't keep your counsel for more than a day."

Bethany put a hand on Jay's arm and tilted her own chin. Titus could be humorless and exasperating when he believed he was right and they were in error. Tonight, *he* was wrong.

"Thank you, Jay," she said. "I believe I shall speak to Father of this posthaste."

"I thought you might want to." He gave her a grin that recalled to her his face when he had been a little boy. His grin faded as he added, "And don't delay, Bethany. I don't want you married to Dunley Morelock either."

"She has to marry someone," Titus put in, his voice still sharp with anger. "And Dunley isn't so bad, once you give the man a chance."

"I have tried," she said. "I even went with him and Father and Sir Asa for a carriage ride one day. He was loud and monopolized every conversation and wiped his nose on his sleeve."

Titus chuckled. "You're describing Sir Asa, not Dunley. You should give Dunley another chance, Bethany. You might be pleasantly surprised."

"Or not," mumbled Jay.

Bethany glanced from one to the other, then walked out of the sitting room. Blast! Dunley Morelock was not as loathsome as his father, but she did not want to marry him. She disliked his lascivious glances and his coarse jests, which were more appropriate for the company of his friends than for a lady's ears. And worst of all, in her opinion, were the rumors that Dunley had played a part in the capture of a smuggler who had been betrayed by his own men and sent to hang. Whispers suggested Dunley Morelock had given his name to the authorities in order to gain control of the smugglers and share in their profits.

She despised the smugglers, who broke the King's laws, but lack of loyalty was the most vile crime she could imagine. She could never marry a man who would betray another. She intended to tell Father that.

Right now.

Three hours later, Bethany was still pacing through the house. Her father had guests that evening, a few men from the village who sought his guidance on a delicate issue of property lines and ancient water rights. Because he took his obligations so seriously, she could not imagine intruding on such a meeting, although seldom had one lasted this long.

She went out on the terrace and stared up at the stars that were poking through the summer's lingering twilight. The whisper of water from the fountain in the rose garden offered music beneath the distant lowing of cows.

Sitting on a stone bench, she came right back to her feet. Her disquiet would not allow her to sit and think. She wandered off the terrace and into the gardens. When she saw the carriages awaiting Father's callers, she turned in the other direction. Mayhap if she walked once around the house, they would be gone by the time she returned to this spot. If she walked three times around the house, would the fairies come and spirit them away?

Bethany laughed. 'Twas thrice widdershins around the church that called the fairy folk.

"What is so amusing on such a lovely night?"

At the unexpected question, she pressed a hand over her suddenly frozen heart. She watched through the darkness as a shadow thickened to become a silhouette that was instantly identifiable.

"Mr. Pennington!" she gasped.

"Did I frighten you?" He held up a pail. "I was collecting some water for my horse."

"The trough is near the stables."

"True." Glancing over his shoulder, he added, "But I heard the water from the fountain in this direction and decided to look at it."

A perfectly reasonable explanation, but she wondered if it were the truth. He had just been looking toward the house, not the gardens.

"You are welcome to enjoy the gardens during your stay here tonight," she said as he walked past her.

He paused. "Aren't you coming, Miss Whitcombe?"

"Pardon me?"

"You were walking in this direction, so I thought I would walk with you as far as the stables." He smiled, and his teeth glittered in the light of the rising moon. "Unless you have changed your mind, of course."

How could he make her feel as if she were the outsider here at her own beloved home? In a tone that would have daunted even Jay, she said, "I have not changed my mind."

"Then come along."

"You give orders easily for a peddler."

He laughed. "Why does that bother you when you ignore all of them?" He motioned with his head. "I'm going this way. Join me if you wish. You know you are curious about the pistol."

Bethany almost asked, Which pistol? Fear washed over her anew. She should not be thinking of her own future now. She should be concentrating on Jay's. Tonight, she had intended to speak with him, hoping to change his mind about purchasing that commission. Instead, she was pouting like a child.

"I *am* curious," she said as she matched his steps along the curving walkway. "What did Father think of it?"

"Your father is most interested in the pistol." He

chuckled. "And he is an exceedingly kind host, offering his wine to a stranger."

"Father enjoys the chance to talk to visitors." She hesitated, then asked, "Is he buying the pistol?"

"You should ask him."

"I couldn't. Jay was about during supper, and Father has been busy all evening." She paused by the stable door that was lit by a single lantern. It was so quiet compared to the times when she came to get her horse to ride. The stablehands must be asleep by this hour. She envied them their carefree rest. "I thought you might be more forthcoming now than you were on the road."

" 'Tis not good luck to speak of a transaction before it is completed."

She smiled. "A bit more forthcoming is all, I see."

Setting the bucket on the ground, Mr. Pennington said, "There is still a matter to be settled between us, Miss Whitcombe."

"And what would that be?"

"The matter of payment for this night's lodging and food."

"You need only deduct what you believe is a fair price from what you ask for the pistol."

"But if your father chooses not to buy, then I shall owe your family for this night's stay, and I believe that Polonius was wise when he said, 'Neither a borrower nor a lender be.' "

"Polonius? Shakespeare?"

"*Hamlet*, act one, scene three, if you wish to be exact."

She stared at him. "You know Shakespeare?"

"What?" He gave a sharp laugh, but she was not fooled. The twinkle had evaporated again from his heated eyes. "You didn't think a simple peddler would know of such things?"

"I have no idea what a peddler should know. To be honest, Mr. Pennington, I doubt if *you* have any idea what a peddler should know."

His hand upon her arm halted her from walking away. He turned her to face him. In the dim light from the stable lantern, his eyes sliced into her like sapphire daggers. "What in the blazes is that supposed to mean?"

"Sir, such language is—"

"To perdition with my language!" His fingers tightened on her arm as she tried to back away. "If you wish me to be courteous, then give me the courtesy of an answer."

She stared up at him. To give voice to her suspicions had been jobbernowl. "If you wish an answer, I shall say that I believe you enjoyed too much of my father's wine. I can think of no other reason why you would mistake my words for a threat."

For a long minute, as she held her breath, she feared he would not accept her falsehood. She should have kept her own lips in check, instead of blurting out her misgivings. Then his hold on her arm loosened to a gentle caress, sending a trill of delight through her. She moved away, shocked, for this was more frightening than his anger.

"Good night, Miss Whitcombe," he said as he bowed his head to her.

"Good night." She had no intention of lowering her defenses again. As she went across the stableyard to the gardens on its far side, she kept her pace slow, refusing to let Mr. Pennington think anything he had said was causing her to run away.

She did not need her life complicated by another impossible man. Father had jested about not wanting her to marry until she was as old as Mrs. Linders, but she knew he wished her settled in a home of her own.

How many times had he said in the past fortnight that she was now a year older than her mother had been upon accepting Father's offer of marriage? *Too many.*

And Titus . . . How could he have suggested it would be an excellent idea if she were to marry Dunley? Her brother and Dunley Morelock had been enemies since they were born within months of each other.

She frowned. Tonight had not been the first time she had heard Titus speak of the Morelocks without his usual rancor. Her older brother was a gentle soul, not at all inclined to jumping into the fray with the French as Jay wished to do. Had he seen something in Dunley that she had not?

Bethany noticed something moving near Mr. Pennington's wagon. Who could it be? She almost chuckled as she saw moonlight on dark hair. *Jay!* It must be her brother. He had not been able to hide his curiosity about what the peddler had in his cart. Even Father's request that he wait until the morning to bargain with Mr. Pennington might not have been enough to keep Jay from poking around tonight.

"Jay, what—?"

A hand clamped over her mouth. Her eyes grew wide as she realized that the moonlight had betrayed her. It was not her brother by the wagon. The man was broader than either of her brothers . . . and he was not alone.

The hand pulled her back against a hard form. The odors of sweat and the sea washed over her. Smugglers! Dear God, what were they doing here at Whitcombe Hall?

She drove her elbow back into the man's stomach. He cursed. She reaimed and swung her arm back harder. He retched, and she pulled away. He caught her before she could run a single step.

"Father!" she cried. "Help me!"

She was shaken viciously. Her eyes blurred, but she heard a shout from the house. She wanted to scream again. No sound emerged from her throat, as she fought to hold onto consciousness. Another shout came from the stables, but she could not understand the words through her ringing ears. Her captor pushed her away. She struck the wagon and fell to her knees, half-blind with the pain along her ribs.

She picked up something and threw it at the fleeing shadow. It missed him, but she heard another shout. Looking up, she saw the wagon moving. She tried to scramble out of the way. What a fool she was! That rock must have been keeping Mr. Pennington's wagon in place.

She tried to gain her feet, but dropped back to her knees as her head spun.

"Look out, Bethany!"

The shout seemed to come from everywhere. She stared at the wagon as it hit a broken cobble and tilted toward her. She struggled to rise. Something slammed against her, throwing her to the courtyard and away from the wagon. She moaned as she hit the ground. The crash of the wagon reverberated around her. Glass shattered, and metal clanged on the stones.

A groan was warm against Bethany's cheek. She twisted to see Mr. Pennington's face only a finger's breadth from her. His eyes were closed, saving her from that potent gaze that even the darkness could not dim. Lines were etched with shadow on his brow. He had saved her. But . . .

She slid out from under him to see his right arm had disappeared under the wagon. She crawled past him and pushed against the wagon.

Hands under her arms brought her to her feet.

"Help me help him!" she cried.

"Let the men help him," her father ordered.

She flung her arms around her father as she stared at the men gathering around the wagon. Men from the stables. Men from Fair Cove. Her brothers. They all stared at Mr. Pennington who did not move. Was he dead? Had he died saving her?

Bethany breathed shallowly as Titus and Jay joined the others and propped their shoulders against the wagon. Veins popped along Titus's forehead as he pushed. When the wagon was raised off the ground, they shoved it aside.

Mr. Pennington groaned.

She knelt beside him. Brushing his blond hair back from his face, she whispered, "Mr. Pennington?"

He did not answer.

Knowing she was bold, but knowing as well that the situation went beyond the canons of propriety, she murmured, "Eric? Can you hear me? Are you hurt?"

"What do you think?" he demanded, before his words vanished into curses. His eyes opened, his glare as taut as his lips. "The wagon went right over my arm." He put his left hand on her shoulder. "Help me up. I have to check the wagon."

Father leaned over him. "Don't worry about the wagon!"

"He must if the smugglers come back!" Bethany retorted.

Jay cried in excitement, "Smugglers? Here?"

Father gave him no chance to get an answer as the men from Fair Cove ran for their carriages and a chance to capture the smugglers who endangered the village. Ordering the wagon secured in the stable, he motioned for several men to help Mr. Pennington into the house. "And send for Mr. Clarke," he added. "He's the best bonesetter in the shire."

*Bonesetter?* Bethany bit her lower lip as she stared at Mr. Pennington's right arm, which hung at an impossible angle. Blast the smugglers and their fingers that tried to lay claim to anything of value. They were almost as bad as their French allies. Worse, mayhap, because they betrayed the law for the weight of gold in their pockets.

She scanned the trees. The gray shadows could hide an army of smugglers. She wanted to rush inside and bar every door in Whitcombe Hall. A curse shattered her fear as she turned to see Titus putting his arm around Mr. Pennington to help him to his feet.

"Easy," Mr. Pennington ordered, then cursed again.

"Is it only your arm that's injured?" she asked.

He stared at her as if she had just been declared mad. "*Only* my arm? You have a wondrous, irritating gift for understatement, Miss Whitcombe."

"Get the door, Bethany," her brother snapped.

She saw something flicker in Mr. Pennington's eyes. Impossible! It could not be amusement when he must be suffering so much pain. Or was this injured arm just another of his half-truths? Shame flooded her when another groan slipped past his rigid lips.

"Right arm," Mr. Pennington said in answer to her father's question. "Down from the shoulder, my lord. I shan't be able to drive my wagon, and I shall—"

"Be our guest longer than you planned," interrupted Bethany. When Mr. Pennington glowered, she offered him no sympathy. He must know that she shared his yearning for him to be on his way.

With care, Titus helped him into the house. Father did not slow as he led the bizarre parade through the kitchens and into the small reception hall by the stairs. Bethany left them long enough to send a lad to the small farm beyond Fair Cove where Mr. Clarke lived. A shudder wracked her shoulders. The last time they had needed to send for the doctor was the night Mama had died almost four years ago.

As she entered the small room that was so well lit the gold stripes threatened to leap off the wall covering, she listened to her father give quiet orders. She clasped her hands before her as she heard him send several men to make sure the smugglers had left the lands of Whitcombe Hall.

"And take guns with you," Father called to them as they scurried out.

"They won't need them."

Bethany glanced, astonished, at Mr. Pennington, who was sitting, his face as gray as the stone walls of Whitcombe Hall, with his right arm cradled in his left hand. Pouring a glass of wine from the decanter her father always had waiting for unexpected guests, she held it out to him.

He grimaced as he glanced at his arm. "My hands are full at the moment, Miss Whitcombe, although I appreciate the thought."

Bending toward him, she put the glass to his lips. He sipped cautiously and smiled as she lowered the glass.

"Thank you, Miss Whitcombe. I owe you a duty for your kindness."

"Repay me by telling me what you meant."

His smile did not waver, but his eyes became hard. "About what?"

"The smugglers." She helped him drink again. "You said something about no need for guns."

"By the elevens!" he growled when wine splattered on the front of his shirt. "Be more careful. This is my best shirt."

"I didn't mean to spill the wine."

"I know." He looked up at her, his face almost as close to hers as when he had shoved her to the ground to save her from the wagon. "I'm not myself, Miss Whitcombe. Forgive my lack of manners."

"And mine. Thank you for saving me."

His smile became ironic. "I have to own I might have thought twice if I had known this would happen." He winced as he shifted in the chair.

"I doubt that."

"You seem to assume that I would risk life and limb for you, Miss Whitcombe."

"An easy assumption when you just did." Bethany set the empty glass on a nearby table and knelt by his chair. "Will you be honest about what you meant about the smugglers?"

He leaned back in the chair and closed his eyes. "Why not? Do you know much of smugglers, Miss Whitcombe?"

"Only what I have heard whispered about the shire."

"Then you should know that they have one universal trait. They know how to hide and stay hidden from any authority that might wish to halt them." He grimaced. "I didn't know a broken bone would hurt like this."

"I'm so sorry, Mr. Pennington."

"Sorry?" His brow furrowed as he demanded, "What do you have to be sorry for?"

"If I hadn't thrown that rock at the smuggler who seized me, the wagon would not have rolled."

"You threw a rock at him?" He started to chuckle, but the sound became a moan.

"He hurt me. I wanted to hurt him."

She was shocked when he rested his left elbow on the arm of the chair and tipped her face toward his. "Your chin is scraped."

"Is it?" She put up her fingers to touch the sore

spot, but pulled them back when they brushed his. "It's nothing compared to . . ."

"Compared to what?"

She smiled as she stood. "That smuggler treated me with the lack of manners I would expect of his ilk."

"Did he?"

Bethany almost recoiled from the fury in Mr. Pennington's eyes. Then she realized it was not aimed at her. How glad she was of that, for his easygoing smile covered a strong temper that pierced through her.

"Where else are you hurt?" he asked.

"Just bumped about." She turned to refill the wineglass. "I've been hurt as badly racing Jay on horseback across a field."

"So you fought back when you knew this man could hurt you even worse."

"I did what I must."

His smile was strained through the pain etching his face. "I'm sure you always do what you must, no matter what you face."

"I do."

He looked past her and out the window at the downs, where even now lanterns wagged as her father's men sought any sign of the smugglers' trail. "I hope that's a vow you still will be able to keep, Miss Whitcombe."

# Three

Something warned Bethany that she was no longer alone. More than once, she had suffered uneasiness while walking in the garden this afternoon as she waited for the time to meet Nana in Fair Cove. She suspected it was no more than her imagination that had been fired by the smugglers' attack last night. She had not expected them to be so brazen. If she had not chanced by, Mr. Pennington's wagon would have been stripped clean . . . and he would be gone.

She should have guessed that Father would insist Mr. Pennington be given one of the bedchambers and be treated like a welcome guest. Both Father and Jay were effusively grateful for how Mr. Pennington had saved her. Titus had said nothing, and she no longer could guess what he thought about anything.

Gooseflesh prickled along her nape. Was someone else here? Turning, she nearly screamed as a man stepped out from behind a copse.

She took a shuddering breath. The tall man was not a stranger. Dunley Morelock would be known anywhere by his ginger hackles. Even from a distance and despite that red hair, he was undeniably handsome, his chiseled features as strong as his massive shoulders. He was dressed, as always, in prime twig, a reminder to everyone that he was the only son and heir of Sir Asa Morelock.

"Dunley, you startled me!" she chided.

Sticking his thumbs in the waistband of his breeches, Dunley Morelock grinned. The expression she detested glinted in his dark eyes. "What happened to you?"

Her face flushed as she touched her left cheek. That very morning, she had discovered it had become a rich tapestry of colors. "It's nothing. I bumped it."

"With help from the smugglers?" He laughed when she gasped. "Bethany, you know nothing stays quiet in Fair Cove."

"Did you hear if any of the smugglers were caught?"

His patrician nose wrinkled. "No, of course not, because that didn't happen."

She sighed. The smugglers had never been so daring. Father had vowed to search every outbuilding on Whitcombe Hall property and had urged his neighbors to do the same. Most would. As for Sir Asa, she was not sure what he would do, for he was even more incomprehensible than Titus.

Walking toward the house, she flinched when Dunley said, "I heard Jay was hurt, too."

"No, not Jay. Eric Pennington."

He put an arm out to block her way. "Who in perdition is Eric Pennington?"

"That language is unnecessary."

He grasped her wrist. "Answer my question!"

She tried to twist it away. When his fingers tightened on it, she gasped, *"Mon Dieu!"*

"What did you say?"

*Dash it!* She must get rid of the horrible habit that had been such a joke even a few months ago when there had been no threat of invasion. "Release me, and I shall answer your questions!"

When Dunley's fingers moved along her arm, she ripped herself out of his grip, wrenching her elbow.

"Stop that!" she ordered when he teased the curve of her ear beneath the ruffle of her straw bonnet.

"Don't be so prim, Bethany."

"I do not want to be pawed." She pushed past him and climbed the steps to the terrace.

Grabbing her hand again, he did not let her slip away. "Who's Pennington?"

"A peddler."

"Peddler? A peddler is staying in your house?"

She drew her hand out of his and went to the door. "Father is grateful that Mr. Pennington saved my life last night."

"When your face was bruised?"

"Yes." She looked toward the stable where the wagon had overturned.

Dunley spat out a profane oath which reddened her cheeks.

She was not sure how to get rid of him. She did not want to go into the house with him trotting after her like a puppy, but there was no choice. Mayhap Titus, who seemed to have become friends with Dunley in the past month, would be about and engage Dunley in some sort of discussion while she . . . While she checked on Eric. Avoiding the temptation to go and do that was what had had her lingering in the garden. The doctor had assured them last night that Eric's arm was not broken as they had feared. Instead, he had wrenched his shoulder fiercely, an injury that would take almost as long to heal as a broken bone.

But she could not avoid checking on Eric any longer, she realized when she saw a motion in the morning room. Jay came running out to grab her hands and pull her into the room that had surrendered itself to shadows with the passage of the sun overhead. The pair of chairs, on either side of a settee placed next to the bay window, offered the perfect place for a conversation.

"Come and hear what Eric was telling me about how the French are moving across the continent," Jay babbled like the bird that had given him his nickname. No one, but Nana and Father, when he was angry, called him by his given name of Warren.

"Yes," Dunley said, his voice as grim as Jay's had been joyous, "let us hear what *Eric* has to say."

Jay gave Bethany a guilty grin, but tugged her toward the chairs by the window. She was grateful that she had this excuse to get away from Dunley.

All thoughts of her brother and her neighbor vanished when Eric rose from the settee on which he had been sitting. Her gaze was enmeshed in his, although she noted that his right arm was hidden in a sling and his color was a decided gray beneath his tan. Even so, a smile slowly curved along his lips as she fought to breathe. She wondered how many ladies he had charmed into buying his wares with that smile, for she could not imagine telling him no now.

"How are you feeling?" she asked, her voice barely more than a whisper.

"As if I had been run over by a wagon." His laugh was gentle. "Actually better than you look, Miss Whitcombe."

"Were her bruises caused by your hesitation to endanger yourself?" demanded Dunley from behind her.

When Eric's gaze flickered from her to Dunley, she released the breath she had been holding. His smile lost its warmth when fingers cupped her elbow. Dunley's fingers! She shook them off.

She should caution Eric about Dunley's temper. She had seen Dunley strike a man from his feet with a single blow. The man had not awakened for so long, they had feared he was dead. But she could not speak of that when Dunley stood beside her.

Bethany said, "Dunley, Eric Pennington. Eric, this is Dunley Morelock."

"Miss Whitcombe was not hurt by my hesitation, but, I'm afraid, by my determination to keep her from being killed." Eric extended his hand.

Dunley ignored it. "So you ended up getting her bruised and obtained yourself an invitation to stay at Whitcombe Hall, Pennington."

"That's true."

"You were a leather-head to think you could catch a wagon."

"Dunley," said Bethany, "Eric saved my life."

Eric grinned when the other man bristled. Resting his right hand on the back of a chair, he winced as the simple motion sent agony through him. The blasted arm might not be broken, but it ached as if it were. "Forgive me," he said, lowering himself onto the settee. " 'Tis the price of being a hero."

"Hero?" Dunley dropped to a chair, then came to his feet again, for Bethany had not sat. "Pushing her away from a wagon is hardly heroism."

"Dunley!" chided Bethany.

He scowled. "I thought I had the right to say what I wished. After all—"

"I believe Miss Whitcombe is disturbed by your strong words," Eric said.

"When will you be leaving, Pennington?"

Bethany's face lost all color as she looked from Morelock to him. Because he was leaving or because Morelock hadn't? *Blasted leg!* His frustration eased when he watched Bethany walk past him to ring for tea.

"I am not sure yet," he replied. "Lord Whitcombe

tells me there have been few traveling merchants around Fair Cove."

" 'Traveling merchant?' " Dunley laughed without humor. "That is a fancy name for a peddler."

"Probably, but a traveling merchant is what I am." He rested his left elbow on the arm of the settee and smiled as he noted the wide arc Bethany kept between herself and Morelock as she came to sit beside Eric. He hid his amusement as Morelock's face grew long with fury.

"Are you in more pain?" she asked, adjusting the sling that threatened to slip from his shoulder.

He almost spoke the truth, that he could not be in pain when she was touching him so sweetly. Yes, he was suffering an agony, but an agony caused by the urge to draw her within the arc of his uninjured arm and sample her lips.

"No more than one should expect," he answered. That, at least, was the truth, although he wondered why he had experienced this need to be honest with her *now.*

"Dunley," Bethany said, "please sit and tell us what you have heard of the smugglers."

Jay cried, "Yes, tell us!" He sat on the other side of his sister and looked up expectantly at Dunley.

Grumbling, Dunley said, "Bethany, I must speak with you. Alone!"

Bethany stood, reluctant to obey even a single one of the orders he fired at her as if she were the lowest servant in his house. "Jay, tea should be here post-haste. If there is anything Mr. Pennington—"

"He shall be fine!" snapped Dunley, taking her wrist and jerking her toward the door. "You need not watch over him like a mother bird."

Bethany pulled free of him. "What is it?" she demanded heatedly when they stood in the hall beyond the door. She was not going farther with him.

"Get that man out of your house!"

"What?" She pressed her lips closed to contain her laughter when she saw his rage. "Dunley, he cannot drive his wagon with his shoulder wrenched as it is."

Dunley shrugged. "He can walk. Get rid of him."

"Mr. Pennington is my father's guest."

"I want him gone, Bethany. I won't have him stealing your affections."

"Stealing my affections? From whom?"

"From me."

She started to tell him that was ridiculous, then realized he might take her answer as a vow that she had a *tendre* for him. "Good day, Dunley."

She feared he would not release her, but slowly his fingers unwound from her wrist. He strode to the door and, not even waiting for the footman, opened it and then slammed it behind him.

Trouble was coming. She shuddered as she had in the garden. As soon as Dunley spoke to his father, she was sure both men would call.

"Is that an example of the welcome around Fair Cove?" Eric asked from the doorway of the morning room.

"Don't judge all of us by Dunley."

"Should I judge the residents by you?"

"Don't be silly." She did not look at him. "Do you need something?"

"Your company for tea." He gestured to where a maid was placing a tray with all the makings for a pleasant tea on a table near the bay window.

She wondered where Jay had gone. He could easily have slipped out of the room while she was speaking with Dunley, but that was not like him. He usually preferred to be in the midst of any hullabaloo.

"Miss Whitcombe?"

At the bafflement in Eric's voice, she forced her gaze back to him. He was smiling as he motioned toward the tray with a grace that suggested he was the host. Again she wondered where he had acquired such polished manners. Other peddlers who had come to Whitcombe Hall had been as rough as the life they lived.

"Thank you," she said, knowing she must say something. She chose a chair across from the settee so there was no chance he would sit right next to her. Being close to him had an odd effect on her, so odd that she found it difficult to think of anything, save that and him.

She reached for the teapot, glad to have something to do other than become lost in her uncomfortable thoughts. When he sat cautiously on the settee, a flicker of pain crossed his face.

"How are you feeling?" Bethany asked, before she could halt herself. "Really?"

He smiled. "Not as well as I let your friend Morelock think, but not as bad as the compassion in your eyes suggests." As she handed him a cup of tea and poured a second for herself, he asked, "Why do you put up with that cur?"

"Because I must."

"You must? Why?"

"Because Dunley Morelock may become my betrothed."

Eric set his cup back on the table. Mayhap he had misunderstood Bethany. No, her ashen face warned that he had heard correctly. "That is preposterous!"

"I agree, but Dunley's father is our neighbor. It would be deemed an excellent match. Sir Asa—"

He should not have assumed that things could not get worse. "*Sir Asa* Morelock?"

"Yes. You know him?"

"Of him." He kept his smile in place, but chose his words with care. "There cannot be many who have failed to hear of Sir Asa's single foray into politics."

She glanced over her shoulder as if she expected both Morelocks to be lurking there. "You should not speak of that around Fair Cove. His actions in berating the prime minister in front of the Prince Regent embarrassed everyone in the village."

Disregarding the blade of pain slicing through his shoulder, Eric reached across the small table to cup her chin in his left hand. Her eyes met his with an honesty he wished he could return. That this lovely sprite could be given to that beast seemed the worst injustice he could imagine. "Last night I told you I was sure you would do what you must, Bethany. I cannot believe that has changed. You will find a way to halt this betrothal."

"Mayhap," she murmured, but she looked away.

"Why mayhap?"

"Titus seems to be in favor of it, and Father often heeds his counsel."

"And not yours?"

Her smile was weak. "Father feels a man knows better in these matters."

"What do you think?"

For a long moment, he thought she would not answer as she stirred milk into her tea. Then she said, "I think I hope you are right."

"That you will find a way to get out of this betrothal?"

She nodded; then her smile grew stiffer. "You ask a lot of questions, Mr. Pennington."

"I have learned that is the way to learn things." He picked up his cup again and took a sip. The blend was not strong, so it was a treat for a man who had become accustomed to the tea in low taverns that was served black enough to threaten to eat right through a cup. "Jay calls me Eric. Will you, too?"

"All right." She glanced toward the window.

He was not surprised when she did not return the offer to call her by her given name. "Do you need to be somewhere just now, Miss Whitcombe?"

"I must meet my grandmother in the village this afternoon." She put down her cup.

"Your grandmother?"

"Don't look so shocked. You haven't had a chance to meet her because she has been visiting in Canterbury."

"But why do you have to meet her? Doesn't she have a carriage?"

Her dark brows arched. "Nana is somewhat eccentric. She does not like to ride alone, so she takes the mail coach."

"A dowager baroness?"

"I told you she was a bit eccentric. She likes the chatter she hears on the mail coach and the people she meets. She has told me, more than once, that to confine oneself to the Polite World is to miss out on some of the most interesting folks there are."

"I look forward to meeting your grandmother."

"Just prepare yourself. She speaks her mind. She is not cruel, but she is honest."

He chuckled. "Every word you say intrigues me more."

A clock rang from somewhere in the house. "I fear I shall be late, because I must give my friend Tryphena a look-in before I meet the mail coach at the inn, so I must ask you to excuse me."

He watched her stand with a grace that teased him to think only of how beautiful she looked. He must not let himself be waylaid from his work. "Miss Whitcombe, would you by chance be going near Mr. Cartman's warehouse while you are in Fair Cove?"

"Tryphena lives not a block in from the shore where the warehouse is." Bethany hesitated, then asked, "Do you want me to take a message to Mr. Cartman for you?"

Eric came to his feet with care, she noted. Did his head still ring with the concussion of the accident, as hers did if she moved too swiftly? Reaching under his waistcoat, he pulled out a package wrapped in brown paper. "I was supposed to deliver this to him when I reached Fair Cove. I have had it with me since I last left London, so there is no hurry." He gave her a wry smile. "On the other hand, I have been carrying it about with me for some time now, and he might be waiting for it."

She held out her hand. "If you wish, I can take it to him for you."

His grin sent something delightful through her heart. "It is not meet that a peddler should ask a baron's daughter to run errands for him."

"You are my father's guest. I can do no less." She chuckled as she added, "And you have been very kind not to remind me that it is my fault you are hurt."

"Not yours, but that of those accursed smugglers, who should have known better than to come here."

She took the package which could not hold more than a sheet or two. "Is that what you and Jay were talking about?"

"No." He chuckled as he rested his hand on the chair again. "He was trying to find out what news I had of the war. It seems your young brother is very determined to go and punch Boney in the nose."

"It's not funny!"

"That he wants to punch Boney?"

"That he wants to go and fight." She blinked back

the tears that came too easily each time she thought of Jay marching off to war and never returning. "He is an air-dreamer if he thinks Father will purchase him a commission."

"I don't think a commission means that much to him. He would go as an enlisted man."

Shaking her head, she whispered, "How can he be so shortsighted? There is no glory worth dying for."

"Are you so certain of that?"

She stared at him as if seeing him for the first time. She could not mistake the quiet conviction in his voice. Although she had seen his face without a smile before, she was sure she had never seen him so resolved as he was now. "If you feel that way," she retorted, "mayhap you should be toting a gun on some battlefield instead of hawking your goods down these country lanes."

"I would be of little use now." He tapped the sling.

"Which is most convenient for you in the midst of this discussion. I hope you did not air your opinions for Jay. He needs little inducement to run away and join the army."

He came around the chair between them. With his hand on the back of it, less than a finger's breadth from hers, he met her gaze without compromise. "I know you do not know me, Miss Whitcombe, but I have done nothing to convince you that I would send a young boy into the maw of war."

"You haven't?"

"Not that I was aware of. If you think differently, will you enlighten me?" His hand shifted on the back of the seat, so the tips of his fingers covered hers.

She fought to breathe past the sudden lump in her throat. Was it her fear for Jay? No, for those tears still clung to her lashes. Or her heart? No, it was throbbing wildly in her chest. Or delight? She should not be delighted with his bold touch, but she could not ignore the truth.

Her voice sounded strangled in her ears, but she managed to say, "Do not think me less than grateful for what you did, Eric, for I know you saved my life, but it is that very type of heroic gesture that Jay sees himself making in an effort to save England from Napoleon's invasion."

"Miss Whitcombe—"

"Please let me finish," she said, not sure she could say what she must if she faltered here. "You must understand that there are many along these shores who would gladly see peace negotiated with that black-hearted Corsican. Livelihoods in the village have been ruined, and those who continue to prosper have thrown aside their honest ways to become smugglers and risk ending their days in a noose. Some of those folks would promise anything to see the war ended."

"I did not suspect to find such sentiment here where you could suffer the brunt of the invasion."

"Don't you understand?" She shook her head and sighed. "That is just what I mean. You see only a glorious end to the war in Napoleon's defeat while those here, who have so much to lose, are willing to consider other alternatives."

"But that is treason!"

"No, it is not treason, for no one wishes to gainsay the government, only to safeguard those who are important to them. When a father looks at his children and realizes they could die in a French invasion, he may change his mind about victory at any cost." She drew her hand from beneath his. "I bid you good afternoon, Eric."

As she walked toward the door, he called to her back, "Miss Whitcombe?"

"Yes?"

He came to stand beside her again. "Do you share their opinions?"

"I do not believe victory at any cost is worth my brother's life."

"You didn't answer my question." He stepped between her and the door.

"If you recall what you said to me last evening, you will know my answer."

His eyes narrowed. "That you will do whatever you must to achieve your ends."

"Yes." She did not wait for his answer, hurrying out of the room before he pressed her to reveal the whole of her plan to keep her brother alive. She could not tell him. Not because she did not trust him, although she had no reason to do so, but because she was not sure herself of what she would do to keep Jay from joining the army.

But she would do something, because she did not want anyone she loved dying for glory as her grandfather had.

# Four

Dust danced in the sunlight that found its way through the narrow windows. Wondering how anyone could work in such a dim place, Bethany closed the door behind her.

She wished she could close thoughts out of her mind as readily. On the way down the hill to Fair Cove, which clung to the strand, her conversation with Eric had played through her head. She was *not* in favor of negotiating with the French for peace, but, somehow, she had found herself arguing for that. What a bothersome man he was! If she did not owe him the duty of being kind to him after he had saved her from the smugglers, she would have been tempted to cut him direct.

With a sigh, she knew she would not have done that, even if she were not obligated to him. Father insisted on treating everyone under the roof of Whitcombe Hall with respect.

"Miss Whitcombe!" Mr. Cartman, who was barely taller than his counter, wiped his hands on a stained apron. "Were you expecting the arrival of a package today?"

"No." She smiled and held out the packet Eric had given her. "Eric Pennington asked me to bring this to you."

"Eric Pennington?" His nose wrinkled, giving him the appearance of an overfed puppy.

"A peddler who arrived at Whitcombe Hall last night."

Mr. Cartman's brown eyes twinkled. "Ah, I understand now. I have heard of the problems up at the baron's house last night and of how a peddler came to your rescue."

"I thought, in return, I would deliver this packet that he intended to bring you from London."

"London?" Mr. Cartman's brow ruffled again.

"I believe that is what he said." She set the packet on the counter. Curiosity taunted her. On her other visits here with Father, Mr. Cartman had been effusive and jolly, not alternately smiling and frowning. Since Eric's arrival, no one had acted as they customarily did . . . except Dunley. She did not want to think of him and his assumption that she not only would marry him, but would be honored to do so.

Mr. Cartman picked up the packet, glanced at it, then smiled. "Ah, I had forgotten about this. Thank you for delivering it, Miss Whitcombe."

"You are most welcome," she said, although she truly wished to ask him what was in the packet. She had not been inquisitive about it until she had seen Mr. Cartman's odd behavior. Although she wanted to wait and see what was within it, she said only, "Good afternoon, Mr. Cartman."

"Good afternoon, Miss Whitcombe." He looked up from the packet to add, "And thank your peddler for me."

Bethany wanted to tell him that Eric was not *her* peddler, but she only nodded as she went back out into the sunshine. She steered the cart she had driven from Whitcombe Hall along the cobbled street that led up from the harbor. She was glad to reach the neat stone house where her best friend lived.

She waved to Tryphena Sullivan, who was working, as she did every day, in the rose garden encircling the parsonage where she lived with her father, Reverend Sullivan. Tryphena stood and waved back, her golden hair catching the sunlight, even beneath her bonnet's brim. There were rumbles throughout the village, asking why a woman as pretty and prettily mannered as the minister's daughter had never married. Tryphena had never spoken of this most private matter, even to Bethany. However, Bethany suspected it was because Tryphena had a *tendre* for Titus. A few months back, her older brother had called on Tryphena several times, and there had been murmurs about a possible marriage. Then Titus had begun visiting Miss Deborah Gillette regularly. Although he spoke more of Miss Gillette's brother, Francis, everyone expected an announcement at any moment.

Everyone . . . including Tryphena. Bethany wished she knew a way to ease her friend's despair, but, because Tryphena never spoke of Titus, Bethany could do nothing.

"I was beginning to wonder if you had forgotten that I wanted to show you the new roses I planted," Tryphena said, wiping earth from her hands as she opened the gate to let Bethany into the well-tended garden.

When Tryphena looked over her shoulder, puzzled, Bethany laughed and leaned over the fence to pull free a vine that had embedded its thorns in her friend's skirt. "I think your roses are becoming as attached to you as you are to them." Roses were everywhere, climbing over the stone wall and up the sides of the house to grasp the thatched roof. Taking a deep breath of their sweet fragrance, Bethany smiled.

"What happened to you?" Tryphena's blue eyes grew as round as her mouth.

Bethany touched her aching cheek. "I'm surprised you haven't heard about the fracas with the smugglers at Whitcombe Hall last night."

"I heard about it." She edged around Bethany to look at the bruise Mr. Cartman had not seen in the dim warehouse or had chosen not to mention. "I didn't realize you were hurt."

"They were chased off before I could be hurt worse." For some reason, she did not speak of Eric's part in rescuing her. She never had been reticent with her friend before, but now something kept her from adding more.

"Your father needs to put an end to these smugglers." Tryphena scowled. "If they become any bolder, they are going to be asking to be appointed to the village council."

"Father tries to halt them, but they always manage to slip away."

"Someone is warning them."

Taking her friend by the arm, Bethany drew her around the corner of the house. She did not want to chance someone overhearing Tryphena. Looking about to be certain no one was lurking, listening to them, she said, "I have thought that as well, and I know Father has been making inquiries in that direction."

"He should make inquiries also into the question of whether they are obtaining help from the French."

"I pray not."

"As I do, but you must have heard the rumor that a boatload of the accursed Frogs was seen just off the spit."

"No!" Ice dropped into the very center of Bethany's heart. "When?"

"Two nights ago."

She shivered, although the day was warm. Two nights ago, Frenchmen may have come to their coast. Then, last night, the smugglers had dared to bring their heinous business right to Whitcombe Hall. This did not bode well.

"Is it more than a rumor?" she asked, hoping Tryphena would put her mind to rest.

Her bosom-bow did not. "Mr. Anderson did not think so. He was quite emphatic that he saw them. He even described the green uniforms that Papa told me are most definitely French."

Bethany clenched and unclenched her hands. Mr. Anderson was a man of somber temperament, not given to bouts of drinking at the pub. If it had been Mr. Griffen or even Sir Asa telling of seeing the boat, she could have discounted the stories as images brought forth by a bottle of blue ruin.

"I wonder if Father knows of this," she said quietly. "That may be why he had some of the gentlemen to the house for a discussion last night."

Tryphena nodded. "Papa was going to go, but Mrs. Caldecott took ill and swore that she was on her death bed." She dimpled. "Again."

Bethany tried to smile, too, but she could not. Odd that Father had heard of these rumors, yet had not cautioned any of them. Mayhap he had reason to believe that Mr. Anderson had been confused about what he had seen.

She made her excuses to her friend to take her leave, remembered to compliment Tryphena on her roses, and quickly went back to the cart. Even though she set the horse to its best speed up the hill, she could not escape her thoughts.

*The French! Here in Fair Cove!*

*Impossible!*

If they even considered coming here, they must be met with every possible resistance. The Frogs could not win as much as a grain of English sand.

Looking out at a sea that was empty in the afternoon sunshine, she saw a bank of fog rising near the horizon. She shivered. A foggy night was the best time for smugglers and for a clandestine invasion of Fair Cove.

She hoped it would never come.

"We will speak of this again, Anson. This matter is not closed."

Eric looked up from where he was perusing one of Lord Whitcombe's books in the quiet book-room. He could not recall the last time he had held a book and had a chance to read it. This one was in English, although many of the books on the shelves were in French and German. Clearly, the baron prided himself on his education. Eric had seen pieces of art in the house that were undeniably French, so he guessed the baron had more hatred for the smugglers who were breaking England's laws than for the French.

This interruption had come at a bad time, because he had let himself get swept up into the story, but he could not restrain his curiosity about who was speaking to the baron in such authoritative tones.

He walked across the faded Persian rug to stand in the shadows of the doorway. Lord Whitcombe had his back to him, so he had a good view of the baron's clenched hands clasped behind him. The man who had clearly irritated Bethany's father stood in profile to Eric.

He knew instantly that this must be Sir Asa Morelock. The handsome features of his son had grown thick with the passage of years, leaving Sir Asa with jowls that hung heavily along his jaw. Gray lined his thinning hair, and he clearly needed spectacles, because he was squinting at Lord Whitcombe. His clothes, Eric noted with an appreciative eye, were as well made as his son's. Mayhap Bethany hesitated to buy a piece of silk that might have been brought to England by an owl plying the Channel, but Sir Asa seemed to have no such scruples. His waistcoat was of elegant silk brocade that caught the light to shimmer with his every motion.

As Sir Asa raised a finger to point at Lord Whitcombe, the baronet said, "We had a gentleman's agreement, Anson."

"We simply had a conversation," replied Lord Whitcombe with quiet dignity. "Nothing was decided about a betrothal announcement."

"Nothing was decided about *when.*"

"That is true, but I shall not be hurried into this. Nor shall I hurry Bethany. Another fortnight shall not matter."

Sir Asa's eyes lit up. "Then it is decided. We shall announce the betrothal in another fortnight."

Eric's respect for the baron increased tenfold when his voice remained calm. "That is not what I said, Asa. I must give the whole of this more thought."

"What thought? You need not give the girl a dowry. My son is quite mad for her."

"There are other matters to consider, some much more important than a wedding between our children before the end of the summer."

Eric edged back into the shadows. He had thought Lord Whitcombe was not considering Dunley Morelock's suit, but it appeared that he was. Mayhap the baron had not noticed how his daughter cringed when Morelock was present.

He waited for the two men to go down the stairs and then slipped out of the room. He needed some fresh air to scour away the distaste left from eavesdropping on the conversation.

*Blast!* He had thought he had given up any illusions of being a gentleman, but here he was, ready to leap to Bethany's defense again. Hadn't he learned anything after last night? The pain from his arm should keep his head clear, but he seemed to be having trouble thinking clearly about Bethany, because images of her beguiling smile muddled up his mind.

He reached the door in time to see a grand carriage being whipped up. He hoped the coachman was skilled, for a single chuckhole could upend a carriage going at that speed. When it disappeared past the gate, he walked in the opposite direction.

Jay came around a wing of the house. Seeing Eric, he waved wildly.

With a smile, Eric walked toward him. Young Jay obviously had something on his mind. Mayhap it would get Bethany off *his*.

"Where are you bound?" Eric asked.

"To do some practice shooting, so I'll be ready." He pulled a gun from beneath his riding coat.

"You hunt foxes with a dueling pistol?"

"Not foxes, but the sly French." Jay's grin widened. "I cannot wait to cross the Channel to make them my targets."

"Let's see how skilled you are." Eric guessed that attempting to convince the lad he should think twice before joining the army would be a waste of breath.

As he walked with Jay toward the gate, he listened to him talk about his determination to serve his country. Similar words rang in his memory. Did every lad harbor dreams of glory?

He pushed that thought aside when they paused by a stone fence. Without comment, he watched Jay fire at a target he had carved into a tree halfway across an empty field. He made some suggestions to the youth to aim lower, because the pistol kicked up on every shot. When he saw how slowly Jay reloaded the gun, he bit his lip to keep from warning him that he could be killed easily if he did not learn some speed in reloading. Unlike when the lad chased foxes across the downs, the French would be firing back in the hope of killing everyone in British uniform.

The rattle of wheels coming along the road brought an expression of dismay from Jay, warning Eric that someone he did not want to see him shooting was coming toward them. Turning, he saw Bethany driving toward them in a small cart. With her was a silver-haired woman who must be her grandmother.

Jay muttered, "Eric . . ."

Eric held out his hand for the pistol. Jay gave it to him with a conspiratorial grin as he stepped forward to assist Bethany out of the cart.

"Welcome home, Nana," he said with a smile.

"What have you been up to, child?"

"Nana—"

"Don't lather me with out-and-outers, child. I recognize that guilty expression. Your father always wore it when he was up to no good. Your grandfather, too, and his father. Must be some sort of strain of unremitting honesty in the Whitcombe line." She patted Jay on the cheek; then her eyes, as dark as Bethany's, turned toward Eric.

He bowed his head toward her. "Good afternoon, my lady."

"Bethany," Lady Whitcombe crowed, "you didn't tell me he was *this* pleasant on the eyes. My girl, no wonder you are as skittish as a man hiding under his mistress's bed when her husband is at the door."

"Nana," Bethany replied, stiffly, "this is Eric Pennington."

Eric wanted to laugh at the dowager's words, but he could not, for Bethany might think his amusement was with her when she held firmly to her dignity despite her grandmother's words. Eccentric? That was no exaggeration.

Lady Whitcombe held out her vein-lined hand. "I am Hannah Whitcombe, young man. I shall never be addressed, under any circumstances, as Nana Hannah. Do I make myself quite clear?"

He bowed over her hand, glad to hide his smile. "Completely, my lady."

"You are better on the eyes than the usual hawkers who wander through the shire." Appraising him without apology, she smiled. "I can see why Bethany is all atwitter today."

Jay chuckled.

His grandmother focused a frown at him. "Don't stand there snickering, child. Take me back to the house. That mail coach did not miss a single stone."

"I would be glad to. Bethany?" Jay asked, holding out a hand to his sister.

His smile did not fool her, Eric noticed, but she handed him the reins. "Thank you."

After he swung up to sit next to his grandmother, Jay slapped the reins on the horse and drove on toward the gate.

Bethany glanced at the pistol in Eric's hand. "I see you and my brother have been getting some fresh air."

"I'm not accustomed to being inside all day."

"You are welcome to enjoy the gardens. The water garden is especially pretty at this time of year."

"Would you show it to me?"

"I should go and let Father know—"

"What trouble your grandmother got herself into?"

She laughed in spite of herself. "You would think a woman of her years would know that the driver of the mail coach would not take kindly to her comments about his driving as well as his personal habits."

"You warned me."

"I did. Nana is one of a kind."

"That is a shame. We could use more plain-speaking people."

"If you will excuse me, I should tell Father all the details."

"He might be busy."

She frowned. "Why do you say that?"

He glanced along the road, and his stance abruptly resembled that of a stag pausing to listen for the hunter. Then he smiled. "You chose the very best time for your call on your bosom-bow. Sir Asa just left. You must have passed him along the road."

She shook her head. "I didn't see his carriage. Mayhap he was not going home."

Eric chuckled. "Do you mean to suggest that he wishes to cause upheavals for your neighbors as well as for your father?"

"What did he say to Father?"

"I was not privy to the whole conversation, but your father looked quite distressed."

Bethany struggled not to smile as her heart leaped with joy. If Sir Asa was disgruntled, it might mean that Father had told him a betrothal between Dunley and his daughter was out of the question.

Not wanting Eric to guess her thoughts, although she was sure he knew exactly why her smile refused to be hidden, she said, "I see Jay convinced you to shoot with him."

"He has a good eye for a lad."

"But?"

"You are right to try to talk him out of enlisting."

"I know that." She let her smile become sincere. "On that, I never have second-guessed myself." She glanced again at the pistol which he held with the ease of a man accustomed to handling weapons. "I hope you are a better shot than he is, so he does not become overconfident."

He turned and aimed across the field. She gasped when, holding the pistol in his left hand, he fired and bark danced away from the tree trunk.

"You need not be so surprised," he said, waving aside the choking gun smoke. "I would be addled not to be able to protect myself and my wares"—he smiled as he glanced at his right arm—"though, you may not believe me when I say that I usually escape such attacks with much less damage to myself."

"Have you been attacked often?"

"The roads along the shore can be very dangerous."

"Smugglers?"

He shook his head. "They seldom bother me, because I have usually found shelter off the road before nightfall. Other vagabonds, who prefer to consider themselves knights of the pad, may not be brave enough to halt a carriage, but see a solitary peddler as an easy target."

"English vagabonds?"

"Who else?"

She ran her fingers along the stone post. "Who else, indeed?" Looking across the field to where it dropped off to the sea, she said, "I heard some disturbing rumors in Fair Cove today."

"Of an invasion force from France floating just out of sight in the Channel?" When she turned to him, her eyes wide, he laughed. "Don't look at me as if I read your thoughts. I know what is on every mind along this shore, for I have heard the uneasy conversations over and over as I have traveled. There is nary a soul here who does not fear that Napoleon will throw his army upon these strands."

"It shall not be amusing if it comes to pass."

"From what your father said during a conversation we had earlier today, I suspect he has a few ideas of his own to welcome the French here."

"Father told you of how he has given arms to the villagers and set up a warning system to fight off any invasion?" She could not be more startled if Eric had told her that he had been named the new king.

"Not so succinctly as you have, but he did say he would be prepared."

Bethany turned away again, berating herself for betraying her father's plans so carelessly. She had cautioned Jay so many times to watch what he said, and then she had revealed the whole to a man she did not know.

His finger under her chin brought her face toward his. The strong odor of gunpowder vanished as she was caught anew by his gaze. As when they had stood on the road yesterday, the glint of humor had vanished from his eyes. The strength of the emotions burning within them unsettled her. He might jest with her brother and charm her grandmother and prattle with her father about matters of little import, but Eric Pennington was more than the carefree peddler he portrayed so well. What was the "more?"

"Bethany," he murmured, using her given name with an ease that suggested he had used it often, "you need have no fear that you have told me something that will undermine your father's efforts to protect his family and Fair Cove. I have traveled far through England, and I have seen similar preparations in every coastal town that faces the continent. It would be more of a surprise if he were not so vigilant."

"You must think me an empty-headed prattle-box."

"No."

"Why not?"

He chuckled. "If you were just an empty-headed prattle-box, you would be satisfied to marry Dunley Morelock, who could send you to London for the Season where you would be able to enjoy the company of other prattle-boxes such as yourself." He edged a step closer. "I see your curiosity. Now let me satisfy it."

"Satisfy it?" she whispered as her gaze settled on his smiling lips. Satisfy it with a kiss? She feared she was quite out of her mind to be thinking so about a peddler, but she could not deny her own thoughts of his arm sweeping around her waist and bringing her mouth to his.

"I have, on occasion, done my hawking in London, although I find the streets too close." He laughed again. "And I find the competition too fierce. I prefer to spend my time walking these country lanes instead of selling from a stand pad in the city."

"But you were recently there."

"Was I?"

She frowned. "You said you brought the packet from London for Mr. Cartman."

"It's not unusual for me to make deliveries months after I receive something like that."

She walked back to the gate, needing to put some room between them. "I would have guessed it would be easier just to have it sent with the post."

"Some folks don't trust the government to take care of things for them, so they decide to take care of them themselves."

Whirling to see he had not moved, she said, "Now *that* sounds like treason."

"Does it?" His smile returned while he walked to where she stood. "Is it any different from your father arranging for a patrol along the shore? I do believe,

Bethany, you need to sort out your feelings on the whole of this."

She did not move as he continued past her and disappeared through the gate. He was right. She did need to sort out her feelings—and not just on the war on the other side of the Channel. On that, she was very sure of her opinions. She wished she could be so sure of what she thought of Eric Pennington and who he might really be.

# Five

Bethany was surprised at how simple it was to avoid Eric in the corridors of Whitcombe Hall. Or mayhap he was avoiding her, for, save during meals, she seldom saw him during the fortnight after her visit to Fair Cove. As the pain in his arm diminished, he was often outside, coaching Jay in shooting or talking to the stablehands or in the garden, hunched down next to the gardeners as he engaged the men in conversation. She saw him deep in discussion with her father and had heard that Nana had invited him to have tea with her twice in the past two weeks.

That was why she should not have been startled when she was summoned to Nana's bright blue reception room to find Eric there, chatting with her grandmother as if they were the best of bosom-bows. He had rid himself of the sling, but she noticed that each move he made with his right arm was cautious. It was apparently still bothering him. She was a bit astonished to discover him there, but not as amazed as she was to see Titus sitting on the gold settee beside him. She had seen her brother even less during this fortnight than she had Eric, for Titus had developed a habit of dining with the Gillettes.

As she entered, she smiled. This room suited Nana. It was vibrant, with no concessions for her age. Whimsical bits of art sat beside the most recent books published in London. Nana had met Bethany's grandfather during a London Season that was still renowned for its elegance. A portrait of her grandfather sitting on a stone overlooking the sea was set over the black marble fireplace where it could be seen through any door in Nana's rooms. For her whole life, Bethany had admired her grandmother's strength, her graciousness and devotion to the Whitcombe family, and her sense of humor.

Giving her grandmother a kiss on the cheek, she quickly obeyed when Nana ordered, "Sit there by those two handsome young men and be a good chaperon for your grandmother who still likes to hear good-looking young men vie to beguile her with courtly promises."

"Nana," mumbled Titus under his breath. When he rolled his eyes, Bethany jabbed him with her elbow. He glowered at her, then rested his elbow on the marble-topped lyre table beside him.

"All we need now is Warren," Nana continued, setting herself on her feet and walking spryly to the door.

"She means Jay," Bethany whispered to Eric.

"I know," he said as quietly. "She talks about him all the time. She is as worried as you are about his plans."

"She knows?"

He nodded.

"And she hasn't stopped him?" She had expected Nana to speak her mind on this as on everything else. Mayhap Jay would heed Nana.

"She hasn't done anything to stop him *yet.*" He smiled and reached for the plate of cakes. "Would you like one, Bethany?"

Titus mumbled something else and stood, going to look out the window that gave him a view across the fields toward the Gillettes' house.

Eric chuckled under his breath. "He seems to be suffering seriously from a case of unrequited love."

"Unrequited? What makes you think so?"

"There has been no announcement from that quarter, has there?"

She frowned and motioned the plate away. "You seem to have acquired my grandmother's unfortunate habit of enjoying gossip."

"A bit of poker-talk can give one intriguing insights into people, and a peddler is expected to bring tidings as well as items to purchase." He smiled. "You never repeat rumors, Bethany?"

From the door, Nana asked, "Where is that boy? Being late is an unattractive thing in a child." She opened the door and peered out.

"I try never to repeat things unless I know them to be the truth," Bethany said.

Eric chuckled. "No wonder your grandmother considers you far too serious."

"She has been speaking to you of me?"

Again, he smiled. "Often."

"If you were a gentleman, you would not have listened."

" 'Tis a good thing I'm nothing more than a peddler then, isn't it?"

Bethany took a breath to retort, but running steps echoed wildly through the room before Jay burst through the door. He reached out to steady Nana, who had been able to edge out of his path, but she waved him aside.

"I am sorry, Nana. I—"

"No damage, Warren." When he grimaced, she patted him on the buttocks as she had when he was a toddler. "Go and sit with your sister. Titus, will you join us, or are you going to continue to brood and be utterly tiresome?"

Nana selected her favorite chaise longue and smiled as Jay handed her a cup of tea. "Now that all of you are here, I must speak with you of a matter of importance. The beating of the bounds is always held the second week of June every year. That is nearly upon us. With your father so busy—"

Eric cleared his throat before saying, "My lady, this sounds like a matter of interest to your family. I would be glad to leave."

"Nonsense." She stretched forward to pat his right arm as if he were no older than Jay. "You shall still be with us by then, and you may be necessary to help me convince Anson that simply because Napoleon is being so beastly is no reason to cancel the beating of the bounds. It is too important to the shire to let a year pass without it. In addition, all the invitations to the ball that evening have gone out."

"The same day?" Eric asked, his eyes widening.

Bethany was glad for a chance to chuckle at his amazement for a change. " 'Tis a tradition in this shire that goes back before anyone can remember. Of course, it is much simpler now when most of the fields in the shire are enclosed. Years ago, people would have to walk nearly thirty miles during the day to make sure all the markers were in place to show where Whitcombe land ended and the king's began. Then they would dance through the night. Now, one need only to go about ten miles to traverse the bounds."

"And still dance through the night?"

"Not until dawn, for we keep country hours here. Not the late hours they do in London."

He lowered his eyes quickly when she mentioned London, and she wondered what he was trying to conceal. She could not ask, not when the others were gathered here to speak of the beating of the bounds.

Titus made no effort to conceal his opinions. "This

whole tradition is a farce. Bethany is right, Nana. The fields have been enclosed for years. What purpose is there in tramping about the countryside in the damp and rain? Let us have the ball alone and enjoy it for once."

Bethany put a hand on his arm. "Titus, the villagers in Fair Cove look forward to this all year. Tryphena was telling me only a few weeks ago of how she was sending to Brighton for special fabric for her gown."

Titus gulped so loudly she was afraid he had swallowed his tongue. Again he stood and went to the window. Dropping to the window seat, he glowered at his hands, which he locked together between his knees.

Bethany wanted to go to him and apologize. She had not intended to discomfit him, but she had not thought the mere mention of Tryphena's name would agitate him so. Why did it, now that he was courting Miss Gillette? Tryphena had been heartsick when Titus had stopped calling, so she had not put an end to his visits. None of this made sense.

Jay bounced to his feet. "We cannot cancel the beating of the bounds this year. I promised Lyle Dudley that I would remember him at each of the boundary markers this year."

"Gently, I hope," Bethany said. "I heard that some of the villagers last year tipped the youngsters upside down at every boundary marker to help them remember where each one is."

" 'Tis better than when I was remembered." Jay rubbed his backside. "Then we had to lean over each boundary stone and have its location imprinted on us with a stick."

"It is a waste of time," Titus grumbled.

"Is it?" Bethany returned. " 'Twould be good for everyone to remember where the paths lead through the woods and away from the coast. Just in case."

"You are right," Eric said quietly; then he smiled at Nana. "And it would behoove me to discover what other hamlets are in this area. Some of them might be eager for a visit from a traveling merchant."

Nana chuckled. "I suspected you would come to that conclusion eventually, my boy. I am glad we all are in agreement, then." She looked at Titus. "All of us, yes?"

Reluctantly he said, "Of course, Nana."

"Good. We all are in agreement."

Bethany nodded, but had no chance to speak as Nana outlined her plans for how the beating of the bounds would be held. No one had a chance to speak, save Nana. Titus's glower grew grimmer and grimmer. Jay's smile broadened.

And Eric, who seemed to be enjoying the whole, leaned back on the settee, his left elbow balanced on the arm. His other hand rested on his knee. When she noted his fingers closing into a fist as Nana spoke of following the old paths through the woods, she stiffened. That slight motion was as unmistakable as a scream. Something about Nana's words disturbed him. But what?

As soon as Nana dismissed them, because she was expecting Reverend Sullivan to call as he did each week at this time, Bethany let Jay and Titus hurry ahead of her out of the room. Jay was eager to begin following Nana's suggested plans for the beating of the bounds. Titus was just eager to be gone. She heard him calling to a footman to have a carriage brought around even as he reached the stairs. He must intend to waste no more time in getting to the Gillette house.

"No wonder everyone expects an announcement." Eric's voice was laced with laughter as he walked with her along the hall toward the rear of the house. "He acts like the bridegroom who is eager to get through the ceremony to have his wedding night with his bride."

"What a charming way to describe it!"

"I warned you I'm no gentleman."

"Now."

He smiled, but it was the coldest smile she had ever seen. "On that, you're right. Mayhap someday I will be able to claim that title."

She wanted to say *Again?*, but instead asked, "What is disturbing you?"

"Making plans for next week, when I need to return to my work."

"If you wish, I can have the women in Fair Cove come here."

"No."

Bethany choked at his brusque response. "But—"

"I am not turning your home into a shop."

"Father would not mind."

" 'Tis not him I am thinking about."

"Nana would be delighted to have even more callers, so she could hear the latest tidings."

"Of that, I am certain. However, 'tis you I am concerned about, Bethany."

"You need not concern yourself with me."

His arm slipped around her waist, drawing her back into an alcove along the wall. "But I have no choice."

"You have the choice of releasing me or of being sorry if you do not."

He stepped closer, backing her up into the narrow space that was rumored to have been a priest's hole three hundred years ago. Mayhap it had been, because no one walking along the hall would see them until coming nearly upon them.

"You are right about that," he murmured, "but I was speaking of the lack of choice I have about keeping you out of my thoughts, Bethany."

"This is unseemly. You should—"

"Yes, I should." His arm tightened around her waist, pulling her up against his chest. Even in the dim light, his eyes glowed like twin stars, teasing her to whisper a wish on that starlight and then letting him make it come true. "I am not Dunley Morelock," he whispered. "You do not need to be frightened of me."

"I am not afraid of Dunley."

"But you are afraid of marrying him and going to live with him and his father. Just the father and the son and you, the bride. Very, very cozy."

She shuddered as he said the words she had not dared even to think. "You do not know what you are talking about. You are a stranger here at Whitcombe Hall."

"After a fortnight at Whitcombe Hall, I have heard many things, including the fact that Sir Asa was most anxious to marry you himself before your father told him that would never come to pass."

She halted her efforts to escape, staring up at him. "Sir Asa? *Mon—*" She bit back the French oath. "Are you out of your mind? You should not heed silly gossip."

"Even when both your grandmother and your father let that fact slip into conversation?" He shook his head. "No, your father may have let it slip. Your grandmother, I believe, intended for me to know that."

"I—I—" She did not know what she wanted to say, but she was certain that she wanted to deny his words. Sir Asa had asked for her hand? She did not understand. Dunley had told her years ago that *he* would marry her when they both were of age. Or had he told her exactly that? Had he said instead that she would be living in his father's magnificent house when she was grown?

Eric's fingers brushed her cheek, and she looked

up to see sympathy in his eyes. "I thought you knew," he whispered.

"I wish I did not know now."

"You need not look so fearful. Your father was emphatic in saying that you would not marry Sir Asa." A slow smile eased along his lips. "On that, I agree with him completely."

"Then, now that you have told me what you obviously felt you must, will you step aside?"

"Do you wish me to?" His fingers quested along her cheek to her ear. A single fingertip traced its curve, lingering behind it. His gentle caress sent a bolt from her skin to spiral deep within her.

The glory of his touch flowed through her. As if it had longings of its own, her hand rose to his face. Her fingers tingled when she touched his rough skin. Nothing had ever been so wondrous—nothing!

"You woo a man to your side with a flash of your obsidian eyes and the promise of pleasure on your lips," he continued in a low voice which resonated through her.

When he drew her toward him, her gaze settled on his lips before rising along the firm line of his nose. She noticed, as she had not before, amber sparks in the azure fire of his eyes.

"You are so winsome, so ready for the battles of the heart," he whispered.

"Eric, I—"

"Tell me that you abhor my embrace, and I will be glad to release you and never touch you again. Tell me, pretty one, but tell me truthfully."

As her fingers combed through his golden hair, she knew she was silly to become a part of his madness. She did not care, for she was lost in the enchantment he spun with his touch, which lured her to make her fantasy of being in his arms, savoring his kiss, come true. His fingers played along her cheek, creating a melody she heard in her heart. As his mouth lowered toward hers, her eyes closed in sweet surrender.

"Bethany!"

She whirled to see Father behind Eric. Her father's face was long with his frown as he gripped her arm. She gasped when his fingers bit into her arm, but he ignored the sound as he drew her away from Eric.

Father's voice was clipped. "I did not expect this."

Bethany whispered, "Neither did I." She had not expected that this emptiness would ache in her when she had been so close to sampling Eric's kiss and then been denied it.

He glared at her, but his words were aimed at Eric. "I demand that you give me your word, on your honor, that you will not attempt to kiss my daughter again."

"You have my word as a peddler," Eric answered quietly.

Bethany glanced at him. She must be wrong. She could not have heard a mirthful undertone in his words. As she faced her father, she feared her yearning for a single kiss had possessed her like a curse. Never did she think anything through to its conclusion. If she had paused to think, she would have known that the cost of this pleasure was far too high.

Father snapped, "And I trust I need not remind you, Bethany, of how you should behave."

"I shall endeavor never to forget what I should do." Her strained voice startled her as much as it must have her father whose eyes grew round in surprise. She wanted to retract her cold words, but it was too late.

"Good." He released her, tugging nervously at his rumpled waistcoat. "I do not have time to make sure you have a watchdog every minute."

"What has happened?" she asked. For the first time, she noticed the scent of horseflesh and salt on him.

His clothes were not wrinkled from having worked hard at his desk, but from riding for hours.

"I was called away with the tidings of a confirmed sighting of French soldiers on the shore not far east of Fair Cove."

"Father, we have heard that rumor dozens of times before."

"This was not a rumor."

Eric asked quietly, "How do you know?"

Father frowned at him, but said, "Because one of the soldiers was captured. Now, at long last, we shall learn everything they have planned."

# Six

The morning mist refused to acknowledge the sunrise. Gray twilight clung to the ground, leaving everything damp and chilled, even though the sun had come up out of the sea more than an hour before.

Bethany's shoulders shifted under her shawl. Once the mist drifted back out to sea, the day would grow warm, but, for now, she needed her shawl's warmth. She stood on the front steps of Whitcombe Hall and watched the people gathered in what had been the inner bailey when the hall had been called a castle. There must be more than three-score villagers and residents of the shire gathered in the courtyard, but it was preternaturally silent.

Although almost a week had passed since the capture of the French soldier, a sensation of disbelief still gripped Fair Cove. Rumors had skulked around the village for months about the possibility of an invasion, but this reality sent waves of fear, as savage as a winter storm tossing the ocean upon the strand, through every resident.

"Have they convinced him to say anything?"

Hearing the question she knew was not directed to her, she turned to see Jay speaking to Eric. "Not that anyone has said," Eric answered. His face was somber as he looked across to the gate, where more people were wandering into the courtyard.

"If he has not revealed anything by now," Bethany said, "it seems there is little reason to believe he will anytime soon."

Eric's eyes narrowed as he walked over to her. Because she stood on the steps, she had to look down to meet his gaze. Her attempt to smile froze into an uncomfortable grimace when he answered, "It is clear that you have never had to endure a single hour in a cell, eager to taste the sweet flavors of freedom again."

"You speak as if you have had the experience of being in prison."

"I speak as a man who has come to like the breeze on his face and the sun highlighting his path." He rubbed his right shoulder and grimaced.

"You are so anxious to get back to your work?"

"Don't think me ungrateful for your family's hospitality, but it is the life I chose."

She smiled, although it took all her strength. It had been almost a month since Eric had saved her from the smugglers. In that time, the smugglers had remained out of sight, sneaking about to do their dirty tasks, and Eric had sneaked into her thoughts. She was no more successful at banishing him from her mind than Father had been at stopping the owls.

Jay leaned toward them. "I hope the authorities do not come to collect that Frog while we are out beating the bounds."

"I had guessed they would be here as soon as word reached them." She frowned. "How long can it take for a message to reach Dover and a detachment to arrive in Fair Cove?"

"Obviously at least this long." Eric chuckled. "I suspect some of the officers have been lured to London to rid themselves of the boredom of being in garrison. If the commander of the garrison is not there, no one may be willing to make a decision."

"About retrieving an enemy prisoner? What can there be to decide? Mayhap they are all witless."

Before Eric could reply, Jay snapped, "I know you despise the idea of me joining the army, Bethany, but you do not need to disparage them like this."

"I was not—" She sighed as he stomped away. Looking at Eric, she sighed again.

"He is young," he said quietly.

"And I fear he will not get older if he becomes a soldier." She put a hand on his arm. "Eric, he respects you. If you were to speak to him of being more sensible, mayhap he would heed you."

He put his hand over hers, out of view of the others. "When a man wants something so much, no one can talk him out of it."

"He is only a boy."

"I know, but I am not only a boy."

She stared down into his eyes as he lifted his hand off hers. His fingers slid beneath her shawl to stroke her arm before gliding up along her shoulder. The morning no longer seemed chilly as she closed her eyes, wanting to relish this pleasure which she craved in her dreams . . . and when she woke.

When he whispered her name, she opened her eyes to find he had climbed the narrow steps to the one just below her. Again she had to look up into his eyes. As his fingers curved down over her shoulder to inch her toward him, the day's mist vanished as she was caught up in the golden light sparkling in his eyes.

Suddenly he stepped away.

"Bethany! Isn't it a grand morning?" Nana waved to her from the pony cart that was rolling to a stop in front of the house.

Bethany glanced at Eric, knowing he must have heard the cart approaching while she had been lost in his spellbinding touch. She wanted to say something, anything, to keep this moment from ending, but as he turned to speak to Jay who bounced up the steps, she knew the magic had already ended.

Again the day was gray and damp and clammy. Wrapping her shawl more tightly around her, she walked down the steps. She realized that more than a dozen of the usual leaders was missing. They must be with Father in his office on the ground floor of the Hall, discussing why the authorities had not come to get the prisoner.

Now that Nana had arrived, the beating of the bounds could begin. In short order, Jay led the way out of the gate, as if he were the baron instead of the younger son.

Bethany lingered behind, hoping to see which group Eric was leaving with. They would not be able to be alone, but she would enjoy the chance to walk through the woods with him.

Tryphena rushed up and gave Bethany a big hug. "It is finished," she said with a wide grin.

"The dress for tonight?"

She nodded. "It is the most perfect gown ever made. I cannot wait to dance in it." Without pausing, she asked, "Where is that peddler I have heard so much about?"

Bethany looked around. Where *was* Eric? He had been here only moments ago. Trying to keep her sigh silent, she guessed he had left while she was greeting Tryphena. "I am sure you will have a chance to see him somewhere along the bounds this morning."

She let her friend's chatter surround her as they walked out the gate and turned toward the shore, where the first marker was set on the very edge of the strand.

The sun began to pierce the mist, jeweling the landscape as if dozens of fairies had sprinkled their dust upon the grass and the stone walls. The markers themselves became dull as the dampness was rubbed away when the children beating the bounds for the first time tried to read the inscriptions. The lettering had almost disappeared beneath the assault of the sea wind and rain through the years. Laughter marked each time a child was remembered at the markers with a swat on the backside or by being held upside down while reciting the landmarks that led to this stone.

What had been a cluster of people at the beginning thinned as the day wore on and the miles wore off determination to walk the full length of the bounds. Some lagged behind, while others rushed ahead to be done quickly so they could get ready for the evening's entertainments at Whitcombe Hall.

Bethany guessed she and Tryphena were somewhere nearer to the leaders than those who had dropped their pace to a stroll, because they matched their steps to the pace of Tryphena's words, which showed no sign of slowing down until she had chanced to mention Titus.

"He did not choose to take part in the beating of the bounds," Bethany said.

"I guessed that when Jay led the way." Tryphena gazed along the path that led steeply up the next hill and toward the wood that sheltered it from the sea.

"He never mentioned anything about not coming." Bethany kicked a pebble ahead of her. "I am sure he will be at the ball tonight."

"Your father would not be pleased if he were not."

She grimaced. "Father will not be pleased that Titus is not here today. He expects all of us to take our duties as seriously as he does his." Glancing at her friend, she said, "I am sorry, Tryphena. I know you hoped to see him today."

"Do not fret on my behalf." Tryphena smiled gently. "It would be worse if Titus pretended to feel something he does not."

"He does not seem to believe that. He scurries away like a guilty child whenever your name is mentioned."

Tryphena stopped by a stone wall that wove an uneven path across the hillside as if it were a piece of thread abandoned by a playful kitten. "He does?"

She nodded. "Did he do something to hurt you?"

"Other than deciding to call on Miss Gillette instead, no. He always has been the epitome of kindness." She took Bethany's hand and squeezed it. "Please stop fretting over this. Titus was kind to give me a look-in as he did. I realize we have long been friends, but I realize, too, that it would have been difficult if it had become more because of the differences in his rank and mine. He is a baron's heir, and I am a minister's daughter."

Bethany ran her hand along the uneven stones of the wall. Glad that most of those beating the bounds were either far ahead or far behind them, she tried to think of something to say to refute Tryphena's words. There was nothing, and, if a minister's daughter and a baron's son were not an acceptable match, how much worse was it that Bethany thought constantly of Eric?

"Oh, dear," Tryphena murmured.

"Oh, dear what?" She did not want her friend guessing the course of her thoughts. Mayhap, for the first time, she understood why Tryphena had not confided in her about the state of her heart. Such emotions were too fragile—and too doomed—to share.

"I have down-pinned you when I know how you enjoy this day."

Bethany squeezed her hand. "I am enjoying this day, and I am glad you are coming to the ball tonight. We shall have a grand time."

"We will, won't we?"

She whirled at the voice that was so much deeper than Tryphena's. Unable to halt the shudders that raced down her back, she forced a smile for Dunley Morelock. Beside her, Tryphena tensed. Her bosom-bow loathed Dunley and made no secret of it.

"I did not know you were joining us for the beating of the bounds," Bethany said when the silence seemed to grow painful. Not even the chirps of the birds and the buzz of insects awakening as the sun grew stronger could ease it.

"It is a skimble-skamble thing." He fingered the lapels of his coat, and his nose wrinkled as he brushed away some leaves and twigs from its fine blue wool.

"Speak plainly," Tryphena urged. "We use simple words here, not the silly language of Town."

He scowled at her, but Tryphena did not look away. Why should she fear him? He would not deign to marry a mere minister's daughter, for he had bragged to everyone—so Bethany had heard—that he would gain more prestige for the Morelock family by marrying well. Bethany wished he would take himself to Town. He was a well-favored man with a fair fortune coming his way. Some woman there might be eager enough, especially at this late point in the Season, to buckle herself to him. Then he would be out of her life, and she could . . . Bethany was not sure what she wanted to do.

Yes, she was. She wanted to be with Eric, where they would not be interrupted, so that she might know—just once—what it was like to be in his strong arms as he kissed her.

"Bethany!" Dunley's irritatingly impatient voice tore into her fantasy, shredding it.

"Yes?"

He recoiled from her sharp tone, and Tryphena put

her hand to her lips to conceal a giggle. Dunley included Tryphena in his scowl as he said, "You do not need to snap at me like an old tough."

"If you continue to speak with the Town polish, Dunley," Tryphena interjected, "no one beating the bounds will be able to understand you."

"Anyone with a bit of wit about them shall."

"I stand corrected." She linked her arm through Bethany's. "Mayhap you and I should go to London next Season."

"The pair of us in Town for the Season?" She laughed. "I daresay one of us would make a *faux pas* before the first hour had passed."

"But what wondrous matches we would make." Tryphena flung out her hand, nearly striking Dunley who backed away hastily. "I think a marquess for you and an earl for me. We would not have to settle for the title of anything less than lady."

"Must you always prattle endlessly like this?" Dunley demanded.

"Not always."

Dunley again stared at Tryphena. When she did not continue along the narrow path, he scowled. Bethany almost laughed when her bosom-bow frowned back. She thought that Dunley would have learned years ago that he could not intimidate Tryphena Sullivan. They had all grown up together, and Tryphena knew him for the dastardly bully that he was.

Ignoring their previous conversation, Dunley said to Bethany, "Of course, I came to the beating of the bounds. It is important that the *ton* recall their duties."

"The *ton?*" Tryphena laughed. "Are you about to journey to London for a Season, Dunley? Mayhap you can find a destitute duke's daughter who is desperate to marry you."

"I do not need to go to London to find a bride."

Bethany swallowed her sigh, while Tryphena fired her an apologetic smile. Trying again to smile, she said, "I did not see you at Whitcombe Hall."

"I got a bit of a late start. I cut across the fields to catch up with you."

"You needn't have bothered."

" 'Twas no bother. I wanted to be certain that I could spend today with you."

"Why?"

"Because it is a day we both shall want to remember the rest of our lives."

Bethany exchanged another glance with her friend. Tryphena's eyes were wide with a dismay that echoed the feeling that raced through Bethany. "Why?" she asked again.

"Because tonight, when you and I are dancing together and being toasted, we—"

His name was shouted again from the top of the hill. A man was gesturing to him. When Bethany squinted and put her hand to her forehead to shade her eyes, she still was unsure who stood up there. She could not imagine who wanted to see Dunley, but she was grateful that he was called away. Nodding in response to his mumbled excuse, she released the sigh she had been holding.

"How do you bear him?" Tryphena asked.

Bethany stared at the friend whose words echoed so closely the question Eric had asked her the day after he had arrived at Whitcombe Hall. Her answer was the same. "Because I must."

"Your father is a reasonable man. I cannot believe that, if you ask him to reconsider, he would force you to marry that uncouth cur."

She smiled. "You are quite blunt about your opinions of him."

"As you should be. Lord Whitcombe should not be considering a match for you with Dunley."

"I don't think he is any longer."

"No? Papa told me that Sir Asa came to speak to him about officiating at the ceremony."

"What?" She dropped to sit on the wall.

"Oh, mayhap I should not have said anything."

Bethany shook her head. "No, 'tis all right. I would have learned about this sooner or later."

"I thought you understood that was what that dolt Dunley was babbling about."

"Babbling about?" Coldness surrounded her in a cloud of horror. "He thinks we are going to be toasted tonight, when our betrothal is announced." She rose. "Excuse me, Tryphena. I have to return to Whitcombe Hall and speak with Father posthaste."

"Do you want me to go with you?"

She started to say yes, then shook her head. "If Dunley sees you, he may not guess that I have skipped the rest of the beating of the bounds. Then he won't come looking for me."

"I will make sure he sees me at the crest of every hill and just before I turn every corner."

Bethany gave her a quick hug. "Thank you so much."

"Good luck. I'll be praying that your father will heed your pleas."

"I will, too." Gathering up her gown to an unseemly height, Bethany climbed over the wall.

She waved to Tryphena before hurrying across the field. Glad for her high-lows, because shoes would have been ruined in the still-damp grass, she breathed a sigh of relief when she reached the trees on the far side of the field. Now there was no chance that Dunley would see her.

She held her dress close to keep it from being

snatched by the briars growing under the trees. This must be Mr. Griffen's copse. He did little to maintain his land, preferring to spend his time at the inn near Mr. Cartman's warehouse.

Her heart slowed its frantic pounding as she rushed through the wood. The shadows were like furtive breaths of cold air, but she shrugged them off. Nothing could be icier than her heart at the thought of marrying Dunley Morelock.

Suddenly, Bethany's hand was grasped. With a cry, she tried to pull away. She could not let Dunley find her here alone. She was not sure what he would do in his determination to force her to be his bride.

A familiar laugh halted her panic. She looked up into Eric's sparkling eyes. When he motioned for her to continue among the trees with him, she smiled.

He did not release her hand, and she did not draw it away. Sometime in the last week, she had accepted the fact she was as much of an air-dreamer as Jay, but, for this moment, when the mist still jeweled the tops of the trees, she wanted to delight in this simple, but forbidden, pleasure of his fingers enclosing hers.

Eric smiled when she knelt to look at some small, yellow blossoms peeking from beneath last autumn's fallen leaves. He squatted next to her. "Is this why you came into the woods, Bethany? To admire the flowers?" He held out his hand.

"Did you consider that I simply wanted to catch my breath after the long walk?"

"I can understand that, for you make me catch my breath."

She stared at his hand, but did not put her fingers on it as she rose. Tryphena's commonsensical comments echoed through her head. Why was it so easy to accept that there could be nothing between them when he was not nearby? Standing close to him like this, she forgot the obligations of rank. All she wanted was to hear his laugh and discover the flavor of his lips.

He picked one of the blossoms. As he stood, he handed it to her. She placed the flower in the band of her bonnet.

"Thank you," she whispered.

"I did the flower no favor."

"By plucking it?"

"By letting you place it so close to your face, for its beauty dims."

Even though she wanted to linger, she said, "Thank you for the flower and the compliment, Eric."

"But?"

"But I must hurry back to Whitcombe Hall."

"Is that where you are hying to like a frightened rabbit seeking its hole in a hedgerow? When I saw you at a near run across the field—"

"Did anyone else see me?"

He frowned. "Are you skulking away from someone?" He held up his hands. "No, let me guess. Did you encounter the inimitable Dunley Morelock?"

Bethany wanted to pour out the truth to him, but she was afraid of what else might flow from her heart when she opened it to reveal her terror at the idea of marrying a man she knew she could never love. "Eric, you still ask far too many questions."

"And you still seldom answer any of them." He chuckled as he looked around. "I will know these woods intimately by the time we are done with this tramp through them."

"You are in excellent spirits," she said, startled by how easily he accepted that she no longer wished to speak about the previous subject.

"Why not? The sun is out, and so am I." His fingers rose to brush a strand of her hair back under her bonnet. "And I am here with a lovely lady who makes me forget how many miles we will be walking in a circle today."

Edging away a step before she gave in to the temptation to move closer to him, she walked toward an abandoned stone wall that was nearly as tall as her shoulder. It was pitted from rain and wind.

"Now where will you run to, Bethany?" he asked from behind her.

She glanced back at him, then turned to her left. If she recalled correctly, this wall did not run far in this direction. Some said it had been raised to keep ancient raiders out of a castle that had otherwise disappeared from the downs. Others whispered that the ancients had built it to hold in the dark gods who lived in the forest. She did not believe either. She suspected it was the forgotten curtain wall that once had been part of the larger defenses of Whitcombe Hall.

When she reached its end, she stared at an impenetrable barricade of briars that reached almost as high as the wall. She did not remember this from the last time she had been through this greenwood; then she realized that the last time had been more than five years ago. With Mr. Griffen's neglect of his land, the thickets were reclaiming it.

"Shall you storm back in the other direction or plow straight through?" Eric leaned against the stone wall and smiled at her.

"I have not yet decided."

"Your errand must be one of great urgency if you are even considering going through that." He fingered the fabric of her sleeve. "You shall quite ruin this pretty pink gown."

"As you have your shoes?" She pointed at his footwear which was marked by drying salt stains. "Did you walk out into the sea to begin the beating of the bounds?"

"Jay told me there is a legend that the first marker is now hidden beneath the waves a few feet offshore."

She laughed. "So you are the one they convinced this year to wade out and look for a marker that never existed?"

"I did not go far. Your younger brother is not adept at keeping a somber expression while playing a prank."

"If you were with him, you should be miles from here by now."

"I thought to see how you were faring, Bethany."

"I am doing fine." She started to walk back along the wall, but he stepped in front of her, blocking her way. "Eric, I have no time for this."

"For someone who avers that she is doing well, you seem to be frightfully perturbed." He laughed again and backed her toward the wall. When she gasped as she bumped into it, he said, "You must not be thinking clearly if you do not have time for this." His fingers brushed her cheek.

She gasped again, this time in delight at the sweetness flowing through her. She found herself gazing up into his eyes, captured like a rabbit by a sly fox. Her eyes closed as she leaned toward him, longing to know the fiery power of the passion ablaze in his eyes. When he did not lower his mouth to hers, her hands paused as she was lifting them to be wrapped around his shoulders.

"Is something wrong?" she whispered. *Yes!* She could not rid herself of this longing she must ignore.

Instead of replying, he took her shoulders and pressed her against the wall. She stared at him, astonished at his rough action. He had always treated her with gentleness. Not like Dunley, who had no patience with her questions.

Lightning seared her when his gaze explored her face with tender yearning. When his hands caressed her shoulders, outlining their curves with warmth, she started to pull away. But his hands tightened.

"No!" she cried.

"No?" he repeated with an arching of his eyebrows. His expression bespoke his disbelief louder than the single word.

"I promised Father to—"

"To recall how you should behave, and you have been behaving quite well, serving his interests well, as a daughter should, in the beating of the bounds." He gave her a wry grin. "*I* promised not to attempt to kiss you."

"But—"

"So I shall not attempt it. I shall do it."

He swept her up against him as he captured her lips. All her fantasies of this moment vanished, weak shadows compared to this glory. The tip of his tongue brushed her lips, sending quivers of sensation to the very tips of her toes.

As close as they were standing, she was unsure if the shivers were only hers or if his desire was as uncontrollable. She should push him away, but she slid her hands along the strong muscles of his arms.

He enfolded her to him as his lips found hers again. Everything she wanted was in his kiss, for it offered her as much rapture as it demanded. His fingers stroked her back, sending tingles twisting along her spine. As her hand curved along his nape, his thick hair caressed it.

Eric sighed when Bethany suddenly pushed herself out of his arms. An expression of alarm stole the last glitter of delight from her eyes, which closed again when he bent to kiss her cheek. Her fingers clenched at her sides, warning him of how hard she was fighting her craving—*their* craving. How he would love to wrap himself around this sensual woman, but to do so would bring her more sorrow. He could not forget that he soon would be leaving Fair Cove.

Today had proven to him that he must go soon. He had managed to keep up with the others on the beating of the bounds, and he had taken note of several places he must revisit soon. His wagon was fixed, and his wares awaited his finding a buyer for them as he continued on his journey through Kent. The message to Cartman was not the only one he had to deliver, so he should not linger a day longer.

Yet . . . He grasped Bethany's arms and tugged her to his chest again. Her soft breasts brushed against him with her swift breaths as he recaptured her lips. Boldly, hungering for her every intriguing flavor, his tongue probed her mouth. Her fingers gripped his sleeves, then slipped up through his hair. He teased her tongue to caress his, and she swayed against him, offering him an invitation to the rapture that would not be interrupted in this green bower.

When her breath grew ragged, he released her reluctantly. He was unsure how much longer he could kiss her before his restraint, which had never been tested like this, failed. He resisted looking into her eyes, but that was a mistake, for he found himself staring at her kiss-softened lips. The anguished need to give in to this craving was nearly intolerable.

He stepped back a single step, then another. Pointing to the right, he said, "I would suggest that, if you are determined to get to Whitcombe Hall, you go that way, Bethany. It will lead you away from where I saw Dunley Morelock stopping every group of walkers to demand if they had seen you."

"Eric . . . ?" She touched his cheek in the lightest caress.

He was not sure he had the strength to step away again, but he did. He would be gone soon. He could not make a jumble of her life by surrendering to this ecstasy. Without another word, he turned and walked away.

Nothing in his life would ever be so difficult.

Except leaving her for good.

# Seven

The ballroom shimmered with candlelight. Eric knew a peddler was as out of place here as a cyprian taking tea with her lover's wife. The baron's guests, each of them dressed with an elegance that made his road-worn clothes look even more threadbare, glanced at him with curiosity as he walked through the magnificent room which sparkled with crystal and gilt.

He took a glass of some tepid lemonade, wishing that Whitcombe would relent on this one thing about the smugglers and serve a decent glass of champagne tonight. Listening to the conversation sifting through the music, he took note of every word, but heard nothing unusual. Somehow, he had forgotten, for which he was grateful, how much time people could spend talking about nothing.

He was on the far side of the ballroom when he heard a familiar laugh from near the doorway. It was not loud or high-pitched, but it cut through the conversation to pierce his thoughts.

Edging around the floor on which no one was dancing, as all waited for their host to lead off the first dance, he stared, unable to halt himself. In the weeks he had been here, he had thought he had admired Bethany's ebony hair and slender features from every possible angle and had become accustomed to her fairy-like prettiness. Today, near the old stone wall, he had touched the lilt of her cheekbones and sampled the medley of delights on her lips. Mayhap there had been no music then, but he had heard it as surely as he did now.

He was sadly mistaken to think he could find nothing new about her to draw his attention, for when he saw her in a white gown with ribbons only a shade darker than the midday sky drawing his gaze to her alluring curves, it was as if he were seeing her for the first time. When she laughed again as she spoke with her father, the sound went right to his heart to swirl about him like the sweetest melody.

Something must have alerted her to his stare. Could it be that she was no more unaware of him than he was of her? What should have been a stolen kiss to ease their curiosity had instead drawn them even closer together.

As her head turned toward him, he would have sworn someone had crept up behind him and forced the very breath out of him. He could barely think as he was enveloped in her soft gaze. The thought that filtered into his mind was of watching those eyes close as she offered her lips to him. How much more he wanted now!

Her father must have spoken to her, because she flinched and looked back at the baron.

Eric sucked in a deep breath, wondering how long it had been since he last had remembered to breathe. His feet wanted to send him lurching toward her, but he turned and walked toward the back of the grand room. When his name was called, he struggled to smile.

"Good evening, my lady," he said, bowing over Lady Whitcombe's hand which was stuck nearly into his face. He wondered how close he had come, while lost in his thoughts, to walking right over her. "You look lovely this evening."

She pulled her silvery shawl more tightly over her dark gown. "Don't waste your flummery on me, young man, when it is quite clear by your expression that you have on your mind someone else, much younger and more attractive to a lad like you, I would think. Are you ready to dance?"

"After this day's exercise, I am more fatigued than anything else."

"Why are you lathering me with this falsehood?" Her face fell into a frown. "I thought you a better man than that."

He should have known better than to engage the dowager baroness in a battle of words when his thoughts were so scattered. "I am a man who is not where he belongs."

"You do look like a shab-rag among these fine peacocks." She tapped his arm with her befeathered fan. "You are excused while you change into something more appropriate."

"This is the best I have, my lady."

Her nose wrinkled as she stared at his rumpled shirt and waistcoat and breeches, all of which showed the wear from his journey about the bounds. "We must rectify that with all due haste."

"Why?"

"You cannot appear at functions at Whitcombe Hall looking like a petitioner."

He smiled. "My lady, despite the kindness offered by you, your son, and his family, I must remind you that I am a petitioner here."

"You are a *guest* here, and no guest of mine appears at the beating-of-the-bounds ball dressed like a laborer."

"I stand corrected." He bowed to her again.

"And?"

Not certain as to what she wanted him to say, he asked, "And, my lady?"

"You are not without some graces, young man. I thought you would recognize when a lady wishes to dance."

"Would you do me the honor, my lady?" he asked, resisting his inclination to look over at Bethany to discover if *she* would be interested in partnering with him on the dance floor. With her, he would not be interested in dancing a country reel, but a waltz, which he knew would be considered scandalous here in daisyville.

"I thought you would never ask." Lady Whitcombe tapped his arm again with her fan as she slipped a hand through his arm.

Even though she had lambasted him for his low attire, Lady Whitcombe's stance as they walked together to the middle of the room dared anyone to so much as whisper about her escort. The rest of her family, save for young Jay, were waiting for them.

He was astonished to see Bethany partnered by her father, then realized he had not seen Morelock arrive. "Where is Bethany's eager *beau*?"

"If you speak of Dunley, he will not be joining us tonight," Lady Whitcombe said. "He apparently had the misfortune to walk through some sort of greenery today that caused him to develop the most excruciating rash."

Eric laughed, but Lady Whitcombe slapped him again on the arm with her fan.

"It is not right that one man should laugh at another's misfortune." Her lips twitched. "Or for one's *faux pas* that leads one into making another."

"I shall endeavor, my lady, not to lead you into less than exemplary behavior."

"I believe I have learned enough over the years to find my way on my own." She turned to greet Titus and his partner.

The rather round brunette facing Titus must be Miss Gillette, Eric decided. No one had a chance to introduce him to her, as the orchestra began to play the music for the first dance.

Quickly he discovered that the pattern of the dance was a parody of their lives. Each time he neared Bethany and it seemed he was about to take her hand as he swirled her through the next steps, others came between them, sending them apart once more. He was careful to keep a smile on his face, because Lady Whitcombe was not the only one watching him closely.

When the dance ended, he edged back as Jay offered to stand up with his grandmother. No one spoke to him while he made his way through the crowd and out onto the terrace.

The fresh air was almost as intoxicating as Bethany's kisses. With a curse, he sat on a bench at the far end of the terrace. He gazed up at a moon that was draped with the last wisps of the lingering mist. How many nights had he spent outside or in some rough byre staring up at this moon and watching the stars pop out in the vast arc of the sky? How many more would he do that?

"I thought you might like this."

His head jerked up at Bethany's voice. His smile became ironic when he saw the glass she held out. If he were to drink, he would prefer it be of her lips, not this overly sweet lemonade.

Standing, he took the glass and sipped. His eyes widened. "That is a fine burgundy."

"You know that Father keeps a few bottles deep in the cellar and brings them out for special occasions."

"Such as the announcement of his daughter's betrothal."

She smiled. "Mayhap, but that will not be announced tonight."

"Your grandmother mentioned Morelock's malady."

"He should know better than to wander about, not watching where he is going."

"His thoughts may all have been of you."

Her smile vanished. "Don't even jest about such things."

"Shall we speak of other things then?" He took another appreciative sip.

"Yes. Are you enjoying yourself?"

"It shall be a long time before I again have the opportunity to attend a ball at a baron's country seat." He smiled as he leaned back against the stone railing at the edge of the terrace. "I must own to being surprised that these folks have so much energy for dancing after spending the day beating the bounds."

"Few of them walked the whole distance as you did."

"And you."

"I did not go the full distance."

"Close enough."

She nodded. "Which is one of the reasons I have come out here, so my yawns would not seem so rude."

"One of the reasons?" He took her hand and drew her closer. When his fingers curved along her cheek, he whispered, "What is the other reason?"

"I've told you over and over, you ask too many questions, Eric." Her voice softened as his hand drifted along her neck to linger on her shoulder.

"Do I?"

Her laugh vanished beneath his mouth as he pulled her into his arms. He had tried to persuade himself that this intoxicating pleasure had been only his imagination, honed by arms that had been empty too long. He had been wrong. As his mouth coursed along her neck, she trembled. Her soft gasp of his name caressed his ear and ricocheted within him, setting his every nerve afire.

Her shriek turned that pleasure to agony. Pulling back, he scowled as Titus grasped Bethany's arm and tugged her away.

"Bethany!" Titus snarled. "Did you take a knock in the cradle? What if Dunley learned of this?"

Bethany shook off his hand. Mayhap she *had* taken a knock in the cradle, but she did not care a rap what Dunley Morelock thought. She was about to say that, then saw a shadowed form in the doorway to the ballroom. Deborah Gillette! The young woman had earned a reputation as the worst prattle-box in the shire.

"Titus, I think it would be for the best if we were to discuss this at another time." She glanced past him, and he looked over his shoulder.

Instead of the smile Bethany had expected when he realized Deborah was waiting anxiously for him, a frown flitted across her brother's face. "Mayhap you are right." His voice lowered. "I trust you will refrain from such behavior until we have a chance to speak of this."

"Titus, you are not my father."

"If Father would—" He clamped his lips closed.

"If Father would what?"

"Another time." He turned and strode back to Miss Gillette.

"Now that's most peculiar," Eric said quietly.

Bethany agreed as she watched her brother motion for Miss Gillette to join them on the terrace. She had thought he would offer his arm, as would be befitting a gentleman who had been calling so regularly on a young woman. Instead, he treated her with the polite indifference of a brother.

"If I didn't know better," Eric continued, amusement creeping into his voice, "I would say that the Whitcombe blood runs cold."

She was glad the shadows hid the blush that must match the heat on her cheeks. Father had warned her to guard her behavior with Eric. She should have heeded him, but instead had let her longings bring her into his arms again.

Before she had a chance to greet Miss Gillette, Jay burst out of the darkness, skidding to a halt. He almost tripped over an uneven stone, but Eric caught him before he could fall face-first onto the terrace.

Bethany put a hand on Eric's arm as he grimaced. He shook it off and massaged his right shoulder.

"Sorry," he murmured. "Blasted arm."

She understood what he could not say in the other's hearing. His weak shoulder frustrated him.

"You should not be running about like that." Miss Gillette spoke the scold as if she were Jay's sister. "Why, I heard just the other day that Mrs. Caldecott rose from her sickbed and—"

Firing Miss Gillette a fearsome scowl, Jay interjected, "Bethany! Oh, good! Titus, you and Eric are here, too." He panted as he straightened his coat. "You will not believe what I just heard."

"The French have agreed to peace?" asked Titus eagerly.

"Peace!" Miss Gillette gasped. "Wouldn't it be wonderful to have peace? I vow I cannot recall the last time anyone spoke of anything but that war and the need to put an end to it. If people would just have good sense and—"

Titus's hand on her arm silenced her as he asked again, "Have the French agreed to peace?"

Jay gave him a withering frown. "You might as well have guessed that the sun was just seen rising on the moon. The French prisoner has escaped."

"What!" Bethany exclaimed.

"You heard me. He is gone."

Miss Gillette murmured, "Oh, dear. Oh, dear."

"How did it happen?" Bethany asked.

He shrugged. "No one seems to know. Mr. Cartman was guarding him today, and he said nothing seemed amiss. The prisoner apparently made no sound all afternoon, but he rarely said much in English."

"Oh, dear," Miss Gillette said again.

She looked at Eric, who was showing an odd lack of curiosity.

He stood and wiped his hands, which had been resting on the stone wall. "Mayhap Mr. Cartman fell asleep," Eric said, looking in the direction of Fair Cove, "and the prisoner took advantage of that."

"Oh, dear," Miss Gillette continued.

Again Jay shrugged, but his mouth was set in a straight line. "It's possible. That accursed Frog bunched some pillows on his cot to make it look as if he were asleep. Now he has run back to his comrades, and he will be able to tell them how poorly prepared we are."

"His comrades?" Eric lost his nonchalance. "What makes you think his comrades are still nearby?"

"Oh, dear. Oh, dear." Miss Gillette's voice was rising to near hysteria.

Jay ignored her dismay. "If they aren't nearby to rescue him, he must be looking for a place to hide. I need to tell Father that, so he can have the outbuildings secured. If—"

A roar of voices came from the ballroom. Bethany

looked past her brothers to see that the dancing had halted. The women still stood in the middle of the floor, but the men had come together to huddle in anxious conversation. Word of the escape must have reached the dancers. The orchestra might as well put away their instruments. No one would return to dancing tonight.

Jay rushed inside, not wanting to miss any of the excitement.

Titus started to follow with Miss Gillette in tow, still bemoaning her apprehension, then turned and glanced at Bethany. He did not speak, but there was no need.

"I bid you good evening, Bethany," Eric said when she hesitated.

Taking her hand, he bowed over it as gracefully as any of the gentleman in the ballroom, again bringing forth the questions she wished would remain silent in her head. Who was Eric Pennington? No peddler she had ever encountered had had manners so polished or had possessed such an obvious level of education. He might be a peddler now, but she doubted he had been born to that life.

What had he done that had been so heinous that he was banished from the Polite World?

# Eight

"Miss Bethany?"

At her abigail's voice, Bethany looked up from the novel she had just started. Vella stood in the bedroom doorway, no smile on her wrinkled face. Before Vella had become her maid, she had worked in the nursery. Bethany could no more imagine Whitcombe Hall without Vella than without the sea wind surging through its open windows.

"Can whatever it is wait a few minutes?" She had been intrigued with this story since the first sentence, and she was only a page from the end of the fourth chapter.

"No, it cannot!"

Bethany closed the book when she heard Nana's voice from behind Vella. It was clear she would not reach the end of the chapter now. She recognized that tone. Nana had something she considered very important on her mind.

She stood. Motioning for Nana to come in, she bit her lip when Nana dismissed Vella. What had happened now?

"Did they recapture the French prisoner?" she asked.

Nana scowled, then said, "I have no idea, but I thought you should know that *he* is leaving."

"He is leaving?" She pressed her hand over her heart. "Jay?"

Nana frowned. "Don't be absurd, child. Warren will not go off to join the army while there is breath between my old bones."

"But you said—"

"I said *he* is leaving. Eric."

"Leaving?" Bethany whispered. Beneath her fingers, she was certain her heart had ceased to beat.

"Tomorrow."

She slowly closed the book and stared down at the gold leaf on its red leather spine. As her knees folded beneath her, she sat again on the chair. From the beginning, she had known that Eric's sojourn at Whitcombe Hall would be only temporary, but that did not ease the grief tightening around her heart.

"Why are you sitting here?" Nana asked.

She looked up.

"The least you can do is make sure he has some food and supplies for the next leg of his journey."

Nodding, Bethany stood. What had she thought her grandmother would say? That she should not waste a second of the few hours she had left with Eric?

"Cook has some packets for him in the kitchen," Nana continued. "You should be certain that he receives them."

"That sounds like a good idea."

" 'Tis an excellent idea, because it is mine." Nana smiled. "Go, child."

"Yes."

"And, child?" Nana's smile broadened. "I would stay far from your father's office. He has a caller."

"I never intrude on Father's business."

"A most disagreeable caller."

Bethany nodded. Nana must mean either Dunley

Morelock or his father. She was not certain which one her grandmother despised more.

She walked to the door, then ran back and hugged her grandmother before hurrying down the stairs. She did not bother to go into the kitchen. There would be time enough—later—to worry about packing food for Eric.

She realized how much she had hoped Nana had misunderstood as she rushed across the garden and then slowed to stare at Eric, who was testing the brake on his wagon, looking under it to be certain it was now working. How skimble-skamble could she be? Nana was never confused about anything. She saw everything with a clarity that Bethany envied.

Eric looked up as she walked across the surprisingly empty stableyard. "Bethany, didn't I hear you say that you were going to finish your book this afternoon?"

"I was reading it until I heard what you were doing."

"Nothing stays secret long in Whitcombe Hall, does it?"

"You intended your leave-taking to be a secret? Why?"

He smiled, but his eyes remained serious. "I didn't intend that. Just a manner of speaking, and not a very good one, if I am to judge by your expression."

"You said nothing of this last night."

"No." He kicked a stone under the wheel so that there was no chance the wagon would roll. "I had other things on my mind last night."

She looked away from his beguiling smile. Mayhap Nana had sent her out here so that she had to face her own unthinking choices. Once again, she had not considered the consequences of listening to her heart instead of common sense. She had been a widgeon to let him steal a few kisses, but she feared he could easily steal more than that. He could steal her heart as well.

"You would be wise," she said, "to announce yourself loudly wherever you go. You do not want to be mistaken for that French prisoner."

"That is unlikely, when I have blond hair and he has dark."

"How do you know that?"

He laughed. "You live so close to the French, and you know so little of them. Most Frenchmen have hair even darker than yours."

"I don't want to know them. I want to know why you did not tell me you were leaving."

"I wasn't sure last night. Your father's men got my wagon's brake put back together just this morning." He patted the side of the wagon. "It is better than new."

"Did you plan to tell me before you left?"

"I was still trying to decide how."

"How about with the truth?"

He frowned. "The truth?"

"Why must you always answer a question with a question?" She slapped the top of the wagon.

When she heard a gentle thump, she stared at a small door that had popped open in the side of the wagon. She saw only a flash of steel and some green wool wrapped around some papers before Eric slapped it closed.

He bent forward so his ice blue eyes froze her half-voiced protests. "Don't ever touch this again," he ordered in a low voice.

"There's a—"

"I know what's in there!"

Refusing to be intimidated, she demanded, "Why do you have a gun hidden in there?"

"Don't ask about things that are none of your business."

Bethany recoiled from his sharp words. "None of

my business? You are hiding only God knows what in there, and you tell me it is none of my business? This is my home. Father should know if you are in trouble—"

"I am not in any trouble," he declared as he laughed tautly. "Save with you. Forgive me, Bethany. The pistol is to make sure no one steals from my wagon. The other things are items I promised to deliver to a village not too far from here. That will be my first stop."

"When are you leaving?" She glanced at the wagon. His explanation was reasonable, but his reaction had not been. This must have to do with the secret he had never divulged. She wished she could figure out what it was.

"Once I am sure the brake will hold the wagon, I can be on my way. It will be good for me to get back to my own life."

A deep voice said, "Tomorrow should be a good day to begin your journey."

Bethany started to greet Dunley, but Eric's laugh halted her. Eric said, "You look better than I had guessed you would. Those spots must be pretty uncomfortable. Do they itch?"

Dunley ignored him, turning instead to Bethany. "I have been speaking with your father, and I do not have time to linger here listening to a babbling *traveling merchant.*" He smiled coolly. "I would appreciate your walking with me to my carriage."

When she hesitated, Eric said, "Go along, Bethany, while I finish loading my wagon. I am nearly done, and I told Jay I would join him for something cool to drink when I was finished. I will see you back in the house."

Taking her arm, Dunley shoved her ahead of him toward the garden. He grumbled, "You let him give you orders as if you are the peddler and he is of the *ton?*"

She did not answer his question. To speak of how she was hurt by Eric sending her away when they had such a short time to spend together would make the situation worse. Dunley did not want to hear how she was weeping inside at the idea of Eric's leaving. So instead of the truth, she spoke of the weather, of the search for the escaped French prisoner, of the recent bountiful catch brought in by Fair Cove's fishermen.

Yet, even as she prattled, keeping the width of the garden path between them, her thoughts were filled with Eric's voice. Over and over, like an endless echo, she could hear him talking about readying the wagon to leave. She guessed that Dunley must know that as well, for he was silent.

They were halfway across the garden, separated from the house by the copse at the edge of the water garden, when she halted in midword as his arm clamped around her waist. She almost shrieked when she was whirled against him.

"Don't, Dunley." She stepped away. When she saw his face grow taut with fury, she backed even farther away.

"You're mine!"

"Yours? We are not betrothed."

"We should be." He reached for her again.

As she spun about to return to the house, he caught her and forced her into his arms again. His lips claimed hers, and she screamed out her denial, but the sound vanished into his mouth.

She could not believe what he was doing when he pushed her toward the ground. She was not a lightskirt to be treated like this! She fought him, but he bore down on her until her knees buckled beneath her.

Leaning over her, he laughed. "Save your strength. If you scream until you are weak, you won't give me as much pleasure."

"I have no interest in—"

"You acted interested with Pennington!"

Although Bethany wanted to fight him, she told herself to be calm. Dunley was furious, and she must take care that she did not rouse his temper, for it was clearly as vicious as his father's. "Dunley, you are mistaken. Think what you are doing. Let me up."

"I am thinking about what I am doing. Finally, I am. I will let you up as soon as you prove to me that I am your first lover."

"Are you mad?" she gasped, staring at him as if she had never seen him. Why had she let Titus persuade Father to consider Dunley's suit? She should have listened to her own heart which had warned her that he was a beast. "Stop!"

"You won't tell me that when we are wed." He laughed again. "Pa says you will take a little training, but you shall learn."

"Not from you!" She pushed him away. Scrambling to her feet, she glowered at him when he caught her arm again. "Shall we see what *my* father has to say about your despicable behavior?"

"And what of yours? Was your walk in the woods with Pennington during the beating of the bounds a part of your usual *rendez-vous* far from your family's eyes?"

She wanted to ask him who had seen Eric follow her into the wood as she returned to Whitcombe Hall, but she knew it was wiser to relent now. Even to ask a single question could be dangerous. "I shall tell Father that I cannot marry you."

"Cannot? Why not?"

"Dunley—"

His fingers dug into her arm. "Tell me, Bethany."

"Dunley, you must listen to me!"

"Name him! I shall rip him apart before your eyes so you can see what happens to the man who dares to cuckold me!"

"No! Dunley, there is—"

His lips clamped over hers painfully. Trying to turn from him was impossible. His mouth slid across her cheek as his hands moved up from her waist.

She had to escape this. She must. She would be ill if it continued. *Eric, why did you let me go with him?*

"Eric? Eric Pennington? I should have guessed! You were with him in the wood."

Bethany pulled back as she heard triumph in Dunley's voice. Had she spoken her thoughts aloud? Faith, she had not realized . . . Seeing his smile become a scowl, she said, "Dunley, no! Eric is not my lover. I was—"

"Be silent, whore!" Taking her arm again, he steered her toward the house.

In horror, she understood what he intended to do. "Dunley, no!" She gasped again. Either he did not hear her, or he chose to ignore her. He shoved her ahead of him into the parlor where her father and brothers sat . . . and Eric!

Her father came to his feet, frowning. Only now did Bethany realize that her dress was marked with grass stains and twigs. Her hair had fallen around her shoulders in disarray. When she looked past him to Eric, she knew, from the fury boiling in his eyes' depths, that there was no way to avoid disaster. She wished Nana were with them. Even though her grandmother could create all kinds of mayhem with her outspoken ways, she now would demand that everyone think before jumping to conclusions.

"What happened to you, Bethany?" Jay asked, staring at her in disbelief.

Dunley gave her no chance to answer. He roared, "Pennington, I want to speak with you now!"

"Then speak with me, Morelock," Eric said calmly as he came to his feet. "What do you want to say to me before I tell you what I have to say to you?"

"I return your whore to you." He shoved Bethany forward so hard that she dropped to her knees in front of her father. Morelock's caustic smile was turned upon Father. "Did you tell her that she should be proud to have taken a lover? You must have thought me a sap-skull to have her bastard foisted off on me."

"My daughter is no harlot." Helping Bethany to her feet, her father added, "I suggest you go home immediately, Dunley, and rethink your insults. Mayhap then Bethany will accept your apology."

Morelock bellowed like a mindless bull. "My apology? Why should I apologize to her when she is a whore?"

"Dunley Morelock, I have warned you once not to speak of my daughter so," Father said in a rigid voice. Jay was getting himself on his feet. Only Titus remained sitting. "Get out!"

"Not until you hear her speak of her shame with her own lips." Dunley ripped Bethany from her father's embrace. "I want you all to hear why *I* have decided I do not want to marry her." With a curse, he thrust Bethany toward where Eric watched in silence. "Tell them, Bethany, how you owned to pleasuring Pennington."

"Eric?" Titus choked out the word, in disbelief.

If someone else spoke, Bethany did not hear. She did not breathe. Only her eyes moved as she met Eric's sapphire gaze. It took every bit of her courage not to lower her eyes, for she feared seeing his fury at being dragged into a battle which was not his.

When he stepped toward her, his footsteps loud in the silent room, he took her hand as a hint of a smile eased his lips' uncompromising line. His other hand curved along her cheek. Softly, so softly no one else could hear, he whispered, "What did he do to you to force my name from your lips?"

"Please don't ask."

He drew a strand of her hair forward. "I need not, for the sight of you so obviously disheveled would persuade any man with a bit of a brain in his head to realize you did not speak of your own volition the words that would ruin both of us."

Both of them? Oh, dear, she had not guessed, in the midst of her fear and anger and need to escape, how her unthinking words could damage Eric, too. If rumors spread that he had seduced the daughter of his host, few doors would open to him and fewer would be interested in purchasing what they would now deem his tainted wares. She gasped, "Eric, don't lie! Tell them . . ."

"That, mayhap, Pennington didn't understand what he was doing?" Dunley chortled and slapped his thigh.

Eric looked past her as he put an arm around her shoulders and stood beside her. "I realized exactly what I was doing." He ran his hand along her cheek in a motion that was so tender, tears flooded her eyes. "Bethany's beauty beguiled me until I was insane with desire for her."

"Eric, no!" she cried out as his words cut through the haze of her distress. A flush climbed her ashen cheeks. Was he out of his mind? To give the lie even the least credence would destroy him.

"Hush, sweetheart. It is too late to deny what happened."

In a choked voice, her father asked, "Eric, are you owning that you seduced my daughter?"

He smiled. "You don't think Bethany seduced me, do you?"

"Eric, please—"

He silenced her by turning her into his arms. She wanted so to put her head against his chest and beg his forgiveness for this bumble-bath. Then he could tilt her head back and delight her with his lips over hers. Then . . .

She was pulled away, and she raised her fist to make sure Dunley did not hurt her—or Eric—again. Her eyes widened as she discovered that it was her father who held her. Slowly she lowered her hand to her side.

Her father did not look at her as he growled, "We made you welcome in our home when you were injured. Is this how you repay our hospitality? By seducing Bethany?"

"Hanging might not be a bad idea," Dunley said with a laugh.

She tensed, but Eric said, "My feelings for Bethany were never meant to dishonor you in any way or to lessen my gratitude to you."

"Yet you seduced her and planned to leave her?"

"Father," Bethany began. He tried to silence her with a fierce glare, but she could not let Eric be punished for a crime he had not committed. "Father, you do not understand."

"I understand well enough."

"Eric's life is elsewhere. Mine is here."

"So you thought you could forget about marriage? I thank heavens that your mother is not here to see this. What your grandmother will think . . ." He shook his head.

Bethany tried to halt them, but tears cascaded along her cheeks. She did not cry for herself, but for her father who was wounded by these ridiculous lies. "Father, it is not as you think. Eric and I—"

"Never meant to hurt this family," Eric said with the same quiet serenity.

"Eric!"

He folded his arms in front of him again, and she noticed his wince. How many more ways could she cause him pain? His face was somber. "Bethany has no wish to shame you or her family, my lord."

"But she has. No man will ever marry her." Father glanced at Dunley, who shook his head and laughed loudly.

"That's not true," Eric replied in the same grave tone. "To protect your daughter's reputation, I shall marry her."

Bethany cried, "No, Eric! Are you insane?"

"Silence, daughter!" snapped her father. "This is not the fine marriage I would have wished for you, but it is clear that you had no interest in such a marriage. I shall arrange for a special license to be issued without delay. Jay, alert Reverend Sullivan." His dark eyes gleamed with rage. "I want no chance of you, Eric, changing your mind in the dawn-light and leaving my daughter with a reputation that cannot be salvaged."

"For heaven's sake," Bethany moaned, grasping Eric's arms. She released the right one when he winced again. She did not want to cloud his mind with pain. He had to think clearly. *Now!* "Stop this before it is too late."

"It is too late already." When he looked past her again, she whirled to see Dunley trying to keep Jay from leaving the room.

"Step aside," Jay was saying, his face pale with confusion. She could not blame him for being baffled when she herself could not even guess how this afternoon had exploded with every emotion from contentment to anger and then had become a disaster.

Dunley pushed him back and snarled, "If you think you can save her name by wedding her to Pennington like this, you're a fool, Whitcombe! Everyone will be curious as to why a baron's daughter is marrying a classless peddler."

"Good afternoon." Father's words were spoken without emotion. "You may rest assured that, once this wedding is completed, I shall discuss with your father my opinions of your obvious treatment of Bethany."

*"My* treatment of *her?"* Dunleys narrow eyes glowed with hatred.

Bethany raised a trembling finger and pointed to the door. "Father asked you to leave. If he has to ask you again, I swear I shall get his shotgun and pepper your breeches with buckshot." When a cautioning hand settled on her arm, she stepped closer to Eric.

Although she expected another volley of insults, Dunley turned on his heel and stamped out the door. The outer door slammed as he left. She shivered, unable to believe that her torment at receiving him was over.

"He shall not hurt you again, sweetheart."

Her head jerked up as she heard Eric's endearment. Then her relief vanished. What had she brought about with her attempt to escape Dunley's heavy-handed seduction? She might have been enthralled by Eric's tempting kisses, and she might have dreamed of his touch, but she knew nothing of him. No, she knew he was keeping secrets behind his charming smile.

When his arm curved around her shoulders, she drew away. She must not allow him to touch her. Not now . . . not when she needed to remain free of the fascinating tangle he created with his eager caresses.

He drew her to one side of the room. She waited for her father to protest. Then, she realized, he saw nothing amiss with a couple about to wed wanting a moment alone.

"Eric, help me put a stop to this!" she whispered. "We cannot get married because of Dunley's tapestry of lies. He invented them to cover his own disbelief that I would not be thrilled to wed him."

His chuckle was devoid of humor. "It appears we shall be getting married as soon as your father makes all the proper arrangements."

"This is ridiculous! Stop it!"

"I can't."

"Yes, you can." She flung out her hand. "Just walk out the door and never come back. That will end this."

His palm followed the line of her jaw, and she fought not to savor the rapture flowing through her. It had betrayed her before; she must not let it betray her again.

Quietly, he asked, "Do you want me to leave here and never come back, Bethany? Do you want me to leave you with a ruined reputation?"

"But I have done nothing to ruin my reputation." She gripped his arms and wished she could shake some sense into him. He always had been so reasonable. This was the wrong time to change. "Why won't you tell Father the truth?"

"He has no reason to believe me when his daughter whom he has always trusted has owned to being my paramour." He gave her a wry smile and tipped her face up, gently. "It won't be so horrible to be married to me, will it?"

She pulled back. "You intend to go through with this? You cannot be serious!"

His voice lowered to a husky whisper that stirred through her. "Very serious, Bethany. For better or for worse, until death do us part."

She took another step back. "Why? Why do you want to marry me? You told me you were eager to leave, that you could not wait to continue your travels."

"Why do you find it so difficult to believe a man would not take advantage of the opportunity to marry you?" His gaze swept over her, and she edged away.

As soon as Tryphena's father arrived with the proper papers, she would be marrying a man she hardly knew—for better and for worse and for all the days of their lives. Every night of those many days, she must share her bed with him. As she looked at his smile, she began to understand just how long that could be.

# Nine

Bethany was not certain if the time flew or crawled past while Father waited for the special license to be delivered to Whitcombe Hall. Sitting alone in her room and being so quiet even Vella finally left her to her own thoughts, she wished she could turn back the clock to the moment when Dunley had asked her to walk him to his carriage.

She would have refused. Then she would not have had to suffer his pawing and been so stupid as to speak Eric's name. Then she would not have had to see the horror on Father's face and listen to Eric calmly owning how he let passion for her overmaster his good sense.

It was all lies. Why could no one else see that?

She leaned her head back against the chaise longue. Mayhap she could have persuaded Eric to change his mind about all this if she had had a chance to speak with him alone again. He had been avoiding her.

A knock sounded at her door. Bethany sat up. Could it be Father? Mayhap *he* had come to his senses and demanded that Eric be honest with him. Uncertain if she could trust her voice, she rose and opened the door.

Her eyes widened as she saw Titus. He had not said a single word to her through all of this. She wanted to put her arms around him and assure him that she had not shamed him or the rest of the family.

"Yes?" she managed to whisper.

"I'd like to speak with you, Bethany."

She nodded, opening the door wider. His rigid movements mirrored her own. Closing the door after him, he walked over to stare out the window that overlooked the gardens. She waited for him to say something, but he remained silent.

The rattle of a carriage announced an arrival. She looked out the other window and swallowed her moan of dismay. It was Reverend Sullivan's pony cart. The special license must have been delivered, and Father had sent for the minister to marry her and Eric.

*No! This was all wrong!*

Edging to her door, she opened it to hear Reverend Sullivan greeting her father. If no one halted this madness, she would be marrying Eric Pennington to right a wrong they had not committed.

"What did you want to say to me?" Bethany asked as she closed the door and faced her brother. "It seems you must be quick about it, for the minister is here."

"Can you be honest now?"

Heat rose along her cheeks as she reached for her hairbrush. Brushing her hair into place would give her trembling fingers something to do. Looking at her reflection in the glass, she knew she had never dreamed of being married in the light blue gown she usually wore for tea when Father had special guests at Whitcombe Hall. The pink roses along the bodice were nearly the color of her cheeks, but, even as she watched, her face became as pale as the white ribbons laced through the sleeves.

"Yes," she whispered, "I can be honest now."

He shuffled his feet as if he were the guilty one. When he raised his eyes, she saw he was uncomfortable with her as he never had been. Tears pricked her eyes. The most horrible legacy of these lies might be that she was ripped away from her beloved family.

"Eric is lying, isn't he?" Titus asked.

"Yes," she answered without hesitation, "but how—?"

"I know you," he stated with the dim hint of a smile. "I am also beginning to know Eric. He doesn't take his vows lightly. He might bend his promise to Father enough to kiss you, as he cannot hide that he wants to do so, but he would never seduce you."

"You do know him."

"So why did you set up this charade? Do you love each other so much that you were willing to chance ruining yourselves this way?"

She placed her brush on the table beside the window. She then opened the window to allow in the fresh air from the garden, but none of the luscious scents could ease her despair at realizing how much easier it was to speak of Eric and herself as lovers than to own to the uneven state of her heart. "I am being honest when I say that love is not why Eric decided to agree to marry me."

He spun her toward him. When she was about to protest, his fierce expression silenced her. With an intense tone she had never heard in his voice, he snarled, "This is no lark, Bethany! Reverend Sullivan's waiting downstairs for you and Eric to stand before him and take vows of fidelity for the rest of your lives. The rest of your lives! You have been rash before, sister, but think before you agree to something as want-witted as this."

"What can I do? Accuse Eric of lying?"

"He *is* lying!"

Stepping away, she reached for the small box sitting on the shelf beside her bed. She opened it. Lifting out a chain with a small gold circle edged with pearls, she said, "Titus, Mother gave me this pendant when she knew she would not live to see me marry. She told me to wear it on the most joyous day of my life."

"Which this cannot be."

"She expected that I would wear it when I was married." Bethany set the box on her bed and latched the chain behind her nape.

Titus stared at her, opening his mouth once, then closing it. He took a deep breath that raised and lowered his shoulders slowly before saying, "You said Eric is not marrying you because he loves you, but do you love him, Bethany?"

Again she found it impossible to meet his eyes. "That is not really important now."

"When will it be important? When you are taking your vows? When you consummate your marriage? When your first child is born? When, Bethany? Liking is not the same as loving."

"Don't you think I know that? Don't you think I have been thinking of little else?" She bit her lip to cage her sob. She wished he would not give voice to the questions which taunted her.

When her brother whispered her name in a broken voice, she turned to look at him. He gently touched her cheek. "Why are you doing this?"

"Because you and Father and Sir Asa have given me no choice."

"You have a choice."

"What choice? To marry Dunley?" She shook her head, drawing away from him. "I told him that I cannot marry him. That was when he started accusing me of taking a lover."

"Why did you own that you had?"

"I didn't! He simply could not believe that I might not want him because he is a lout."

Titus frowned. "You have never given him a chance."

"A chance?" Her voice remained steady, only because she exerted all her will. "To do what? Force me to become his lover in the garden?"

"Dunley would not—"

"Believe I did not want him until he convinced himself that I had been seduced by Eric." She raised her chin. "Titus, you are the one deluded. He would have forced himself upon me."

"You must have mistaken his intentions."

"I believe I have mistaken yours." She walked to the door and opened it. Looking over her shoulder, she saw his face harden as she said, "I thought you cared more about your sister than ingratiating yourself with that disgusting slug and his father."

Bethany did not slam the door in her wake, but only because she wanted to do nothing more to shame her father. Her furious steps faltered when she saw Jay standing near the stairs. How easily she could be furious with Titus, but she was protective of Jay, even more so since their mother had died.

"Are you truly going down to the chapel to be married?" he asked incredulously.

"The chapel?" She had not given thought to where the ceremony would be held. Speaking hypocritical vows of love might be possible in the parlor, but in the chapel . . .

"Father said this must be done right from this point forward." He colored to nearly the shade of his scarlet waistcoat. Offering his arm, he asked, "Will you let me escort you to Father?"

She nodded, then whispered, "How is he?"

"He is not happy." Jay gave her a quick grin. "But he is not as upset as he was. He lectured me for a full hour."

"You? Why?"

"He does not want me to make the same mistake you and Eric have." His brows lowered, giving him the appearance of their father, a resemblance she had never seen until now. "But I am not sure he believes your story, Bethany. I'm not sure I do either."

"Then why . . . ?" She bit her lip to silence the rest of the question. Mayhap her father knew, as she did, that to speak the truth now would mean she could be obligated to marry a man she despised.

He paused as they went down the stairs. Facing her, he said, "I know I would rather have you be Bethany Pennington than marry Dunley Morelock."

"Don't say that!"

"Say what?"

"That name!"

He frowned. "Bethany Pennington will be your name if you do not change your mind."

"I know," she whispered, adding nothing else. She doubted if there was anything else to say.

As he continued down the stairs, Bethany followed. Her gaze was caught by her bedchamber door as it opened. Her fingers clenched on the banister. Not her bedchamber when she returned from the chapel, but hers and Eric's. Before dawn, the man who had courted her with fiery kisses and his lightning-hot touch could be teaching her a far more intimate pleasure. She longed for his caresses.

"But not like this," she whispered.

"What did you say?" Jay asked.

"Nothing," she mumbled. How could she tell him about her thoughts? They would label her a wanton as Dunley had. Yet how could she think of anything else?

Mrs. Linders was waiting at the bottom of the stairs. Bethany appreciated the housekeeper's attempt to smile more than she could say. When Mrs. Linders held out a handful of flowers, she said, "A bride should have flowers."

"Thank you," Bethany whispered as she took them.

"Father said to hurry." A hint of a grin loosened the tightness of Jay's lips. "He is not worried that Eric will run out on you, but something has him concerned. He has two footmen watching the front door and one on the others."

Bethany understood what her brother did not. As Jay walked beside her toward the back of the house where the small chapel had been the site of many Whitcombe weddings, baptisms, and funerals, she stared at the flowers. Father was worried about the Morelocks.

She was surprised, now that she thought of something beyond her despair, that Sir Asa had not called already. Or had he, and she had not taken note? Impossible! No one could fail to take note of Sir Asa Morelock. He would not allow that.

Clasping her icy hands more tightly around the flowers, she asked, "Is Nana coming to the wedding?"

"Of course." Jay glanced at her with surprise. "Why are you asking?"

"She has not come to see me."

"Because," Nana said in her most no-nonsense voice as she stepped out of another passage to stop right in front of them, "I have been searching every inch of the attics for this." She held out a lace mantilla that had yellowed with age nearly to the color of Eric's hair.

Bethany tried to shake that thought out of her head, but it refused to be budged. Her fingers trembled as she reached for the lace.

Her grandmother shook her head. "Jay, go ahead, and let your father know we are on our way."

"Yes, Nana." He disappeared along the shadowed hall.

Nana set the lace on Bethany's hair. "I dreamed of you, my only granddaughter, being married in a grand wedding in a gown of white silk."

"Father would not allow me to wear white silk now."

"Not the silk, no, but the white?" She smiled. "You must love him dearly, Bethany, to go through this charade to keep him from leaving."

"Do you think that is what this is?"

" 'Tis as good an explanation as any, I believe."

"But it isn't the truth."

Nana's wrinkled hands grasped her shoulders. For the first time, Bethany realized she had to look down to meet Nana's eyes. Her grandmother had been such a formidable force in her life that she had not noticed when she had grown taller than Nana.

"My dear child, don't you realize that the truth is no longer important? Everyone has made up his or her mind what that truth is, and nothing you or Eric might do will change a single mind an iota."

"The truth is always important."

"Bah! That's your father speaking at his most pompous." Nana laughed at Bethany's gasp of amazement. "Even he knows that truth has many shades other than black and white." A frown flitted across her face. "Or he would if he paused to think about all this."

"If the wedding is delayed—"

Nana wagged a finger in front of Bethany's face. "Do not try to twist my words, child. Your father has given this matter much thought, and he has not changed his mind."

Bethany nodded as Nana drew the veil over her face. Titus might have chided her for being unthinking, but he could not ever say Father was.

Walking with her grandmother along the hall, she shivered as she paused by the chapel door. As soon as she stepped through it, she would be beginning a new life, one she had never imagined. No, she had imagined being in Eric's arms—far too often her mind had drifted in that direction—but she had never envisioned herself exchanging marital vows with him. And what would happen after the ceremony . . . ? No, she must not think of that, because, if she did not marry him, she feared a quick betrothal with Dunley would be arranged.

Bethany stepped back when the door opened. Nana went in, motioning for her to stay where she was. Candles burned on every surface within the chapel, their flames keeping the sunlight from reaching far past the stained glass. Instead of being empty, the chapel was filled with the household staff and Tryphena. Bethany wanted to rush forward and take her friend's hands and ask her to help find a way out of this jumble. When she saw no one standing by the altar, her heart thudded against her chest. Where was Eric? Had he—? She did not want to consider any of the reasons he might not be here.

Instead, she looked at her father who stood in the doorway. Her eyes widened when she realized he was dressed in his very best dark coat and pale breeches. When he held out his arm to her, her fingers trembled as she put them on his sleeve. He put a hand over hers and patted it as he had when she was a child and needed comforting. How she wished he would gather her up in his arms now as he had then and twirl her about until her unhappiness vanished into laughter.

A door opened at the far end of the chapel, and Reverend Sullivan stepped out. Her stomach leaped like a rabbit racing across an open field when Eric followed him toward the altar. The candlelight burnished his golden hair and his bronzed skin. His shirt was neatly pressed. An unstained waistcoat of a pale blue peeked out from beneath a dark coat that was as formal as her father's. If his boots had not been the scuffed ones he always wore, she would have been sure a stranger stood beside Reverend Sullivan.

Until she looked into his eyes. Even though so much of what she saw there was baffling, as always, the twinkle that brightened them when he looked at her was irresistible, tempting her to forget all the reasons why this marriage ceremony was wrong and to consider all the ways it could be so very right.

"Bethany," her father said quietly, "it is time."

She nodded, again unwilling to trust her voice. Tearing her gaze from Eric's, she glanced at her father. She had not been sure whether he would be smiling or frowning, but puzzlement claimed his expression.

"It will be all right," he said.

"I know." She managed the two whispered words.

As Father led her toward the altar, everyone rose from the stone pews and turned to watch. She ignored the temptation to laugh when she realized how different this was from the wondrous wedding she and Tryphena had envisioned she would have in this chapel. As she looked from her father to her brothers, now seated in the foremost pew where Nana sat beside them, a beatific smile on her face as if she had arranged the whole of this, then on to the gently smiling countenance of the minister, she wanted to apologize for snaring them in this web of delusion.

Her gaze went again to Eric. To him, she owed the greatest apology. In order to save herself from a horrifying life with Dunley Morelock, she was ruining his. He had every reason to despise her. Mayhap that was why he had been avoiding her. He had wanted to savor his last few hours of freedom.

Warmth washed over her as Eric smiled so gently she knew her fears had been silly. His smile reached within her to melt the ice around her heart. Gasps rang through the chapel as he stepped down from the altar and walked toward her.

Father's arm grew rigid, and Bethany knew he was wondering, as she was, if Eric was walking away to leave her in shame even now.

But Eric paused in front of them. Bowing his head toward her father, he said, "Thank you, my lord."

Father blinked, then nodded. Lifting Bethany's hand off his arm, he placed it in Eric's hand. She had thought her father would say something to them, but he stepped back.

When Eric entwined her fingers with his as he led her to where Reverend Sullivan waited, she whispered, "You do not need to do this."

"But you must." His smile grew cold. "If you do not marry me today, I suspect you will be marrying Morelock tomorrow."

It required all her strength to still the quivers in her voice. "I know, but you were planning on leaving to return to your life."

"Now I guess I shall be staying to make my life here." He sighed, but that glitter remained in his eyes. "If I refuse to save your family's reputation by marrying you, your father will take target practice with my backside as you threatened to do to Morelock."

"If we told Father—"

" 'Tis too late for the truth."

"It is never too late!" She was distressed that he was echoing Nana's words. Had all of them gone crazy?

Before he could answer, Reverend Sullivan called, "Shall we begin?"

Bethany looked expectantly at Eric. This was his last opportunity to tell the truth, but he acted as if he had no qualms about this mockery of a marriage. Mayhap he truly was mad. Had she traded a life with Dunley for a life with a madman? Glancing at his fine clothes, she shivered. Or did he have another reason for agreeing to wed her? A peddler should not aspire to wedding a baron's daughter, but she was more and more sure that he was no more a peddler than she was. He had some reason for behaving as he did. She wished she had some idea what it might be.

When he tugged on her fingers to draw her toward the altar, she forced her leaden feet forward. Reverend Sullivan regarded her steadily, and she wondered if he was ashamed of what he must see as a straying lamb in his flock.

The minister took her other hand between his. "Will this man make you happy, Bethany?"

"Yes," she whispered, hoping the witnesses would translate the blush on her face as embarrassment. Instead she was flustered by Eric overhearing her owning to the minister what she had never said to him. Although she was not sure that she loved Eric Pennington, being with him was endlessly thrilling. He teased her and forced her to keep up with his quick wit. When she despaired, he offered her compassion and dared her to face her problems head-on. The aura of mystery surrounding him tantalized her. And his touch . . . Her bones threatened to melt like sweets left in the sun as she thought of how this ceremony would end. She would be in his arms and his mouth on hers. Later—

"Then, Bethany," the minister said, interrupting thoughts which brought more heat to her face, " 'tis time to say your vows with this man you love."

She glanced at Eric. To hear the pastor speak of love with such ease unsettled her. She wanted to shout that she was not in love with Eric, but she remained silent. Nana was right. Eric was right. It was too late for the truth. It was too late for anything but marrying a man she barely knew to begin a new life she could not envision.

# Ten

Bethany answered when required as Reverend Sullivan read the marriage rite. She kept her gaze in the center of his surplice until he asked, "Who gives this woman in marriage?"

"I do," her father said.

She looked at him in astonishment. She could not mistake the emotion in his voice. Not embarrassment, not anger, not even relief, but quiet pleasure. She gazed into his eyes that were so like her own. A sob caught in her throat. For whatever transgressions he believed she had committed, her father had forgiven her.

He kissed her cheek. "I hope you will be happy with Eric, daughter."

*I hope so, too.* She prayed she had not said those words aloud. No one must hear the doubts clamoring within her.

Eric repeated the wedding vows in a clear voice, but hers trembled as she promised to love him forever. When he took her left hand in his, she gasped as she watched him slide an ornately twisted ring onto her fourth finger.

"Where did you get this?" she blurted out.

He grinned. "A good peddler always has every kind of gewgaw on his wagon, even things he could not imagine needing himself."

Reverend Sullivan smiled as he pronounced them man and wife and added, "Congratulations."

Bethany's fake smile made her face ache as she thanked him. She was glad for anything which gave her an excuse not to look at Eric. At *her husband!*

His hand on her arm warned her that he refused to be overlooked. He brought her to face him and said softly, "Bethany Pennington. A wife is something I did not expect to find when I offered you a length of silk in exchange for a night's lodging for me and my horse."

As he rubbed his finger over the wedding ring, she whispered, "I am so sorry that—"

"Sorry?" With a laugh, he tugged her into his arms. He lifted aside her veil. His lips stilled her answer as he teased her to recall the rapture of stolen kisses. When his tongue surreptitiously teased the corners of her mouth, his breath swirled through her mouth.

She struggled not to dissolve into the seductive fire. As he raised his lips, his fingers caressed her cheek, lingering on the curve of her mouth. She could read the craving in his eyes. A quiver ran along her back.

"Don't look so frightened," Eric teased. He kissed Bethany lightly again, resisting the need to claim her lips until every yearning within him was sated. "I shan't be an ogre of a husband."

"You shall be only as impossible as you've been up until now?"

He laughed, hoping his hoaxing would ease the fear in her eyes. "I suspect you may be right."

His efforts were in vain. Her smile was brittle when her family came forward to congratulate her. He stepped back to give them a moment alone as a family and to let him observe how the baron reacted. Whitcombe's rage was gone. Instead, relief seemed to surge through his father-in-law.

Father-in-law!

*You are a leather-head.* The condemnation was not in his own voice, but it might as well have been. He knew that marrying now was probably the most witless thing he had ever done. The devil was sure to demand his due, but not marrying Bethany would have been far more stupid. He could not let this ceremony change his plans. The others would have to understand that he intended for his name to protect Bethany against the Morelocks. It was the very least he could do for her.

"Shall we share a drink from the bridal cup?" he asked in a light voice which masked the truth he must never speak, even to the woman who shared his name.

"Bridal cup?" Bethany repeated. When she looked at Eric, she saw sympathy in his eyes. Fury laced through her. Pity was not what she wanted from Eric Pennington. She realized, with a jolt of dismay, that she had no idea what she did expect from him . . . and from the life they must have together.

"There are refreshments for everyone in the morning room." Nana waved at all the witnesses, shooing them out of the chapel like a farm wife shooing her chickens ahead of her.

Tryphena remained sitting in her pew. She stood, and Bethany went to her, leaving Eric to speak with her father and the minister.

Taking her hands, Tryphena smiled at the same time she blinked back tears.

"Are those tears of joy?" Bethany asked.

"How can you ask that?" Her friend's eyes widened as she whispered, "Is it true what is rumored in Fair Cove? Did your father force you to marry this peddler?"

"My father would not force me to marry against my will." Bethany repeated the words which she had said so often, and she longed to believe them. Mayhap Father would have acquiesced if she had flown off into a pelter about marrying Eric, but she was certain he would have insisted she marry someone else without delay.

Tryphena's smile returned. "Then it is as I guessed when we were beating the bounds. You have a deep *tendre* for this man who saved you from the smugglers."

"You thought that?"

"How could I not have?" She laughed quietly. "You glow like the first star each time you speak of him. He must make you very happy."

"He does." Bethany was relieved to speak the truth. Even though she was unsure about loving Eric, she was certain that her life would be empty without him in it. She flinched and glanced back at the altar. He had said his life would be here now, but for how long? So many times, he had spoken of his love for his free life upon the country lanes.

When an arm encircled her shoulders, she looked up to see Eric's smile. Somehow, she managed to introduce him to Tryphena without bumbling over her words too often. He was as gracious to Tryphena as if she were the daughter of the king, which was no surprise. Eric treated everyone with respect, save for the Morelocks.

"Your grandmother told me quite imperiously that we should not delay joining the others in the morning room." He gave her a rakish leer. "Mayhap she thought I would spirit you off to have you alone even before the first toast was raised to our marriage."

Bethany had seldom blushed before Eric arrived at Whitcombe Hall, but she knew she must be doing so now, for heat surrounded her. He laughed and winked at Tryphena who giggled as they walked out of the chapel.

Or had she reddened? When his fingers played along her arm, the sweet blaze raged within her.

They neared the morning room. From it came joyous voices. When Reverend Sullivan and Tryphena continued into the room, Eric slowed.

"It is too late for second thoughts," Bethany said, her voice falling flat again.

"You are wrong about that." His finger stroked her cheek. When she did not look at him, his thumb ran along her jaw before tilting her chin up. "I am filled with second thoughts, Bethany."

"As I am." She gave him a wry smile. "An annulment might not be so easy when we have acknowledged that we cuckolded the parson."

"Such language!" He tapped her nose. "But an annulment was not among the second thoughts on my mind now."

"And what is?"

"This."

His kiss was gentle, asking her to give him only what she wanted to. She wanted to give him everything. She pulled back with a gasp, frightened by her own cravings to make this marriage more than a sham built on lies.

Rushing into the morning room, she could not escape the truth. The one bit of truth she had refused to speak, just as Eric had refused to speak of how they had shared no more than kisses. She was falling in love with Eric Pennington, who continued to be the very husband she had longed for—a man of courage and honor. A man she could admire at the same time she could love him.

"Have you misplaced your bridegroom already, sister?" Jay crowed, warning her that she had hurried headlong into the room without considering the consequences . . . yet again.

"No." She looked back to see Eric in the doorway. His face held a smile appropriate for a man who had made a good marriage that day. "There he is."

"We are waiting for you two to share the bridal cup, so we can enjoy the cake." He pointed to the table where a multitiered cake was decorated with flowers and doves. It was wildly extravagant and totally wrong for this hurried wedding.

Then she realized that Nana would not be denied some parts of this celebration. No wonder, she had not seen her since the wedding was announced. Her grandmother had been busy making all these arrangements.

Affixing a smile in place that was the twin of Eric's, Bethany said, "Then I shall have to make certain you wait no longer." She went to the table, hoping to appear nonchalant.

Jay's chuckle warned her that her anxiety was visible. She prayed that they would guess her nerves were simply those of any bride, for she did not want to let anyone suspect her thoughts.

She cursed her fingers which trembled as she reached for the bottle of cider waiting by the cake in the center of the table. Glad that Father had not served wine, which would make the day even more stressful for all of them, she pulled at the cork. When it did not move, unreasonable tears of frustration bubbled against her lashes. Broad fingers covered hers, and she looked over her shoulder to see Eric's smile.

"How do you expect me to open it if you grab it away from me?" Color washed from her face as she heard the abrupt silence which followed her heated words. They were not words a bride should be speaking to her husband minutes after the wedding rites.

Eric acted as if he were immune to the startled glances, although she knew how little was missed by his keen eyes. "I want to help. Nothing more."

"All right." She handed him the container and reached for the crystal goblets. Keeping her eyes on the cider as he poured it was easier than meeting the amusement she was sure would be in his gaze. Or worse, she would see the desire which taunted her into ceding herself to passion. A quiver raced through her, warning her how feeble her defenses were against the longing he instilled in her just by standing so close.

The cider splashed into her goblet as conversations resumed. Hearing Jay jesting with Titus, she tried to smile. She had almost succeeded when loud footsteps sounded on the floor beyond the morning room.

Again conversation vanished. Eric put a hand on her arm, but she did not want to move from his side as Sir Asa Morelock paused in the doorway and scanned the room. Even with the passage of years, Sir Asa had not lost his commanding presence. The black remaining in his gray hair was as dark as his eyes, and the breadth of a face that was falling into jowls was diminished by his wide shoulders. It was easy to imagine him browbeating the prime minister . . . both figuratively and literally.

Father went to the door. "Sir Asa, I did not expect to see you today."

"No?" Sir Asa burst into the room, Dunley trailing him in silence. When his father pointed a wide finger at him, Dunley glowered. "This want-witted son of mine has told me only in the past hour that he decided not to marry your daughter. What do you know about this?"

"Isn't it better they discovered that before they spoke their vows before Reverend Sullivan?"

"What do they know?" Sir Asa snarled a curse.

Nana snapped, "Asa Morelock, I will ask you to refrain from using such oaths in my home. If you wish to continue to speak so lowly, I will ask you to leave."

He started to retort, then stared past Nana to the table and the cake that was set in its very center. His eyes narrowed as his gaze swept the room.

"Don't say anything," Eric hissed under his breath.

Bethany glanced at him, then lowered the cups to the table. She would never quail before Sir Asa again. No longer did she have to listen to his comments of how happy she would be when she married his son.

Faster than she had guessed he could move, Sir Asa leaped forward and grabbed her arm. Before he could tug her toward him, Eric's fist struck his wrist with a sharp whack. Sir Asa screeched, but released her.

"Bastard!" Sir Asa cradled his wrist as he glared at Eric. "I shall break you in half!"

"No!" Father stepped between them, even though he was a head shorter than either man. His voice was calm. "You were not invited to this wedding, Asa."

"Wedding?" Sir Asa stared at Reverend Sullivan. "Whose wedding?"

Eric put an arm around Bethany. When she stepped farther within that haven, he smiled. "Our wedding. Bethany is now my wife."

"I told you!" Dunley cried. "She took that damned peddler for her lover. She is nothing but a doxy."

"Be silent!" roared Sir Asa.

Dunley crouched like a beaten pup. Astonished when pity washed over her, Bethany was about to speak, but Eric's squeezing of her shoulders silenced her.

Not that anyone would have heard her, for Sir Asa continued to bellow, "Bethany was to be Dunley's wife. You agreed to that, Whitcombe."

"He did not," Nana said quietly. "He would not be so witless."

"Mother." Putting a hand on her arm, Father said, "Do not speak of what you do not know."

"Do you mean to tell me that you considered for even a heartbeat giving your daughter to those beasts? Mayhap your wife did not tell you what—"

"Mother," he repeated. "This is gentlemen's business. Let us handle it."

"I would if I thought you would not get yourself into another complete pickle."

"Mother!"

Bethany touched her grandmother's arm. When Nana glanced at her and nodded, she knew that Nana understood what could not be said aloud. To engage her son in a brangle now would only lengthen this uncomfortable situation.

Reverend Sullivan came around the table, his hands folded in front of him. "It may ease your dismay, Sir Asa, to realize this is not unusual. Even if Dunley and Bethany had been formally betrothed, a betrothal can be ended upon the agreement of both young people."

"Dunley did not—"

"Dunley did break it!" asserted Bethany, unable to be silent any longer.

"Impossible!" Sir Asa pointed a thick finger at his silent son. "Speak up, you useless excuse for a man!"

Dunley flushed, the ruddiness visible even beneath his sun-darkened skin. He shot a vengeful glare at Bethany. "I do not want her when she has been letting that lowborn peddler tumble her."

"You idiot!" his father screeched. "You were supposed to bring her home. We were supposed to have her."

Bethany's fingernails bit into Eric's arm. When he loosened them, giving her a grim smile, she leaned closer to him. She had not wanted to believe him when he had said Sir Asa wanted her more for himself than for his son. When she glanced at her father, she saw realization dawning in his furious eyes. He looked at her grandmother, who nodded sagely.

Father's face grew as ruddy as Dunley's. Beside him, Jay edged forward, his hands in fists. Even Titus was scowling. Mayhap he had finally realized the caliber of the men he had been betwattled into believing.

Father glanced at Bethany and smiled an apology. She wanted to smile back, but she could not while the Morelocks infested their home.

Sir Asa had not yet fully vented his ire. "Your daughter is a trading dame, Whitcombe, who deserves no better than a man who has taken airs to call himself a traveling merchant. Who knows how many men she has pleasured? Or do you know and hope to get her a name to save your own. Pennington! Who the hell is he? He is so pitiful a man that you could foist your whorish daughter off on him!"

Stepping forward, Eric said in an unruffled voice that did not match the enmity in his eyes, "Bethany has known no man before me, I assure you. You would be wise not to slander my wife because she chose to become a Pennington instead of a Morelock. I shall not debate the obvious intelligence of her choice." He smiled. "Do not make me so angry that I shall be forced to teach you a lesson before my wife and her family."

"You? Teach me a lesson?" Sir Asa snickered. "I could break you with my bare hands!"

"Do not be so sure of that."

Bethany screamed as Morelock lunged at Eric. Hands grabbed her. Tugged back against Dunley's chest, she struggled to escape. She saw her father motion to one of the footmen, but screamed again as Sir

Asa's wild blow went wide. He whirled to face Eric who had moved easily out of the way.

Eric smiled as Sir Asa came at him. At the last second, he stepped aside and put out his foot to trip Sir Asa, who fell against the table with a crash. The wedding cake teetered. The top two layers tumbled to the floor, one striking Sir Asa on the head. With a laugh, Eric took the cider and poured it over his head.

"To wash you off, Sir Asa," he jeered. "If you're going to act like a child, that's how you should be treated."

With a roar, Dunley shoved Bethany aside and raced forward, his fists raised.

"Enough!" shouted Whitcombe. He elbowed Dunley aside and reached for the shotgun a footman held out to him. "My daughter warned you if you came back here without your manners, she would see your backsides filled with buckshot. It will be my pleasure to do so, if you two do not take your leave at once."

Shaking his head, Sir Asa rose. "You would not dare."

"Do not push him to find out." Reverend Sullivan's deep voice rolled across the room. "Put that away, Anson. There shall be no more fighting. This is a wedding, not a brawl." He held out a hand to Bethany. When she went to him and put her left hand, with her wedding band glittering on it, on his hand, he placed her hand in Eric's. "Remember these words. 'What God has joined together, let no man put asunder.' Do you understand?"

Sir Asa swore. "Bethany was supposed to be a Morelock. The people of Fair Cove are going to learn about this faithless whore!"

"Get out!" ordered Father. She stared at him, astonished by the breadth of his rage, then noticed her grandmother was beaming with pride. "Get out of my home, Sir Asa Morelock, and never enter it again until you apologize to my daughter, her husband, and the rest of my family."

Nana added, "We shan't despair if you decide *not* to apologize, Asa."

"Mother . . ." Father groaned, then smiled as she smiled at him.

With another curse, Sir Asa stormed to the door. He motioned for his son to follow.

Dunley shot a venomous scowl at Bethany before doing so.

As if there had been no interruption, Nana went to the table and picked up a knife. She pressed it in Bethany's numb fingers.

"Cut the wedding cake, my child." She chuckled. "Or what is left of it, at any rate, so we may all enjoy some of Cook's best frosting."

Bethany stared down at the knife, but could not lift her hand to cut the cake. When Eric's fingers covered hers once again, she looked up at him. She owed him more than her sanity, which would have been in jeopardy at the Morelocks' house. She owed him her life.

With false levity, her father urged, "Go ahead, Bethany. It is time we truly celebrated this wedding."

Hours later, when the last guest had departed and Nana had expressed the last of her many, far from subtle hints that the bride and groom might wish to be alone, Bethany was silent as she walked along the hall to the bedchamber that would be hers no longer. She fidgeted with the lace of the wedding veil that she must return to Nana and listened to Eric's footfalls behind her.

She wanted to ask him what he was thinking. Mayhap his thoughts were as jumbled as hers.

He took her hand as they reached her bedroom door. "I know it is tradition for the groom to carry the bride over the threshold into the bridal chamber." He rubbed his shoulder. "I hope you will understand; that would not be a good idea."

"I understand." *None of this was a good idea,* she added silently. She went into the bedchamber that was exactly as she had left it hours before, save for the lacy nightgown waiting on the bed. She flinched when Eric closed the door behind him and sat on her bed as he slipped off his coat.

Eric Pennington was her husband. He had every right to share her bed.

He frowned and kneaded his shoulder carefully.

"Is it worse?" she whispered. She did not trust her voice to speak louder.

He smiled wryly. "The temptation to teach Morelock a lesson was too sweet to resist."

"Eric, what you did was . . ." When he looked up at her hesitation, she said, "It was stupid!"

"As stupid as your telling Dunley Morelock that we were lovers?"

"I know I was witless to whisper your name when—" Terror raced along her spine.

He stood and, placing a finger beneath her chin, brought her face up to meet his furious eyes. "He shall never threaten you again, or I shall have the pleasure of taking him apart piece by piece. Not even this blasted shoulder shall halt me."

She put her fingers over his on her cheek. Just touching him strengthened her. "Please do not speak so."

"Do you harbor some affection for Morelock?"

She shuddered. "Neither father nor son, but, Eric, your determination to protect me has led you to do another very foolish thing."

"Marrying you?" He shrugged. "Bethany, to be honest, at the time, the idea of rescuing you from that ogre seemed a fine idea."

"You do not love me!"

"You do not love me, either." He sat on her chaise longue and tugged off his left boot. Again he massaged his shoulder. "Dash it! I am beginning to believe this will never be the same."

Kneeling to pull off his other boot, she said, "Nothing will."

He took her by the shoulders and drew her up between his knees. His smile echoed the longing in his expressive eyes as his lips touched hers. "You are a good wife to help me like this."

She gasped and pulled away to leave him grasping nothing but air.

He stood and padded toward her in his stockinged feet. When she backed into the bed, she moaned in horror. His eyes widened in shock when she cowered away from his outstretched hand. "Why this sudden timidity? You have never been averse to my touch."

"We were not married before," she whispered.

He sifted her hair through his fingers. "Bethany, we *are* married now." With a sigh, he picked up her nightgown and placed it in her hands. "Ready yourself for bed, Bethany, while I go to my room to gather some pillows and blankets."

"What?" She was certain she had heard him wrong.

"I doubt you wish to share yours." His grin became self-deprecating. "You should hurry and change if you do not want to tempt your husband beyond what a mortal man can endure. It should not take me long to sneak to my room and get what I need for tonight and the morrow."

"You are leaving?"

"Only for a few minutes."

"But, I thought—"

He grasped her shoulders. "Bethany, you are what you are, and I am what I am. What sort of future can I offer you?"

"That is something we should have considered before we spoke our vows."

"I did. When I am certain you are safe from the Morelocks and their machinations, I will ask your father to petition for an annulment of this marriage."

"But you said you were not thinking of an annulment."

"I said I had no second thoughts about one. I know it is what we must do." The back of his hand caressed her cheek. "There is no place in my life for you and certainly none in yours for me. The time you have to endure this should be short."

"Short? You are leaving?"

"Yes."

"When?"

"Right now."

"Right now?" she choked. "Where?"

He smiled. "To get some pillows and blankets."

Grabbing a pillow off her bed, she flung it at him. How dare he mock her like this! Her life was turned upside down and inside out.

He caught the pillow and tossed it back on the bed. "Bethany—"

"I have heard all I wish to hear of your flummery, Eric Pennington! I wish I never had chanced upon you that day you walked into the shire." She walked toward the dressing room.

"Do you? Do you really?" he asked to her back.

She halted, wanting to believe she had truly heard pain in his voice. His hands on her shoulders slowly turned her to face him.

Gone was his ironic smile. Gone was the twinkle of

merriment in his eyes. Gone was everything but a sorrow that struck her more fiercely than the smugglers had.

"Do you?" he asked again in a raw whisper.

She shook her head. "No."

"Nor do I. Our lives may be a mull, but I would not trade a second of this jumble for anything when we can share this." With a groan, he pulled her into his arms and captured her mouth beneath his. She answered his longing with her own. When he released her so suddenly that she swayed back against the bed, she saw the glitter of craving in his eyes. He fingered the lace on the nightgown with another gut-deep groan.

Then, cursing under his breath, he walked out of the room.

He would be back.

She wished she knew what he would do then. She wished she knew what she would do.

# Eleven

Bethany was surprised to wake up alone in the morning. She had not thought she had slept, but apparently she had dropped off long enough for Eric to slip out of the room. After ringing for Vella, she was as silent as her abigail while she dressed. She saw Vella glance at the chaise longue on which a folded blanket and pillow were neatly stacked. Still, she said nothing. There had been enough lies in this house, but she could not speak the truth. She was not sure why. She only knew her heart ached within her like a broken-winged bird's.

Going down to the breakfast room, she hoped to be late, so she could avoid her family. Instead, when she paused in the doorway, she found them waiting for her, as unspeaking as Vella had been. Was this her punishment for hypocritical vows? To lose the closeness of her family?

*Were those vows so dishonest?* taunted the small voice in her head. She tried to ignore it.

She wondered where Eric was, because he was not in the breakfast room. She could not ask her family, for they would consider her a very odd bride not to know where her husband was the morning after their wedding.

When she could delay no longer, Bethany walked to the table. Neither Jay nor Titus met her eyes. Did they think she had been altered by her marriage? Mayhap they were right. Nothing could ever be the same in the wake of the lies and counterlies which had bound her life to Eric's.

"Good morning," she whispered, kissing first her father's cheek and then her grandmother's.

"Sit here beside me," Nana urged.

Nodding, she obeyed. Her grandmother patted her knee, out of sight of the others, in a motion so kind that Bethany feared the gathering tears would not stay in her eyes.

When a bowl of porridge was set in front of her, she asked, "Jay, will you pass the sugar, please?"

"Of course," he answered, without lifting his gaze from his food.

She wanted to ask why he refused to look at her, but said only, "Thank you." She understood his bewilderment, because she shared it.

When she had stirred some sugar into her porridge and dipped her spoon into it, she raised the spoon, then lowered it, the porridge untasted. Her family was intently eating. She tried to think of something, anything, to say that would sweep aside the despair smothering them, but no words seemed right.

Her fingers clenched on her spoon as a shadow crossed the table and draped her in velvet darkness. As she raised her eyes to meet Eric's, she wondered how, even in the midst of all this madness, she could have forgotten how handsome he was. Tawny lights danced in the sunlight caressing his hair as her fingers longed to do. Gone was the gray tinge from his accident; a tanned glow had returned to his face. A yearning to touch him afflicted her, but she kept her fingers tightly wrapped around the spoon.

Eric bent and kissed her on the cheek with a composure which gave no suggestion that there had been anything strange about their wedding and wedding night. "Good morning, my dear wife."

"Good morning, Eric," she said, her voice quivering. She could not halt her hand from reaching up to brush his freshly shaven cheek.

He turned his head and pressed her palm to his lips. The motion was not inappropriate, but the fire burning in his eyes was intensely intimate. She could not doubt what he was thinking. He regretted, as she did when he touched her so sweetly, that their marriage was one of appearance only.

Sandwiching her hand between his, he asked, "I trust I did not disturb you when I left the room this morning. You were asleep, and I did not wish to wake you *then.*"

In spite of her attempt to curb it, at his slight emphasis on that single word, suggesting he had awakened her at other times during the night, a blush oozed up her cheeks to heat her face. "No, you did not disturb me this morning."

"Come here, my boy," ordered Nana. "As you are part of this family, you should know by now that I expect to be acknowledged with a kiss on the cheek by each of my grandsons each morning."

With a chuckle, Eric kissed her proffered cheek.

Father glanced at them as he lifted his cup of coffee. "Sit down, Eric. As Mother said, you are now a part of this family. You need not wait for an invitation to partake of a meal."

"Thank you," Eric answered as he sat beside Bethany and across from her father. She did not doubt that he meant far more than the two simple words usually conveyed.

While the men spoke about the futile search for the French prisoner, they managed a casual air that Bethany could not copy. She toyed with her breakfast food until she heard her father say, "Eric, I am assuming you will be staying at Whitcombe Hall."

"For the time being."

"The time being?" she asked.

He smiled at her, but she was not bamboozled. That odd intensity had not left his gaze. "You and I must discuss our future at a time when we can speak in privacy, my dear wife."

"Yes, yes," her father said with an odd impatience. "That, of course, is your business. What I want to know now is, are you interested in joining the strand patrols, Eric?"

"The nightly patrols?"

"Yes."

He chuckled and smiled at Bethany. "Not every night, Anson."

Bethany had been about to ask her father about the patrols, but Eric's answer silenced her. He was enjoying this hoax far too much. Yet, if she denounced him, she would have to own that Eric intended to annul their marriage. She was not sure what her father might insist upon then. She could not believe he would wed her to Dunley, but everything seemed so peculiar.

At the end of the meal, she asked, "Father, may I speak with you a moment? Alone?"

He glanced at Eric, then said, "Of course. Eric, I will meet you in the stables in a few minutes."

"No hurry." He brushed Bethany's cheek with another kiss.

She fought her body that slanted toward him, wanting more than this chaste salute. Taking a steadying breath as he walked out of the room with Jay, she forced her fingers to unclench at her sides.

Nana herded Titus out of the room, chatting to him about Miss Gillette. His ears were a blistering red as she asked some pointed questions about his plans.

As their voices faded, Bethany was surprised when her father took her hand. He peeled her fingers back from the fist she had formed again without realizing it. Patting her hand, he smiled.

She smiled back. It was easier than she had guessed. She was tempted to throw her arms around him and spill the truth—all of it. She had not been Eric's lover, not before the wedding, not after, but she feared she was falling in love with a man who had already told her that he was going to leave her.

"I hope you and Eric are going to be happy, Bethany," Father said.

"We will try to be," she answered, hoping her reply sounded more assured to him than it did to her.

Her father's relieved smile told her what she should have known. He had been as uneasy as she about this breakfast. Although she guessed neither Father nor Nana believed any longer that she and Eric had been lovers before the wedding, she knew they would find it unimaginable that she had slept by herself last night.

"You are disturbed about Eric joining us for the nightly patrols, aren't you?" her father asked. "There is not much danger of doing more than tripping over something in the dark."

"The smugglers—"

"Will give us a wide berth. They do not want to be discovered by accident when we are on the lookout for the French to come ashore again. Eric has the instincts he learned while traveling through England to help him guide his patrol."

"His patrol? Are you planning to have Eric lead a patrol?"

"Not overtly, at first, but Jay could use some overseeing on his patrols. He respects Eric. It will work out well." He smiled. "After all, Bethany, if you trust Eric enough to give him your heart, I can trust him enough to keep track of your rambunctious younger brother while we guard the shore from invasion."

"Yes, of course," she said, not knowing what else to say. Again she had had the chance to be honest. Again she had hesitated too long.

"Oh," her father added, as he turned to leave, "your grandmother wishes to go into Fair Cove today. Do you mind taking her?"

She almost asked why he wondered, when she drove Nana into the village so often. Then she guessed he had thought she might be worried about facing censure from the villagers. She wondered what tales were racing through Fair Cove, but did not ask.

"Of course, Father. Let Nana know I am willing to drive her into Fair Cove whenever she wishes."

"You are a good child, Bethany." He bit his lip, then added, "And a brave one."

She said nothing as he walked out. She might be able to baffle her father with half-truths, but she could not do the same to herself. There was no reason to remain cowering behind the walls of Whitcombe Hall to hide from the lies the Morelocks might be spreading when she was living a lie herself.

Tryphena was coming out of a shop on the hilly street leading up from the sea just as Bethany opened the door. When Tryphena stuttered a greeting, Bethany stepped back out into the sunshine.

"Is my grandmother inside?" she asked.

"No, I think I saw her talking with Mrs. Caldecott in the apothecary's shop."

"Mrs. Caldecott?" Bethany chuckled in spite of her disquiet at the strain in her bosom-bow's voice. "I trust she will keep Nana busy for hours with her list of ailments."

"Your grandmother seemed to be doing most of the talking, for once."

Bethany's smile faded. No doubt, Nana believed she had more reasons to complain today than even Mrs. Caldecott. "That is quite a change."

"Lots of things are changing." Tryphena slipped her basket over her arm.

"Lots?" Bethany smiled tightly. "I had not thought one simple marriage could change all of Fair Cove."

Tryphena sighed. "There are some hateful things being said about you and that peddler you married."

"That peddler's name is Eric."

Putting a finger to her lips, Tryphena slipped her arm through Bethany's. She led the way back down the hill as she said softly, "I know that, but I did not want everyone to know what we spoke of."

"What else would we speak of?" Bethany's laugh was brittle as she noticed the surreptitious glances in their direction as they walked toward the shore. " 'Tis the same topic I wager everyone else must be speaking of."

"There is a difference." Tryphena smiled. "I am happy for you and Eric. I could see at the wedding celebration that you have much affection for each other."

"Could you?"

Tryphena pressed a hand over her heart and sighed. "He was so like the hero in one of the books you have lent me. He jumped to your defense with a fervor that can come only from a loving heart. When the people in Fair Cove see that, they will not heed the horrible rumors."

"What rumors?" She paused at the edge of the pebbly beach.

"I do not want to repeat them."

"Then you are most likely the only one." Bethany patted her friend's hand.

"When you bring Eric to the church picnic at the end of the month, everyone will see that Dunley's rumors are simply a result of his jealousy."

"People will choose to believe what they wish, no matter what any of us do. I truly believe that Dunley has come to believe his absurd assumptions."

"His father told him that he would be marrying you. He cannot believe he will not." She hesitated, then said, "Please do not take this the wrong way, but I suspect Dunley cannot imagine that you would choose a penniless peddler over him, the son of a baronet who is full of juice."

"You may take this any way you wish. I would have chosen any man over Dunley." Bethany smiled again.

"Even his father?"

She shivered, although the sun was warm. "I don't want to talk about that."

"So that rumor is true!"

"Eric assures me it is." She glanced back at the village. "I should go and see if Nana is ready to leave."

"Be careful, Bethany."

"I will." *More careful than I have been so far.*

Bethany sat by her bedroom window and watched the fog swirl as if being painted across the downs by a madman's brush. From below, she heard the clang of the clock in the foyer. It was two hours past midnight. Father had assured her that Eric would be home before midnight. When Jay had come home, more than an hour ago, he had told her that Eric wanted to check the stables and should be in straightaway.

Standing, she turned to see Vella asleep in a chair by the door. She gently shook her maid awake and sent her to bed in the small room on the other side of the dressing room, not wanting to chance Vella waking to discover Eric sleeping on the chaise longue.

Bethany tried to read, but the words blurred in front of her tired eyes. Even her favorite book, which had comforted her during her mother's illness, offered no respite from the worry.

Going to the window, she unlatched it and swung it open. The damp air surged in, but she paid it no mind as she tried to see through the mist that was interwoven with a tapestry of gems from the moonlight that did not reach the ground. She strained to hear, but no sound came except the distant motion of the waves upon the shore. She leaned her head against the casement.

Where was Eric?

Tears rolled thickly into her eyes as an ache in her chest warned that her fear had clamped around her heart. Her heart that longed to belong to Eric.

She pushed away from the window. Exhaustion! It must be only exhaustion that teased her with this delusion. She could not have her husband in her heart. She barely knew the man, but, as she thought of his slow, deep kiss before he had left this night, she knew the only one who was deluded was Bethany Whitcombe—Bethany Pennington. That beguiling light had been in his eyes when she had responded wholeheartedly to his kiss.

Hearing a door open downstairs, she rushed to her own door, but it was only one of the servants. She went back and sat on the bed, taking the book with her. Reading would make the time go more quickly and give her an escape from her thoughts.

She hoped.

* * *

Bethany frowned as she woke to find her blankets wrapped tightly around her. She did not recall when she had fallen asleep, but she had been deep in a dream. In it, she had been with Eric. His kisses, bestowed among the dappled shadows by the shore, had sent pulses of delight through her.

Unsure of what had wrenched her from sleep, she sat and rubbed her eyes. Seeing a silhouette move on the ledge outside her window, she bit back a scream. Who had climbed up here? Only a French fiend would be so desperate. Mayhap it was the prisoner who had fled from Fair Cove. Or was it a smuggler chased here by the shore patrols?

Leaning across her bed, she stretched a trembling hand out to Eric. When her hands found nothing on the chaise longue, her fear deepened. Where was he? From the lack of light, she knew the moon must have set. He should have been back hours ago.

She wanted to call out to him, but could not. Even a whisper might alert the man on the window ledge that she was awake. The window rattled softly, then opened wider. Swallowing her scream, she strained to find Eric. He must be there.

She gripped one corner of his blanket. It was there, but not her husband. In a breathless whisper, she called, "Eric? Eric, where are you?"

No answer.

The shadowed man was framed by the window. Slipping from her bed, she inched across the room until she could pull a pair of scissors from her sewing box. They were a poor weapon, but she would not let the French blackguard into her room. Her breath plugged her throat. What remained in her chest burned, but she did not release it.

The man boldly swung through her window, landing with cat-like quiet on the floor. When he started to walk past her, she aimed the scissors at the center of his back.

Her hand was caught in a vise as she was shoved against the wall. Her breath exploded from her, but the sound was muffled against a warm palm. When her fingers became numb, the scissors fell onto the bed. She took a deep breath so she might scream, but she choked on it when the scissors were held up in front of her face.

She heard a soft laugh. "This is hardly the greeting I expected from my dear wife."

"Eric!"

Tossing the scissors into her sewing basket, he grinned. "I thought you would be sleeping at this late hour, Bethany."

"Obviously." Fear augmented her burst of fury as he released her. "Where have you been?"

"Walking along the shore."

"Until this late hour?" She paused as she heard the clock clang three times. "Jay was home more than two hours ago."

"I had a few other places to check, as Anson had requested."

"Father told me you would be home by midnight."

He smiled. "He clearly knows these downs better than I, for I think I walked halfway to Brighton before I realized I was going in the wrong direction."

"But why did you sneak in this way? You could have been killed."

"I wasn't." He sat on the chair and tugged off his boots. Stifling a yawn, he shrugged. "I did not want to wake you. Why don't you go to sleep?"

She sat on the bed, her knees refusing to hold her. "Just like that? I do not expect you to tell me whom you have been with while your wife sleeps, but it seems that a lie would be appropriate at a time like this."

Standing, he stretched luxuriously before reaching for the buttons on his shirt. "Jealous, Bethany?"

"No!" She did not want to guess how close he was to the truth. After dreaming of being in his arms, she had not expected her happiness to come to such a quick and painful end.

He slid the shirt along the wind-burnished skin of his back which glinted in the moonlight with sweat. When she turned away, overmastered by the sight of such strong masculinity when her defenses against him were so fragile, he pulled on one of the new nightshirts Nana had purchased for him.

"It was your decision to make this a marriage of convenience," he said.

"Convenience?" she gasped. "A marriage of *inconvenience*, don't you mean?"

He gripped her shoulders, pulling her to her feet and away from her bed. "My dear wife, I recall that it was for your convenience, or at least the convenience of your reputation, that we wed."

"Are you going to hold that over me for the rest of our lives?" She tried to squirm away, but his arms tightened around her, holding her against him. That she wanted to soften against him and savor his touch vexed her more. "I have told you more than once that Dunley was the one who named you as my lover. Mayhap you should go and inflict your company on him."

"As cantankerous as you are being tonight, I might consider it if he was not on his way to London."

"He's on his way to London?"

"To find another bride, I suspect." His eyes narrowed. "I hope you will not be too distressed by that."

"You are despicable! I should hate you."

He bent forward so that his mouth was only inches from her ear. The pulse of his breath moved her hair and sent waves of unadulterated desire cascading over her. Closing her eyes, she delighted in the sensations that should have been perfect, but were wrong. When he spoke, she swallowed a moan of yearning which would complete the betrayal of the secret she hid in her heart.

"Sweet Bethany, whose eyes are like brilliant candles burning in the dark, you do not hate me."

"Mayhap you should go to Town with Dunley. You could use those flowery phrases to thrill the ladies."

"I would rather stay here and thrill you."

Edging out of his arms, she went to the window and closed it. "I see there is no sense in continuing to ask why you did not want anyone to know the time when you sneaked back into the Hall tonight."

He reached for his pillow and plumped it. "Be a good wife and let me sleep."

"Just like that?"

"Just like that."

Bethany asked herself what she had expected. He had told her that he was not going to tell her why he had come in this way. His shoes were covered with sand, so mayhap he had wandered far and gotten lost. That did not seem right. He was a peddler. He should know how to find his way.

As she stepped toward the bed, her nightgown tightened at her throat. Turning, she looked at Eric who was grinning at her as he held it. His hair was silver in the moonlight, but the blue of his eyes was lost in shadow as he drew her back toward him.

Bringing her to lean over him, he framed her face as he whispered, "Don't wonder about me, sweetheart. Just be my darling Bethany. Be safe in the cocoon of oblivion you've spun for yourself. I want to know that you're safe here when I cannot be with you."

"Safe?" Her voice was as low as his. "Is anyone safe

now? I feared you were that French prisoner sneaking into the Hall to kill us."

His smile tightened as did his hands at her waist. "That Frenchman has no interest in you. All he wants now is to get back to France, if he is not already there." Releasing her, he urged, "Go to sleep."

Her fingers lingered on the rough texture of his cheek. "I still do not understand why *you* are sneaking about."

"And?"

The impatience in his tired voice aggravated her so, she retorted, "I do not know why you once tried to steal a kiss from me whenever you could, but now . . ."

Seizing her elbows, he tugged her down next to him. He pinned her left hand against the blanket as he lifted the other against his chest. An involuntary gasp of pleasure burst from her lips as the unyielding muscles moved beneath her touch.

He pushed aside her sleeping cap to let her hair flow out like an ebony river. Brushing it aside, he teased the crescent of her ear. As she shivered with the power of his heated breath, she pressed closer.

A matching desire in his voice, he whispered, "My sweet Bethany . . . my sweet, sweet Bethany."

She wanted to answer, but sighed as the tip of his tongue outlined her mouth which hungered for his kisses. She wove her fingers through his hair, drawing his mouth over hers. Her breath mingled with his as his tongue sought to explore every luscious secret in her mouth.

She moaned with regret as he raised his lips from hers. Opening her eyes, she used a single fingertip to trace the strong line of his nose and the uncompromising curve of his lips.

"So soft you are, sweetheart," he whispered. "How

sweet it would be to hold you with your skin against mine!"

"I *am* your wife." She steered his mouth back to her.

Instead of kissing her, he sat, his back to her. She reached out to touch his back, but halted her fingers when he said, "I have had a long day, dear wife. Why don't you go to bed so I can sleep?"

"If that is what you want." She was not sure what else to say. Mayhap she had done something wrong, but how could there be anything wrong about something which was so glorious?

When he seized her arms again, she gasped as he growled, "Can't you realize that what we want sometimes is the very thing we cannot have?" He pulled his blanket over him.

She stood before it could whip out and strike her. She did not bother to speak, for she guessed he would not answer her. Why should he? She knew the answer as well as he did. What she did not understand was the reason. She feared it had to do with what had kept him out so late and had convinced him to scale that treacherous wall to her window.

But what could it be? She could not guess.

# Twelve

Bethany was silent as Eric handed her out of the carriage in front of the Gillettes' home. The grand country estate had been built less than a hundred years before, but had been designed to look as if it had stood on this outcropping overlooking the sea as long as Whitcombe Hall had. Every window was ablaze with lamplight, and other guests were mounting the dozen steps that led to the elegant double doors.

She would rather be anywhere else but this gathering tonight, however, Titus had told his friends that the whole family would be in attendance. She had considered begging off, saying she did not feel well. That would only create talk that she was with child and start more rumors about why she had wed Eric.

She could find no fault with his appearance tonight. Again he wore the well-made clothes he had donned when they were married. With his hair neatly trimmed and combed, he could be a fine gentleman visiting from Town, for now he even had polished shoes to match his other finery.

"Do I pass your inspection, dear wife?" he asked as he handed her to the ground. "Or must I suffer a curtain-lecture for some inadequacy?"

Jay chuckled and jabbed Eric in the side. "She can be a nag."

"Warren, watch yourself when you are among the

Beau Monde," Nana chided. "Come here, and escort your grandmother in."

Whitcombe gave them a sympathetic smile before following his mother and younger son up the steps. Titus had arrived on his own at least an hour ago.

Eric drew Bethany's hand within his arm. "You did not answer me."

"You had best accustom yourself to stares," she said as she lifted the hem of her pink dress to climb the steps with him. "You shall endure many tonight."

"We both shall."

"Yes, we both shall."

His finger under her chin tilted her face toward him. "I know I should tell you that I am sorry, but I will not be dishonest with you when you know how glad I am that we can share this."

He whirled her into his arms so swiftly that her feet stumbled on the steps. His arms kept her from falling as his lips found hers. As his kiss deepened, demanding that she give herself to his passion, her fingers climbed his arms to wrap around his nape. He pulled her even closer when they touched the skin beneath his high collar.

His breathing was as uneven as hers when he set her feet back on the stone riser. She gazed into his eyes, then reached up and brushed that recalcitrant lock back from his brow. With a smile, he offered his arm. She put her hand on it as she walked with him up the last few steps.

When she glanced behind them and saw no one, he chuckled. "I did not kiss you to create a public spectacle."

"I am sorry. I thought—"

"What you are wise to think, but I kissed you because I could not resist, not because I wanted to cause more talk. There should be enough already."

"More than enough."

He laughed again, so freely that heads turned as they entered the Gillettes' hexagonal foyer.

Bethany handed a footman her shawl, then slipped her hand onto Eric's arm again. She had not been in this home since the new black walnut paneling was added to the staircase that rose to separate in two directions to reach both wings of the house. A parade of portraits of Gillettes, past and present, followed the curve of the banister, but she did not notice them as she saw how many eyes were focused on her and Eric.

Her own gaze was caught by Nana's. The slightest lift of her grandmother's chin told her to act as if the stares were not of the least concern. When Eric squeezed her fingers gently, she knew she had all the allies she needed.

Holding out her hand to Mr. Gillette, she smiled at the man who was even rounder than his sister. He was a quiet person, so she had been surprised when his garrulous sister had persuaded him to have this evening's rout.

"Good evening, Miss—Mrs. Pennington," said Mr. Gillette in a rumbling voice.

"May I introduce my husband, Eric Pennington?" Bethany smiled.

Eric did the same, but was sure his expression resembled a grimace. He had met Francis Gillette before, although he had not realized it until now. That bass voice he had heard as Gillette had heard his. He hoped his was less distinctive, for that night neither of them had seen the other's face, but had only spoken.

"Good evening, sir," he said, waiting for Gillette's reaction. This could be the ruin of everything he had worked for.

"Congratulations on your wedding, Pennington."

Gillette's smile was as broad as his belly. "Miss Whitcombe has been eyed by many men around here, so you should count yourself very lucky."

"Very lucky." Eric relaxed his taut shoulders, then realized Bethany's fingers were digging into his arm. He might be able to hoax the others, but not her. *Blast it!* In spite of his efforts to let her know no more than she must, somehow, she sensed aspects of him that she must not.

As he spoke the proper words to Miss Gillette, he was aware of Bethany's wary glances at him. She could not know what was wrong, only that something had bothered him. Now he must make certain she did not discover what.

Guilt pierced him, startling him anew. He had forgotten about that emotion in recent months . . . until Bethany had come into his life and made him feel many things he had not thought he would experience again. He had not guessed he would be fighting a battle *inside* himself to keep from telling her every secret he must keep from her and everyone here tonight.

"If you wish to leave, Eric . . ." she began as they entered the grand salon where the evening's entertainment would be held.

"No, that would cause even more poker-talk."

She frowned at him, puzzled. Let her think he was concerned solely with salvaging her reputation from the muddle left by Morelock's jealousy. As the other guests swarmed toward them, he responded politely when he was introduced to each one. He took note of each name and of who stood beside whom, a skill that was as natural to him as breathing, but said little.

When he offered to get Bethany something cool to drink before the quartet began to play the first selection, she seemed pleased. Her smile faded when he left her by the chairs as he crossed the vast expanse of the gilt-covered room.

He was sweating as if he had raced from Dover to Penzance. He had been in other situations that were even more dangerous than this one, so he knew it was not fear that gripped him. It was the unrelenting battle to keep from gathering her up in his arms and throwing away good sense as he put an end to this marriage of convenience by giving free rein to his need for her. Had that longing compelled him to offer for her when he could have found another way to protect her from the younger Morelock?

*You are a leather-head.*

Those words had rung through his head since that day when he had foiled Morelock's plans for Bethany, but now he wondered if the jest was on him. He might have been a fool to leg-shackle himself to her, but he was a greater fool to let her sleep alone night after night.

He glanced at the fruit punch sitting on the table. With a curse, he walked past it. Gillette must keep something stronger elsewhere in the house. If so, he would find it. Mayhap a bottle of wine would erode away this craving. He doubted it, but he intended to find out before he did something truly foolish.

Bethany sighed as she offered yet another excuse for her missing husband. Where was Eric? She was torn between fury and anxiety. It was not like him to leave like this. Was it? She almost laughed aloud. She could not guess what Eric might do, because he was still almost as much a stranger as on the day she had met him.

Mayhap he had gone outside to escape the glances that had followed her as she sought him throughout the room. Stepping out through a French door, she took a deep breath of the warm air. Her shoulders ached as she let them sag. She had not guessed how stiffly she had been holding them.

Going to the edge of the tiny garden, she looked at the high hedge that separated it from the rest of the gardens. She sighed. Eric was not here. She had no choice but to go back inside and pretend nothing was amiss. It might be simpler if she knew whether something truly was amiss.

"Good evening, Mrs. Pennington."

Bethany whirled. The snide emphasis on her name could come only from Sir Asa Morelock. This was not the enemy she had feared meeting in a moonlit garden, but Sir Asa could be as dangerous to her as the French. As if she had no concerns, she walked toward the house. "Good evening."

"Where is Pennington?"

She wanted to curse his ability to find her weakest point with such ease. Instead she smiled. "Father has spoken frequently today of how he looked forward to acquainting his new son-in-law with Whitcombe Hall's neighbors." When his smile became a scowl, she hoped she had not pushed him too far. She should be more careful than she had been with Dunley. "You can find them inside."

"Inside?"

She saw the glitter in his eyes. She had been a widgeon to own that she was alone. She tried to shrug, but her rigid shoulders refused to move. "I came out here to let Titus know Miss Gillette is looking for him," she lied, for she had no idea where her older brother was. "Father has not wished me to be by myself—"

"Since you anticipated your vows with Pennington?"

"—since the attack by the smugglers," she continued in a taut voice.

"Is that so?" His feet crushed flowers as he stepped toward her. Laughing at her dismay, he said, "I wish to speak to you now, Bethany."

She motioned toward the house, hoping she could convince him to leave the garden before he destroyed all of Miss Gillette's flowers. "Why don't we—?"

"Why don't we do what?" He grasped her arm. When his other hand inched along her shoulder where it was bared by her gown, his smile broadened. "Where is that warmth you offered to Pennington instead of my son?"

Bethany laughed, so he could not suspect the depths of her distaste. Then, he would press his attack. "You should not listen to the lies spread about Fair Cove."

"Lies? You owned to taking Pennington as your lover."

"Dunley devised that lie." Batting aside his hand, she stepped away from him. "He and you are the only ones who believe that ridiculous out-and-outer. My family and my husband and everyone else know the truth."

As he laughed, his arm encircled her waist. "We can prove to everyone that my son was not lying."

"Prove?" She tried to back away.

"That you truly prefer a Morelock to a penniless peddler." He gripped her chin, pushing her face back so her mouth was beneath his.

With a shriek, she struggled to break free. It was as useless as trying to move Whitcombe Hall. Turning her face away, she evaded his mouth. His fingers dug into her as he forced her lips back toward his.

She struck his face. When he reeled back, a shorter form stepped out of the shadows. She clenched her hand against her lips to silence her scream as she saw a fist whip forward. Sir Asa collapsed to the ground.

In disbelief, she watched Jay walk toward her, shaking his fist. She ran and threw her arms around him, then stepped back. "Did he hurt you?" she asked.

"I was about to ask the same of you."

"I am fine."

"As I am." He grinned. "Better than fine. *Mon Dieu,* I have been itching to do that since he was so nasty to Father when you and Eric were married."

"Watch what you say!"

"About your wedding?"

"No, the French. You might be mistaken in the darkness for the escaped prisoner."

He laughed. "Then I shall endeavor to speak only German oaths from now on." Rubbing his knuckles, he asked in a more somber tone, "What were you doing out here with Sir Asa? You should know better, Bethany!"

"I came out here alone. I was looking for Eric, and I know how he enjoys the fresh air." She took his arm, tugging him away from where Sir Asa was shifting groggily. "You cannot tell anyone about this."

"If you did nothing amiss—"

"I did not, but I fear what Eric or Father might do if they were to hear of this."

"Give Sir Asa another taste of his own cruelty, I suspect."

She lowered her voice so no one might hear it but Jay. "Did Sir Asa see that it was you who hit him?"

"I don't know. I was not sure it was him until just before my knuckles found his chin." He grimaced. "He has a dashed hard chin. Mayhap if his head were not so blasted hard, he would not be so bacon-brained and would accept that you and Eric are married forever and ever."

Bethany could not halt her flinch at Jay's words. To be honest and reveal that Eric planned to annul their marriage would add more oil upon the already fierce fire simmering behind barely polite smiles.

"Then say nothing of this to anyone," she urged. "No one."

"But, Bethany, if others knew how Sir Asa treated you—"

"And how you treated him, we would both be hailed." She smiled sadly. "You are a hero, Jay, and I appreciate it more than you can know, but I do not want Eric hurt in avenging me."

"I floored Sir Asa with ease. Eric should be able to—"

"You surprised him. He is no fool. He will not be surprised again." She tightened her hold on his arm. "Please, heed me on this, Jay. For once, both of us must think something through clear to the conclusion before we make a decision that could have horrible results."

Slowly he nodded. "All right."

"Thank you," she whispered.

"It shan't be easy." He glanced over his shoulder as they walked to the door. "I would like to regale everyone with this tale."

"Mayhap you are growing up more than I had guessed."

"Mayhap I am, and mayhap you will remember that when I speak to you next about joining the army."

She shook her head. "I cannot change my opinion on that, because I am looking forward to getting to know the man you will be, Warren Whitcombe. I hope I have many years to find that out." She did not add as they entered the room that tonight made her more certain than ever that Jay should not buy a commission or enlist. His determination to be a hero could lead him to death. The last thing she wanted in her family was a well-decorated hero whose last medal was given posthumously.

The echo of her father's laughter followed Bethany up the stairs. He and Eric had spent the time on the short journey from the Gillettes' home debating how Francis Gillette had managed such sensationally good luck at cards that night.

She had not gone to look for Eric in the card room off a back passage, away from where the more sedate entertainments were being held. The gentlemen played for high stakes, and she had not suspected that Eric would be able to afford to play in such company.

Shrugging off her cloak, she entered the bedchamber that was no longer a comfortable retreat, for Eric had invaded every aspect of it—her dressing room, her favorite chair, her small collection of treasured books. Every aspect, save for her bed.

"You are oddly quiet," Eric said as he followed her into the room and shut the door.

"I have nothing of import to say."

"Not of the musical choices tonight?"

"Why speak of them when you were not there to hear them?"

"I thought the chance to sit at the board of green cloth with your father and his neighbors was an opportunity I should take advantage of."

"Take advantage of? Is that your only reason for joining them?"

"Do you think I was trying to avoid you?"

"No."

"Do you think I was trying to avoid the gossip?"

"Mayhap."

He smiled as he drew off his coat and loosened the

neatly tied cravat at his collar. As he tossed it onto a table, he again resembled the peddler who had first greeted her with such a roguish smile.

"You are right, Bethany. I had no interest in recounting the details of our courtship, for I was not sure what tale you were spinning for your friends." He folded his arms on the high back of a chair. "And I would be want-witted not to take advantage of meeting the *élite* of this area." His smile vanished so quickly, she blinked as he added, "And I would be want-witted not to know of the incident in the garden."

"In the garden?"

"When your brother gave Sir Asa a facer."

Her hands clenched beneath the cloak draped over her arms. "Jay vowed to say nothing of that."

"He didn't, but he could not hide the pride in his every step tonight. When I chanced to see Sir Asa come in from the garden and take his leave with unparalleled speed, I guessed the two events might be connected."

Her smile was cold. "So you allowed me to confirm it for you by tricking me."

" 'Twas no trick, simply a good guess." He came around the chair. "What I cannot guess is why your brother felt compelled to darken Sir Asa's daylights."

"It is over. Jay and I agreed not to discuss it."

"Sir Asa is determined not to let your wedding vows halt him from his plans to seduce you, is he?" He laughed without humor. "And why should he be bothered by your wedding vows to me when he would not have been bothered by the vows you would have spoken with his son?"

She turned away. "Eric, it is over. I do not want to discuss it."

She folded the cloak over the back of a chair and reached for her nightgown on the bed. When Eric's broad hand covered hers, she longed to lean her head back against his chest as his arms enveloped her. He drew her hand back and lifted it to his lips. She melted back against him as he teased her fingers with the tip of his tongue. A moan fled from her lips when he traced the center of her palm with fiery kisses.

Whirling, she found the welcome she longed for on his lips and in his arms. As her arms arched up his back, she smiled when he raised his mouth and looked down at her.

"This is very nice," she whispered.

"Yes, very." He traced her lips with his tongue. When she sighed with eager surrender, he added, "Much better than arguing over why you don't want to tell about that madman's attack on you."

She pulled away. "Attack? Eric, you are making something out of—"

He spun her to stand in front of her cheval glass. Tugging at the lace on her right sleeve, he pointed to where it had ripped away. "Something out of nothing? I think you are trying to make nothing out of something, Bethany. The only question is why."

He ran his fingers along her cheek, then down her neck. When they brushed the curve of her breast above her gown, her hand rose to his. Not to push his questing fingers away, but to keep them against her, so this ecstasy would not end.

"Because," she whispered, "I did not want you to get hurt by that beast."

"Bethany, I can take care of myself."

"I know, but I do not want you hurt because of me." She closed her eyes as his fingers played across her bodice. "Because I love you."

His hands were snatched back as if she had struck him. Turning her to face him, he gasped, "Are you out of your mind?"

"Yes, mayhap I am, but I know for sure that you are in my heart."

"You sweet, naïve fool."

When he walked away from her to peer out the window, she bit her lip. So many things she wanted to say, so much she wanted to ask. If she let even a single word past her lips, she would not be able to halt all of it from spilling out. She already had said too much, but she did not regret being honest. The truth had gnawed at her for too long.

"You know," he continued, "that this marriage is only temporary."

"I know."

"So you should know better than to tell me that you love me."

"You make it sound so simple."

"It has to be." Eric swung the window open. Mayhap the remnants of the day's heat would ease the chill that had settled on him. He could not delay saying what he must any longer. Bethany's heartfelt declaration made this even more difficult to do. "I must be gone for a few days," he said as he looked up at the stars.

"Gone?"

"Yes. I told you there were some other deliveries I had promised to make." He sat on the sill and saw that she was sitting, too, but on the bed. If he went to her and pressed her back into that wide mattress . . . No, he must not.

"Will you be returning?"

Her simple question drove a shaft into his heart, and he fought to pay no attention to the pain. He must not heed that organ which could betray him far too easily when he gazed into her colorless face. It would beseech him to ease her fears by telling her the truth . . . all of it. The truth of how, each night, he had leaned back on that chaise longue, which was a foot too short for him, and listened to her try to sleep. Even when she had found escape from the need tangling them together in a snare neither could flee, he had not been so fortunate. Then he had been taunted by the soft sounds of her breathing while he imagined her breath coming quick and uneven as he swept her into his arms and held her in her bed.

"Eric?"

How long had he been lost in his thoughts of making her his? He was finding it more and more difficult to push aside those fantasies that he could make come true if he went to her now.

Standing before he could let his own thoughts seduce him, he clasped his hands behind him. Only then, when he was sure he could keep his fingers from reaching out to touch her, did he say, "Of course, I shall be returning. What sort of man do you think I am that I would abandon you?"

"I don't know what sort of man you are, Eric." She came to her feet slowly.

He silenced his groan as she stepped toward him. Moving back to keep the distance between them the same, he heard laughter. Not from her, but from his own thoughts when he considered how his tie-mates would be amused by his resistance to this sweet pleasure. He was acting like a young miss just out of the schoolroom, afraid of the very idea of the devastating power of the desire in her breathless words.

"You don't know me, yet you say that you love me?" he asked. "That makes no sense, Bethany."

"Nothing makes sense any longer. Nothing has made any sense since you came into my life." Her voice softened to a husky whisper. "Nothing but being in love with you. Eric, I have tried to turn aside this longing in my heart, but it will not heed me. My heart is yours. Mayhap it is senseless, but I do love you."

She put her hands on his arms. He shook them away. When she stared at him with anguish in her doe-like eyes, he struggled not to succumb to the fierce longing to soothe her despair and to ease his own craving for her. To stand so close to her and to be aware of her with every inch of him was an exquisite torment.

"I will see you before week's end, Bethany," he murmured as he walked toward the door.

"Eric?"

"What?" he asked without turning.

Entreaty filled her voice. "I thought you were going to kiss me before you left. I mean . . ."

His face hardened as he seized her shoulders. Staring into her shocked eyes, he demanded, "What do you expect of me? I was not lying when I told young Morelock that your appealing charms are urging me to madness. If I hold you and kiss you, my dear wife, I doubt I could be halted with just that."

"And if you were not?"

He stared at her in disbelief. His hands slipped up from her shoulders to cup her face. If he had chanced upon her even a year ago, he would not have hesitated to accept this invitation, but he was not the man he had been a year ago. Too much had happened to change him.

He released her and walked to the door. He did not look back as he closed it. If he did, he might never leave.

# Thirteen

Bethany tossed a pebble into the stream. Her hope that a walk across the summer leas and into the woods would ease her aching heart had come to naught. As when she had tried to ease her fear about Jay entering the army, she had found no comfort.

Picking up another pebble, she threw it into the water. The splash sent a ring flowing outward, but it disappeared into the rippling stream as if it had never existed.

She pushed herself to her feet. A hint of hysterical laughter tickled the back of her throat. After she had dressed Jay down for not thinking before he acted, she had blurted out the truth that she loved Eric. She should have paused to remember what he had told her the night of their wedding. He had married her solely to give her the protection of his name. Nothing else.

Tears weighed heavily in her eyes, but she refused to let them fall. Eric had been gone for over a week. Mayhap he would be waiting for her when she returned to Whitcombe Hall. She must not let her hopes rise wildly, for she wondered how many more blows her heart could endure.

Dampness struck her face. Not from her tears, but from the gray skies.

Glancing upward, Bethany muttered, "*Mon—Ach*

*du lieber Himmel!*" She smiled, then grimaced as more rain fell.

Suddenly, the rain came down as if a wave had erupted up out of the sea. The brim of her bonnet collapsed as it was drenched. Lightning flashed. When thunder sounded only seconds later, she flinched.

Mr. Griffen's house was not far away. She would seek shelter there. Pulling her shawl up over her head, she hurried between the trees. The wind followed, twisting her skirts around her legs.

The stone house was almost invisible, as gray as the sky. A broken plow was set next to a ragged stump. Two buckets, one of them with missing slats, waited next to the well that was edged with moss. She ran to the front door as a double bolt of lightning lit up the sky.

She pounded on the wood; then, when she got no answer, she peeked through the window. Was someone moving in there?

Pushing her soaked hair back under her bonnet, she hurried around to the back of the house. She would not stand in the rain while waiting for Mr. Griffen to shake off his blue ruin fog. She would wait out the storm in his barn.

Bethany faltered when she saw some motion through the storm. Was someone else seeking shelter in the barn? At least, it would give her someone to commiserate with while she waited for the storm to pass so she could go back to Whitcombe Hall and change into dry clothes.

The hoot of an owl sounded near her. Had it been confused by the dark clouds into thinking night was coming? She had never heard of such a thing. A burst of fear threatened to strangle her. Could it be a signal? From whom? To whom?

Her ragged breath was as loud as a shout in her ears

as she lifted her skirts to flee. Suddenly, as if bursting from the depths of her most horrid nightmare, two forms appeared.

French soldiers!

She stared, as she backed away in one slow step, at the green and black pantaloons visible beneath the heavy greatcoats. When one man pulled a pistol from beneath his coat, she saw the flash of chevrons on the green sleeve of his uniform.

He smiled, the dark eyes above his gaunt cheeks narrowing. She wanted to beg him not to slay her, but she knew how useless her cries for mercy would be. Even if she screamed, she could not depend on Mr. Griffen to come to her aid. The man's fingers opened and closed on his gun, as if he were trying to decide what order to give.

She dared another step backward—bumped into something hard. Her arms were grasped and jerked behind her. Pulling against the strong grip, she looked over her shoulder to see another French soldier. She screamed.

"Silence her!" ordered the man with the gun. He spoke French brazenly.

A hand closed on her throat.

"Do not slay her." The officer muttered something under his breath, then added, "Just keep her quiet. You heard the captain's orders."

Bethany did not say anything because she wanted to let them think she was unable to comprehend their language. That way, they might reveal something that could lead to *their* capture . . . if she escaped alive.

The Frenchman with the gun came toward her with such stealth that his passage barely moved the underbrush. Now she understood how he and his comrades had been able to sneak so close to the village. She started to lean away from him as he put out his hand, but her head struck her captor's broad chest.

A slow smile spread across the soldier's full lips. Catching her chin in his palm, he forced her head up. Horror burned through her as she saw the obvious lust in his gaze as it slipped over her.

She wanted to snarl that she would prefer either of the Morelocks to a French pig, but she must remain silent.

"Do you live here, *mademoiselle?*" the soldier asked with a heavy accent.

She shook her head.

"Then you must have been spying on us," he announced as if he were judge and jury and executioner.

She shook her head in fervent denial.

"You wish me to believe you just happened to be walking through the rain?" he continued. With a laugh, he switched to French, "Bring her to the captain."

Fear slashed Bethany as she was pushed toward the barn. She spun about to flee, but saw a gun in front of her face. She walked toward the barn. Mayhap if they thought she was browbeaten, she might find an opportunity to escape.

She pushed back her wet hair as she stepped into the gloomy barn. Odors of animals and rotten hay fouled the air; but she paid that no mind as she stared at the five men crouched in the center of the floor. When they did not look up, she saw they had a sheet of paper on the floor between them.

A map? Sweet heavens, they were planning an invasion. Fear clamped around her as she realized they could not let her go. She could describe each of these men, save for their leader who had his back to her, to her father.

The captain, who wore a cloak tossed back over one

shoulder to reveal his epaulets, spoke so lowly that his whisper was lost beneath the drips of water coming through the thin thatch of the room. His men nodded, so intent on his words that they had not looked up.

She sensed her captor's impatience. More than once, he cleared his throat, but the captain waved him to silence. She could not doubt that the matter he was discussing was of the most vital importance.

She closed her eyes and whispered a silent prayer. A soft sob escaped her tight lips at the thought of never seeing Eric's face once more, of never knowing again the pleasure of his touch. How ironic that the answer she had sought during her walk was being provided this way! She *was* glad she had not delayed in telling Eric that she loved him.

The soldier jerked her away from the door, and she gasped as she stepped into a puddle.

"Be silent, *mademoiselle,*" he growled.

*"Mademoiselle?"* came the captain's low voice. As he stood and faced them, he continued in French, "Who in hell have—?"

"Eric!" Bethany choked out. Disbelief twisted through her. Above his green uniform with its garish epaulets was the face she had seen so close to hers when he kissed her. "No, Eric! Not you!"

Tersely, he ordered, "Release her!"

The soldier cursed and pushed Bethany away from him. She simply stared. As if in the midst of an appalling dream, she took a step toward Eric, who was dressed in a French officer's uniform. Looking from one face to the next, she saw the Frenchmen were as shocked as she was.

"Do you know this woman, Captain Pellissier?" asked the man who had captured her. "She must be a spy."

"I am not a spy!" Bethany cried in French. She refused to be killed without knowing the truth. All of it must be revealed now. She must know why Eric was wearing this hated uniform.

Grasping her arm, the sergeant whirled her against a stall. He held his pistol up against her chin. "Be silent, Englishwoman."

"Sergeant LeBec, put that gun away!"

As the gun was lowered, Bethany looked past the sergeant. *That man could not be Eric!*

The captain motioned for her to come closer. Continuing to stare at him, she tried to force her feet to move.

"Release her, Sergeant!" he ordered.

"I am not holding her, sir." LeBec gave her a sharp shove forward. "Go, woman! Captain Pellissier wants to talk to you. Find your tongue, for he shall have no patience with your muteness."

"Sergeant, cease your threats," the captain said, his French even more free of accent than hers. "She is frightened almost to death."

When he took her hands, she moaned. The ripple of rapture sweeping along her skin told her that her eyes had not been deceived. This man who wore the elegant French lancer's uniform was Eric Pennington, her husband, the man who held her heart. She could not mistake his beguiling touch for any other's, for her fingers knew the warmth of his.

"Eric?" she whispered. "Why are you wearing this uniform?"

He had no chance to answer.

One of the men squatting by what was unmistakably a map asked, "How does this woman know you, sir?"

Eric raised Bethany's left hand and pressed his lips to the gold band on her finger. "She is my wife."

"Wife?" choked out Sergeant LeBec. "Why is your wife here in England?"

"Because I am English," Bethany fired back.

"Hush," Eric murmured. "Do not make this worse."

Although she was unsure as to how it could be made worse, she nodded.

"Captain Pellissier, you have an English wife?" Sergeant LeBec asked; then he laughed as his gaze raked Bethany again. "But what bridegroom is interested in politics when he has a bride as fair as this one?"

"Enough, LeBec," Eric ordered, his gaze not leaving hers. "Join the other men."

The sergeant hesitated. When Eric repeated the order in a sharper voice, the man stomped over to the others. They bent their heads together, staring at the map before them, but Bethany knew the topic of conversation was their captain's unexpected bride.

*Captain!*

Awareness of betrayal swept through her, bitter as bile and as hot as a flame. Eric had lied about being a traveling peddler. How readily he had duped them! She closed her eyes in agony. If he had been as false about everything, his kisses might have been feigned. He had used their marriage as a way to inveigle his way into her father's favor to gain information on the patrols and betray them.

When his hand brushed her arm, she drew back in dismay. She did not want to delight in a traitor's caress. "Don't touch me!"

"Bethany, you must let me explain," he said quietly.

"Explain? How can you when I see you with *them?*"

"Believe me when I tell you that I never meant for you to find out about this. If—"

"If I had been a good wife, never questioning why you had married me and why I loved you when you hid so much from me, you would never have needed to reveal any of this. You could have gone on betraying my father and his friends"—her voice broke as she added—"and me."

"Sweetheart, it is not as it appears."

Her eyes widened as she fought the sharply edged laugh in her throat. "Not as it appears? *Mon Dieu!*" She shuddered at her own poor choice of words. "Good heavens, Captain Pellissier, how can it be anything but what I see before my eyes? You are a French lancer, a captain!"

"And I am your husband."

"Do not remind me of what shall be my eternal shame!"

He caught her shoulders and brought her up against his chest. His kiss cajoled her into forgetting everything but the delight of his mouth on hers. When her fingers rose, she pulled them back with a moan as they brushed the gold braid of his epaulets.

Pushing herself out of his arms, she wrapped her own around her waist. Her perfidious body urged her to return to his embrace, to forget everything but the pleasure they could share. To surrender to it would mean turning her back on everything else she loved, everything she believed.

His fingers coursed along her shoulders. When he bent to whisper through her ruined bonnet, his breath swirled around her ear, feverish and tempting. "Whether you believe it or not, I shall never betray *you.*"

She faced him, astonished that he still spoke in French. "Why should I believe that?" She kept her chin high, so the tears flooding her eyes could not overflow.

"You wouldn't believe anything I told you, would you?"

"Why should I?"

"Because you love me, Bethany."

"I love Eric Pennington, the man who risked his life to protect me, the man who—"

"The man who delights in touching you." His finger trailed along her cheek and to the corner of her mouth. "The man who aches for your lips." Across her chin, his finger slid past the soaked ribbons of her bonnet to graze the ruffle at the top of her bodice. "The man who cannot sleep when he is alone because he wishes to sleep with you in his arms."

She edged back, then faltered when rain struck her. She was not at the door, so it must be coming through the roof. "Please do not say such things."

"Why not? It is the truth."

"The truth? Do you even know what it is? Our whole life is a lie. Have you enjoyed your game with my heart, Captain Pellissier?"

"Call me Eric."

"Why? Isn't your name Captain Eric Pellissier?"

"Bethany, I am telling you the truth."

"I don't know if I can ever believe—"

His arm surged around her, pulling her up to his hateful uniform again as he whispered, "That I love you?"

"No," she moaned. "Don't tell me that now."

"Because you no longer love me?"

"Because I hate what you are in this uniform."

His hands framed her face as they had the night he had left her alone. Only now did she know he had left Whitcombe Hall to plot its invasion. "I would have done almost anything to keep you from learning about this until a time when the truth would not be painful for you."

"When did you think that would be? When the French Army washes ashore in Fair Cove?"

"Bethany, you must think upon what you are saying. If—"

"No!" She shoved his hands away. Backing toward the barn door, she whirled into the storm as he reached for her.

She heard shouts behind her as she raced into the trees. Overhead, thunder chased streaks of lightning. She did not slow as she ran out onto the road and saw a carriage coming toward her. Waving it down, she glanced back over her shoulder. The soldiers were not far behind.

"Miss Whitcombe?" came a quavering voice from inside the carriage.

"Mrs. Caldecott!" She did not wait for an invitation to climb into the vehicle. Even Mrs. Caldecott's endless litany of ailments seemed welcome today.

As the carriage turned toward Whitcombe Hall, Bethany glanced back toward the woods. The shadows were as empty as her heart.

Everything was so clear in retrospect. Peddling was the perfect profession for a spy. Eric could wander into each village, appraise its defenses in case of an invasion, and learn the names of the village leaders while sharing what he pretended was news from beyond the town.

But he was not a peddler. He was a French captain, sworn to conquer England for that dirty Corsican and to destroy everyone who tried to stop him, including her family and friends . . . and his very own wife.

She relaxed back against the seat and shut her eyes. She wished she knew what would happen now. How could she explain Eric's absence to her father and her brothers when Eric did not return to Whitcombe Hall? Unlike her husband, she was not skilled at lying, but she guessed she soon would be unless she wanted to watch him hanged as a spy.

# Fourteen

"My goodness, child. What happened to you?"

Bethany wondered if everything was going to go wrong today. She had hoped to sneak into Whitcombe Hall unseen, but as Nana walked toward her, she knew that was now impossible.

"I got caught out in the storm, Nana." She plucked at her dress. "I should go and change."

"An excellent idea." Her grandmother's nose wrinkled. "You are leaving puddles in your wake."

She said nothing as Nana walked with her up the stairs to her bedchamber. She should have guessed from the tilt of her grandmother's chin that Nana would not be satisfied with asking a single question.

Nana sat on the chaise longue while Vella helped Bethany dry her hair and change. Although she had expected Nana to fire a barrage of questions at her, the older woman was silent. She tapped her fingers on the cushions of the chaise longue until Vella gathered up Bethany's drenched clothes to take them to be laundered.

Bethany sat in the chair by the window as she brushed the tangles from her hair. She could not keep from glancing out into the steady rain. What a witless air-dreamer she was! She could not halt her heart from beseeching her gaze to seek the drive to discover if

Eric was coming through the gate. He would not be returning to Whitcombe Hall.

*Ever.*

"Bethany?"

She looked at her grandmother.

"Did you decide what to do about you and Eric?"

"About me and Eric?" Sweet heavens, could Nana know the truth? So little that happened around Fair Cove failed to reach Nana, but this . . . "What do you mean?"

Nana smiled. "I know you have been troubled by your marriage, although I do not know why, for this match is one that should be pleasing to both of you."

"It should be."

"So did you decide what you should do?"

Rising, she set her brush on the table and tied her damp hair back with a ribbon. "Yes, I have decided."

"Yet you sound so sad."

"It has not been a pleasurable afternoon." Bethany did not have to fake a shiver. "It was frightening to be out in the thunderstorm."

"So you sought shelter in a byre?" When Bethany gasped, Nana held up a piece of straw. "Don't look at me as if I have read your mind, child. This fell off your gown."

Bethany took the straw and tossed it onto the windowsill. "I was not far from Mr. Griffen's house when the storm started. He was not home, so I considered seeking shelter in his barn. I swear there was as much water coming through the roof as through the trees."

"So you headed for home?"

"Delivered here safely, thanks to Mrs. Caldecott."

That was the wrong thing to say, she realized, when Nana's eyes narrowed. "I thought you vowed not to speak to Mrs. Caldecott after she aimed her demure hits at you whenever she had the chance at the Gillettes' musicale."

"I thought listening to her insults about my lack of virtue were less intolerable than being struck by lightning." She wished she could ease her grandmother's concern, for she had forgotten until now Mrs. Caldecott's behavior at the gathering. Sir Asa's even more outrageous actions had pushed it completely out of her head. She could not say that, because the truth would distress Nana more.

Nana chuckled. "I have to say I would have made much the same choice myself, although Mrs. Caldecott should recall her manners." Without a pause, she added, "When do you anticipate Eric returning here?"

"I am not sure when."

"Or if?"

She stiffened her shoulders so the shudder rising along her spine would not be visible. "Nana, how can you ask such a question?"

"Because everyone else is, although they are too polite to speak of it to you."

"He had some business to complete. I told you that."

"Any deliveries he had promised to make he could have had one of the servants tend to." Nana raised a single finger. "Do not try to hoax me with out-and-outers, child, by telling me that Eric is unaccustomed to making requests of the servants. You know as well as I that he has not always been a peddler."

"I suspect you are right."

"I *know* I am right." Nana rose, putting a hand on her right hip. When Bethany stepped forward to help her, Nana waved her away. " 'Tis just the weather, child. The dampness gnaws at my old bones just as curiosity gnaws at my mind. As it does at yours."

"You are wrong, Nana. I am not curious about where Eric is."

Instead of the frown Bethany had expected, Nana chuckled. "Good. Mayhap you are coming to trust that fine man you married instead of acting as if he had abandoned you."

Trust? She almost laughed, too. She must have given some answer, because Nana kissed her lightly on the cheek, told her to come down for tea in a few minutes, and left.

Bethany sat on the chaise longue and looked at the pillow that was propped there. With a moan, she pressed her face against it and wept.

Bethany hoped she had washed away all the dredges of tears from her face. As she came down the stairs, she was glad that the house seemed empty. She did not even meet a servant as the distant rumble of thunder heralded another storm about to descend upon Whitcombe Hall.

Going into the small parlor, she was surprised that no one else was there. She glanced at the clock on the mantel and realized she was a half-hour early for tea. In her determination to be certain no one noticed she had been crying, she had misread the clock outside her room.

She went to the window and stared at the blackening clouds stitched with white needles of lightning. This storm looked to be even more ferocious than the earlier one. She hoped Eric had better shelter than Mr. Griffen's leaky barn.

"Stay safe," she whispered. "And far from here."

"Bethany?"

She whirled from the window and stared at Titus, who stood in the doorway. Even though the day's heat was close and stifling, he wore a dark brown coat and a correctly tied cravat.

"You startled me," she said.

"I am sorry about that. I am glad, however, that you are alone."

She was not sure whether to laugh or cry at Titus's relief. Yes, she was alone. Completely alone.

"Can I get some advice from you?" he asked as he drew the pocket doors closed.

"Of course, although I am not sure how valuable my advice is at the moment." She sat on the settee. When thunder thudded against the house like cannon, she shivered. She hoped she would never hear the sounds of real cannon fire aimed at these walls.

"Your advice has always been good in the past." He grimaced as he sat across from her in the chair Nana usually chose. "Better than mine, it would appear." He looked over his shoulder. "Jay told me what happened at the Gillettes' party."

"Nana is upset about Mrs. Caldecott—"

"Not about that old tough. About Sir Asa."

She scowled. "He wasn't supposed to tell anyone."

"Did you really believe our little brother could keep such a coup quiet?"

When he smiled, she gasped, "But I thought you had changed your mind about the Morelocks. I thought you liked them."

"Dunley, yes, and I had hoped I had been mistaken about Sir Asa's ways. It seems I was not." He sighed. "His darker side bursts out of control too often. It is too bad, because he is not an evil man."

Bethany arched her brows, but said, "Sir Asa is not whom you wish to discuss."

"No."

"Is it Miss Gillette?"

"No."

"No?" She sat straighter. "Then whom?"

"Miss Sullivan."

"Tryphena?" Her voice squeaked.

He rubbed his hands together between his knees. "I did not handle that situation well, I am afraid."

"On the contrary, Tryphena seems to understand why you no longer call and bears you no resentment."

His shoulders sagged. "She is a generous soul to be so forgiving."

"She cares for you, and she would forgive you almost anything."

"She cares that much for me?"

"Yes." She looked away. Tryphena could forgive Titus for stopping his visits to the parsonage, but how could she forgive Eric? She wanted to forgive him. She could have forgiven him almost anything . . . except being false with her as he had.

"I look forward to speaking with Miss Sullivan at the church gathering." He hesitated, then asked, "Will you help me speak with her there?"

She smiled and took his hands in hers. "Of course. I would be very happy to do that. But what of Miss Gillette?"

"Others have assumed that she has more affection for me than she does."

"So you will not be calling there as often?"

He shook his head as he stood. "Francis and I remain the best of tie-mates. That will not change."

"That is good."

"It is." He bent and took her hands. "Now tell me what is amiss with you. Are you still worried about that escaped French prisoner?"

"French prisoner? I have given him no thought lately."

"Mr. Cartman said 'tis a waste of time to be searching for him."

"Why does he say that?"

"Said the man must be halfway to Vienna now." He grinned. "Actually he said, if he were the escaped prisoner, he would be halfway to Vienna now."

"I hope he is gone. It will make it much more comfortable for everyone at the church outing."

"Do you think Eric will be back for that?"

"I am not certain when he will return."

"And that is what is bothering you?"

"I miss my husband."

He sat on the settee beside her. "I know that, but I saw you come down the stairs. You looked as if you were trying to hide from the world."

"I wanted a chance to be alone for a while."

"And I intruded?"

"No, you did not intrude. I am glad you came to speak with me, especially about this." Talking about his concern for Tryphena had given her a moment's respite from thinking of how and when she should reveal to her family that Eric would not be returning.

"Bethany, are you quickening?"

"A baby?" The idea of surrendering to mirthless laughter teased her. There could not be a child when Eric had never shared her bed and would not now. "No, I am not pregnant."

"Then what else is wrong?" Titus pinned her in place with his anxious gaze.

"Nothing!" At her sharp answer, he stared at her, so she tempered her voice. " 'Tis something I have to attend to myself."

"With Eric?" Her brother's insight seldom failed him, and it had not now.

"To own the truth," she said, although she was not doing so, "Eric and I had a brangle before he left to make these deliveries. I will be glad when we can resolve it." Mayhap it was not a lie, because she wished it could be so.

"I am certain you will find your differences matter little when you are together again."

Although she wanted to tell him how desperately she hoped he could be right, she said, "I had no idea that you were an expert on marital matters."

He grinned. "I shall get married someday. If I want to be prepared, I have to keep my eyes open now to learn from the mistakes of others."

"I hope you can learn something from me."

With a smile, he walked out of the room.

Bethany whispered, "And I hope I can learn something from you."

She stood and walked down the hall to her father's book-room. The door was closed, so she knocked. Even if he was meeting with the village council, she would ask for a few minutes to speak with him. Titus had come to her for advice because he respected her experience. She needed to speak to her father for the same reason. She was not sure how she would tell him of her problem without divulging the truth about Eric's duplicity, but she needed his calm assurance that she was not alone.

"Come in," Father called.

She opened the door and peeked in. "Father, I must speak with you."

"Of course." He stood and motioned for her to enter. "I suspected you would be here as soon as you heard."

Her heart skipped a beat, sending pain throbbing through her. "Heard?" she whispered. Mayhap she was not the only one to stumble upon the French patrol in Mr. Griffen's barn.

"That I was home." From the stormy shadows by the window, Eric stepped out to smile at her.

Bethany mouthed his name as she stared at him. He was dressed in the casual clothes he had worn when she first saw him. She wondered where his uniform was, then recalled the secret compartment in his wagon. No wonder, he had been so determined that she would not get more than a quick glance at its contents.

"Forgive me for waylaying him on his way to let you know he was home," Father said with a taut smile. "I wanted to hear what news he had gathered while traveling along the shore."

"I am sure he has learned many interesting things." She did not try to keep the sarcasm out of her voice. "Have you shared *all* you learned with Father?"

"Not yet." Eric crossed the room. Taking her hands, he bent toward her as if to kiss her. "Have you?" he murmured.

His kiss was swift, but she sensed the hunger in it. Or mayhap it was no more than her treacherous longing for him.

"Did you think I would?" she whispered, when he pressed his cheek to hers.

"If I had, I would not have been want-witted enough to return here," he murmured against her ear.

Quivering beneath the seductive power of his breath stroking her, she drew back. She could not scold him for such an arrogant assumption when it was the truth. She wanted to curse her heart, which had leaped at the sound of his voice.

Without that horrible, green uniform, his sandy-gold hair was bright, even in the dim light, against the high collar of his shirt. He smiled, and she wanted to smile back, to have the afternoon be nothing but a nightmare brought on by the storm.

She turned to walk past him. He still was what he was—a French spy who might already have sent the message that would initiate the invasion of Fair Cove. If she allowed him to resume his life here, he would continue to use her and the others she loved to gain information for his heinous allies.

Her father intruded, saving her from blurting out the words which did not want to lie quiescent. "Come in, Bethany, and tell me what you wish to say. I suspect your husband is eager to tell you about his adventures along the road."

"It can wait, Father."

"I thought it might." He gave her an indulgent smile as Eric took her hand and drew it within his arm. "We can speak more later, son."

She faltered at the obvious trust in her father's voice. She should tell him, but she was caught by Eric's gaze and knew she could not speak the words that would damn him. She might hate the soldier he was, but she loved the man who had saved her from a horrible life with the Morelocks.

As soon as Eric closed the bedroom door behind them, she said, "You should not have come back here."

"Hush." He went to the dressing-room door and peered in to be certain Vella or one of the other servants was not there. Closing and locking that door as well, he came back to her. His hands settled on her shoulders, not stroking, not urging her to the madness of their love, but offering her solace. "I cannot leave."

Knocking his hands aside, she faced him. The sorrow she had heard in his voice filled his dimmed eyes. "Why? You need more information to sell us out to your evil master?"

"Bethany, forget that!"

"Forget it? How—?"

His arms surrounded her as he silenced her with a kiss. Drawing her close, he refused to let her free herself. She fought the deluding snares of passion, but found she needed their love to erase the fear. She held tightly to him, wanting the forgetfulness which came at the apex of ecstasy.

Abruptly, she whispered, "No." She pushed herself away. "Don't pervert the one thing I thought this war could never touch."

His voice rasped with desire as he whispered, "My sweet Bethany, I am afire with yearning for you. I'm not attempting to seduce you from your loyalties, just into my arms."

"No, Eric, I—" She faltered when he caught her to him and pressed his lips against her neck. As her hair cascaded along her back, he enfolded her in his embrace again. It took all her strength to turn her face away as he bent to capture her lips in the sweet prison of passion. "Not like this."

" 'Not like this?' " he repeated in bafflement.

Stepping away, she winced as she backed into a chair. "Why are you doing this? You are not French, although you speak as if you are."

"As you do." A swift smile raced across his lips. "Your father has given you an excellent education, Bethany. Did he teach you other languages, too?"

"We all speak German and can read Greek and Latin."

"I'm impressed."

"As I am," she replied with the same sarcasm she had used before. "Did you receive a classical education as well while you were learning to be a peddler?"

"I learned to speak French and English from my mother who was half-English." He clasped his hands behind his back and sat on the windowsill. "I learned to be a peddler when I escaped from the prison where I was a prisoner of war."

She choked, "A prisoner of war? Here in England?"

"Not exactly, for the prison hulks float offshore." His gaze turned inward. "You cannot guess what a man will do for a chance to see the sun upon his face again. When I managed to get free, I took to this life upon the road, wanting to get my surfeit of sunshine. In the year since, I have struggled to get the odors of death and sickness out of my senses. I want to be able to close my eyes and not see the ragged remains of men who are only half-alive, for they have lost all hope of escape from that torture." His hand cupped her cheek. "I pray you never will understand what it is like, sweetheart."

She faltered, wanting to despise him, but also longing to draw his head down against her breast as she whispered to him that the nightmare was over. "I had no idea."

"I know you guessed I was hiding my past from you. That is part of what I have hidden."

"The rest is that you are spying for the French." She must not allow her love for him to persuade her to forgive him.

"My nation was pleased when I managed to get back with the help of some smugglers who ply the waters between England and France. My connections with them made me even more valuable to my government." He smiled. "I was offered a promotion and this opportunity to help bring the war to a quicker end."

Standing, she folded her arms in front of her. "I want you to leave."

"Why?"

"Eric, if you are caught, you will not be sent back to prison. You will be hanged. If you are here when you are arrested, my brothers and father could be hanged, too." Tears glistened in her eyes as she whispered, "Go, before they hang you."

"But, sweetheart, no one knows but you." When she flinched and would have turned away, he caught her shoulders. "I know you will not betray me."

"I should!"

"You won't."

She nodded, with a sigh. "You are right. I will not tell anyone the truth because I want to keep you alive. I love you."

"You should know you were right this afternoon when you said I had intended to abandon you here," he said softly.

Looking away, she tried to force back the tears which threatened when she whispered, "No, Eric, do not tell me the truth now. Let me believe the lie that you cared for me."

He captured her face between his hands and brought it up so she might look into his. His lips touched her forehead fleetingly, but could not ease the deep ruts of heartache creasing her brow. Tasting her icy cheeks, he said, " 'Tis the truth that, while I honestly married you to save you from those dastardly Morelocks, our marriage also allows me to stay here without creating questions I could not answer. When I learned I must stay here a while longer, I could think of no better way than by being your husband." A hint of a smile strained the taut line of his mouth.

"You could have broken the brake on your wagon again."

"I could have."

"Instead you chose to break my heart? You are nothing but a—"

"A French bastard. I know. You have called me that more than once today."

"I have not!"

"If not aloud, at least in your mind." His arm

around her waist kept her from pulling away. "Listen to me!"

"No! I have heard all I wish to hear from you, Captain Pell—"

He silenced her with a kiss. He lifted his head only enough so he could murmur, "I thought I had it figured out so well. I would marry you to save you from the Morelocks; then I would leave. I would have arranged for word to be sent back to you that I had been killed in some sort of accident, and you would have been free to go on with your life."

"You would have left me to mourn, you mean."

"You were not supposed to fall in love with me, Bethany." He sighed. "Nor I with you. When that happened, I knew I was caught in my own trap. The charade was becoming real. Since our marriage, I woke every night I was in this room and watched you sleeping all alone in your bed."

"You woke to go to meet with your fellow spies!"

He nodded. "Yes, I did."

"And to let the prisoner escape?"

"That was managed while you were enjoying the beating of the bounds. Jay thought I was walking with you while I went into Fair Cove to oversee that. I was on my way back when I chanced to see you going into the woods."

She closed her eyes and sighed. "So you could learn where Mr. Griffen's buildings were."

"I shall not be dishonest with you, sweetheart. You did point me to a possible rendezvous spot, and I did wake up, night after night, to meet with my men and their allies, the smugglers. But, night after night, I delayed a few minutes longer in going to a meeting because I was caught up in the splendor of the moonlight illuminating your beauty as you slept. I ached to remain here with you, to wake you up with my kisses, to make you my wife in truth. Yet to seduce you and leave you was too cruel even for me, so I knew I must keep to my original plan to arrange an annulment."

"You are not cruel, Eric. You are . . ." A reluctant smile swept aside her fury, mellowing it to the familiar irritation when his warmth urged her to forgive him once again. "You are infuriating!"

"I am a man involved heart-deep with a woman and with a cause. I cannot have both, and I cannot decide between them." He tangled his fingers in her dark hair. "I know I cannot leave you here unprotected."

"Dunley and Sir Asa—"

"Are only two of your enemies." He took a deep breath and released it through tight lips. "You need to realize, Bethany, that the night I arrived here, the smugglers came here to teach your father a lesson about interfering with their work."

"Father?" she gasped. "He is in danger?"

When she was about to push past him, he sat her on the chaise longue. "I have warned him."

"How?"

"One does not need to be involved in espionage to hear such rumors." He gave her a wry smile. "I can now tell you on my first night here I thought my men had come to speak with me, and you had interrupted them by my wagon."

"But they were the smugglers."

"Yes. It shocked me when I confronted my men about their stupidity in coming here and I learned they had obeyed orders to stay away from any of the houses along the shore. I guess you were quite the hero in keeping the smugglers from their mischief."

"Do you know if they plan another attempt against Father?"

He shook his head. "Not for sure, but I have ordered my men to alert me to anything they might learn. What they haven't been able to discover is who is giving the smugglers these orders. I have urged caution because I do not want to lose the alliance with the smugglers."

Coming to her feet, she said, "You must leave, Eric, before you play a part in destroying my family."

"Bethany, I won't leave you to your enemies' lack of mercy."

"You *are* my enemy."

He stood and started to speak. Then he closed his mouth. Nodding, he said, "Very well, Bethany. I can see the sense in your suggestion. Give me until the end of the week to make up a good excuse that will not endanger you or your family. Then I will leave."

She nodded. For if she spoke, she would beg him to stay.

Lifting her hand to his lips, he kissed each finger. She leaned her head on his chest as she had longed to do and listened to the uneven beat of his heart. This was not easy for him, nor was it for her. She had wanted him to be honest with her, but she could not be completely honest with him now. She did not want him to go.

"I wish this could be different," she whispered.

"As I do. You have no idea how much I regret that we have had to meet as enemies."

"When you leave this time . . . will you come back?"

"If I can, sweetheart."

She flung her arms around him, knowing how lonely she was going to be. She could not betray Eric. No matter what, she would keep his secret hidden in her heart next to her unending love for him. When his mouth slanted across hers, she tried not to think what that vow might cost her.

# Fifteen

"Have you heard, Bethany?" Tryphena rushed up to Bethany as soon as her friend entered the parsonage to leave her family's three baskets of food with the others brought for the outing after the blessing of the fishing fleet.

Bethany drew off her gloves and bonnet, setting them atop one of her baskets on the long table. "Heard what?"

"About the French soldiers?"

She wished she had left her bonnet on, for it would have hidden an expression that must not be allowed to betray the truth. Eric was supposed to leave on the morrow, but he still had not told her what excuse he had concocted. Were these soldiers meeting him? She knew she should ask him, but she did not want to know. She must not be the one to speak the wrong word that would send him to hang.

"More French soldiers?" she asked.

"Mr. Griffen said he saw some in his barn earlier in the week."

She laughed. "While he was in his cups?"

"He said he was frightened sober by the very sight."

"I know I would be." Eager to change the subject, Bethany said, "Tryphena, Titus told me he was anxious to speak with you."

"Did he?" Her friend's face brightened.

Slipping her arm through Tryphena's, Bethany steered her toward the door. She laughed and ran back to get her bonnet. She tied it under her chin, then took Tryphena by the elbow and hurried outside. She should not be afflicted with guilt when she was making her friend happy, but she was. Thankful she had this excuse to change the conversation from the French soldiers, she wondered what she would do when the subject came up again. As it would, for everyone in Fair Cove knew of the danger surrounding them.

They just did not know that the leader of the French spies was in their midst.

Bethany shook off that nagging thought. Today might be her last day of happiness for a long time, and she wanted to enjoy it. "Titus asked me to smooth your meeting." She chuckled. "I believe he wants to make this day special for both of you."

Tryphena giggled. "I hope it will be."

It did not take long for Bethany to find her brother among the crowd, because he stood right next to Eric. Her heart always seemed to lead her back to her husband. She hoped his would someday lead him back to her.

She smiled when Eric put an arm around her shoulders as they laughed together over Tryphena's story of her father's nervousness in anticipation of the blessing of the fishing fleet. Last year, a storm had blown up just as he was being rowed out to the boats, and he had been swamped and had had to swim back to shore.

"That is why this year," Tryphena said with another giggle and a guilty glance toward where her father was speaking with Lord Whitcombe and Mr. Gillette, "he is going only as far as the end of the pier. He figures he can get back to dry land on his own two good legs if a storm threatens."

"I don't think he needs to fear rain," Eric said, glancing up at the sky where only a few wisps of clouds marred the perfect blue. "Tomorrow mayhap. Today is the perfect day for rowing out to the boats."

"Mayhap you can convince him of that." Tryphena dimpled. "I could not."

"Shall we find a good place to watch the blessing of the fleet?" asked Titus.

When he offered his arm to Tryphena, Bethany smiled at her friend before glancing at Eric. She thought he would follow them, but he held back.

"To give them a bit of privacy in this crowd," he murmured as they walked along the street toward the strand. "Courting requires it, you know."

"No, I don't."

He chuckled. "True. We never did have a chance to enjoy those longing looks and heart-deep sighs the poets write about. You should thank your family for sparing you from that, sweetheart."

"You have a decided lack of romance about you."

"For what I am?"

Her smile faded. "Eric—"

"I know a peddler is supposed to hear songs of the road in the rolling of his wagon wheels, but I am afraid I only hear the passage of miles."

Bethany shook her head, grinning. Eric enjoyed his disguise far too much. Although she should be angry that he was poking fun at her neighbors, she wanted to treasure these moments they would have before he must leave.

She rested her head against his shoulder as Reverend Sullivan walked out onto the pier. The fishermen, including several she had heard her father deride as smugglers, stood on the decks of their ships that bounced lightly on the choppy waves. Nothing was as simple as she had wanted to believe. Mayhap it never had been.

The ships raised their sails as each one was blessed for another season and prayers were offered that each would have safe passage on the fickle sea. Soon the harbor was speckled with more than a dozen earthbound clouds that floated with the breeze. Children ran along the beach and out to the pier, with a trio of dogs following and barking wildly. The youngsters threw wreaths of flowers onto the waves. Cheers rose as the garlands broke apart to surround the boats with blossoms. Two dogs jumped into the water to splash about, then swam toward shore.

"That is a lovely ceremony," Eric said quietly. "I have never heard of such a blessing."

"Reverend Sullivan brought it with him when he came here from Devon. I believe his father was approached by his parishioners there, and that is how it began. It is a good excuse for a feast day."

"And some of that excellent wine that seems to have a habit of falling off French ships and coming ashore not far from here."

"Apparently you already know some of the smugglers well. I have heard that tale repeated by everyone from the minister to Mr. Cartman . . ." She stared at him. She had delivered that packet to Mr. Cartman at his warehouse. For the first time since that day, she wondered what had been in it.

"Don't ask about what I cannot tell you," he said, his voice abruptly grim.

"Even if you made me your messenger?"

"I had no other choice. You were coming to Fair Cove. I was hurt."

"But to betray—"

"You betrayed nothing and no one." He brushed

her cheek with his fingers. "Mr. Cartman *is* allied with the smugglers who are your father's nemeses and, as far as he knows, so am I. He knows nothing more."

"And Reverend Sullivan?"

He shrugged. "If he is out and about at night, is he ministering to the townfolks or doing the devil's own duties? I don't know. It's not my task to uncover all the smugglers, just to arrange a meeting with their leader."

Bethany glanced around, wondering if anyone was taking note of their hushed words. The people closest to them were busy with their own conversations. She stiffened when she saw a tall form pushing through the crowd toward them.

"Eric," she said, trying to keep the panic from her voice, "Sir Asa is walking toward us."

"So I see."

Hearing the strain in his words, she realized he was looking in the opposite direction. He put an arm around her and led her through the crowd, heading closer to the pier.

"Eric, are you going to confront him?"

"Him?"

"Sir Asa." She pointed to the baronet striding toward them.

The oath that Eric spoke under his breath was in English, which astonished her. She had thought he would revert to French when he was distressed. Or had he been part of a silly game as she and Jay had been? She remained silent as he guided her toward where her father was deep in conversation with the minister.

"Stay here," he said in not much more than a whisper. "I will be back when I can."

"Eric—"

His kiss was to silence her question, but it brought

to life the desire that refused to be quiescent. When his breath snagged, she knew he was finding it as hard to resist as she was. He gave her the swift smile that made happiness swirl about within her, then he was gone.

She greeted the minister, glad that he and her father welcomed her into their conversation. She chatted with them as gaily as if her cares were as distant as the thin clouds over the sea while she watched Sir Asa continue past. The glower he fired in her direction warned that she would have to evade him and be cautious during the rest of the day.

She hoped Eric would, too.

Eric carried the basket Bethany had packed out of the minister's house. This day was turning out better than he had had any right to expect. Good! Mayhap this ridiculous assignment was finally coming to an end. Although he did not have the answers he had been sent here to find, he had made some steps toward gaining them amid this convivial atmosphere. Lord Whitcombe might not drink smuggled French wine, but the villagers did not share his patriotic fervor. Two casks had been stored in the shadows of the warehouses farther along the strand, and many elbows had tilted back again and again. Mouths that opened for wine also opened with information, and he had been happy to listen to all the men had to say amid their boasting.

He slipped his fingers through Bethany's, and she glanced up at him with a smile that was more intoxicating than any wine. If things had been different . . . How many times had he thought those words? If things had been different, he might never have chanced to meet her. If things had been different, he would not have to see the fear dimming her luminous eyes. If things had been different, he would not be sleeping each night on the chaise longue. Instead, he would be beside her in her bed.

Whoever had said it was better to be left than never to have been loved must have been a simpleton. As he was, for he had no solution for the dilemma that kept them apart. Mayhap, if he had been honest with her from the onset . . . No, he had been sworn to keep this mission secret.

But this day did not need to be ruined.

He smiled as he said, "One problem has been solved . . . at least for us."

"And what problem is that?" she asked. "Could I hope there has been a court-martial of some sort, and no one in my family is now serving in the military."

He grinned at her wistful wish that he was no longer in the army. She had taken to this deception with an ease that astonished him. "Not that problem, for I have done nothing worthy of being brought up on such charges." He swung their hands between them as they climbed to a hillock at the edge of the woods. "I just heard that Dunley Morelock has decided the British navy needs his assistance."

"Are you certain? The navy?"

"That is what Reverend Sullivan told me and your father. He seemed certain that we would be pleased." He drew her down to sit beside him on the grass. "Why do you look so distressed?"

"I would not wish such a life on anyone. I have heard it is harsh beyond measure."

"Worse than the life he endured here with his father?"

She sighed.

"Take care, Bethany," he said as he set the basket beside her. "Sympathy for Dunley nearly betrayed your brother into persuading your father to arrange for you to marry him. Do not let it betray you now."

"I know, but I hope he finds the navy to his liking." Biting her lower lip, she said, "And I hope his decision does not influence Jay."

"Except to stay away from the military."

"Yes." Her hand covered his on his knee. "Eric, it is more important than ever to keep Jay from entering the military." Putting her head down against her hand, she whispered, "I cannot bear the thought of you and my brother on opposite sides of the same battlefield."

He stroked her hair as he gazed at the people scattered across the rolling hill. So complicated this had gotten, so quickly.

"Sweetheart, I told your father that I would not sell him the pistols."

She raised her head. "Why didn't you tell me that before?"

"Because it was only yesterday that I had that conversation with him. I told him the truth—that they were mine and I did not want to part with them."

Tears jeweled in her eyes, and he cursed the circumstances that had brought them to this. He started to speak, but she turned away to take the cloth off the top of the food basket.

Curving his hand around her chin that stuck out in defiance of him, he delighted in her silken skin. She did not resist when he tipped her mouth toward his.

"I am not hungry for the nuncheon in that basket," he murmured.

"Cook prepared—"

"It is probably delicious, but not as delicious as your lips, sweetheart."

Her fingers combed up through his hair, and he was sure he would explode with his craving. Her caresses—so tender and so innocent and yet so thoroughly captivating—drove him to near madness.

When she stiffened, he frowned. "What is wrong, Bethany?"

"Sir Asa."

"Sir Asa?"

"He is watching us."

"Don't worry. He knows better than to get too close." He smiled. "If you are worried, I could send for Jay to guard you. Sir Asa must have learned by now who laid him low with such ease."

She rolled her eyes. "I want to forget that night."

"As I do." He drew a piece of cake out of the basket. "I wasted that evening I could have spent with you, being miserable because I did not want to be falling in love with you."

"Is that why you left me alone? I thought—"

"That I was out plotting mischief?" He shook his head. "I had more problems than I could handle without adding more. It would have been so much easier if you were a shrew who hounded me with dozens of demands."

"I could be."

He laughed. "I have met your grandmother, so I know you have strong-willed women in the Whitcombe family."

"Who seem to marry pigheaded men."

"True." He held the cake out for her to take a bite. When she leaned toward him to sample the cake, he captured her lips instead.

The cake fell from his fingers, forgotten, as he drew her to him. When her hands slipped along him, pressing her against him, he knew he had found where he wanted to be.

It was his misfortune that he did not belong here now.

* * *

The strand was light with brands as fiddle music challenged the sea. Bethany laughed as the music ended. Seeing Tryphena glowing with joy when she gazed up at Titus, Bethany wanted to continue to spin about in the blithe dance. They did not need music.

The musicians, two fiddlers and a drummer from the village, called for a break. Nana smiled as Bethany sat on the ground beside her chair.

"It may have been a most mistaken thing to assume he would select the Gillette girl for his bride," her grandmother said.

"So you would not be averse to such a match? Tryphena has been concerned that, as the minister's daughter, she should not aspire to wed Titus."

"Nonsense!" Nana patted Bethany's hand. "My dear child, how can you ask that when I did not protest when you announced your plans to marry?"

"My situation was different. If I had not married—"

"Bah! Did you think anyone truly believed those tales the Morelock boy was repeating?"

"Yes."

Nana smiled with reluctance. "All right, mayhap a few beef-heads did, but your family and your friends—all who matter—know you for what you are." She led Bethany's eyes to where Eric was laughing with Jay. "And we know what Eric is."

"You do?" She closed her mouth before she could betray Eric with her astonishment.

"He is a man of strong loyalty and honor. He reminds me of your grandfather." Her smile wavered. "I trust you will have more time together than we were given, but, no matter how much time you are granted, you must not let a single day pass without telling each other what your love means to you. If Titus can see his way to share that joy with Tryphena, I would not stand in their way."

"I'm glad."

"After all, a minister's daughter would be a good addition to this family that seems to be too often in trouble of late."

"Do you speak of me, Nana?" Jay asked, bending to give her a kiss on the cheek.

"A guilty conscience, Warren?"

He grimaced as he always did when she called him by his given name. "I am a young man now, Nana. I believe a guilty conscience is part of growing up."

"You have been listening to your father's lectures too long." She motioned to Eric. "Tell him, my boy, that growing up means learning from one's guilt not to make the same mistakes again."

"I believe that is true," he said with a smile.

Jay laughed. "I don't make the same mistakes twice. I make new ones."

"Then you should learn from others' mistakes," Nana said, her tone abruptly serious.

Jay's smile vanished. He glanced from Bethany to Eric and then back to his grandmother. "You need not constantly repeat that, Nana. The mistakes that Grandfather made I know well. What you should recognize is I know that."

"Jay," Bethany said softly, "this is supposed to be a day of joy, not of anger."

"I would be joyous if just one of you other than Eric would comprehend what I think."

Bethany stared at Eric as Nana replied to Jay. She did not hear Nana's words. What had Eric said to her brother? She had been so honest with him earlier today about her fears for her brother and her husband being on opposing sides of this war.

When Eric held his hand out to her, she hesitated.

She did not want his touch to bewitch her into putting aside her fear for Jay.

"The music is beginning again," Eric said quietly. "Will you stand up with me, Bethany?"

She nodded, although she would have preferred to ask him to explain himself. The brangle now going on between Nana and Jay had no place for her, because neither of them would listen to her when they were in such a pelter.

As they walked to where the thin grass had been beaten into the ground by the dancing, Eric said, "Jay may think I understand him, Bethany, but you do not understand me."

"I understand what you are."

"Bethany—"

"No, let me finish." She lowered her voice. "You are a soldier, so you share Jay's dream of a glorious victory for those you fight for."

"There is nothing glorious about what I do. I despise it."

"Yet you fight."

"I must be ready to defend what I believe is right." He brushed his fingers against her cheek in the way she loved. "However, I do not see it as the path to glory. I have been trying to persuade Jay of that, too."

"He said you understood him."

"I do, for I was once as idealistic as he is." The fiddles squawked as they were being tuned, and he smiled. "I wish they would play a waltz or two."

"You know how to waltz?"

"It is quite fashionable in Paris."

Her eyes widened. "Take care what you say."

"I speak only as others have." He drew her past the dancing area and toward the shadows by the church. "Shall we?"

"Shall we what?"

"Dance."

"The waltz?"

His arm around her waist brought her to his chest. He whirled her about a few steps, smiling. "How I would enjoy moving with you to that gentle music, you in my arms, each motion as one."

"Eric . . ." She sighed with delight as his mouth glided along her neck while he continued to guide her through the steps of the waltz. The music from the fiddles and drums did not match their steps, but it did not matter.

When his hand moved up her back, bringing her up against him, she knew why no watchdog would approve of such a sensual dance. She did not care. This might be the last night they had together, the last chance they had to be in each other's arms. She released his hand. Pulling his mouth down to hers, she tasted the hidden curves within it. She swayed against him, lost in the melody that merged them together in this splendor.

He stepped away, and she moaned a denial. She did not want this kiss to end.

"Come with me, sweetheart," he whispered.

"Where?"

He frowned. "Away to where we do not have to worry about that cur's eyes on us."

She looked over her shoulder and saw Sir Asa standing at the edge of the dancing area. He was not watching the dancers, but straining to see into the shadows. Had he seen them? No, he could not have, or he would have intruded even more than he had.

Clinging to the deepest shadows where they could move without being seen, she glanced up at Eric. His smile was gone, and, even in the dim light, she could see what was in his eyes. She needed no more lure than the promise of ecstasy to follow as he led her toward where the carriage was waiting.

"We are going back to Whitcombe Hall?" She smiled, hoping tonight would be the wedding night she craved.

He shook his head with regret. "I have only time to tell you good night."

"Good night? Here?"

"The moon is new tonight, and I must meet . . . friends." His tongue coursed along her ear before he murmured, "I do not want to hurry away from you, sweetheart, but I want you safe behind the walls of Whitcombe Hall before I leave."

"But tonight may be the only time we have."

"If all goes as I hope, we may have other times."

Her eyes widened. "Eric! What have you learned today? Is the invasion—"

"The only invasion that matters to me right now is how you invaded my heart." He leaned her back against his arm.

"Eric, if Sir Asa is watching—"

"Let him realize what his cruelty cost him." He smiled. "And won me."

She smiled in return. Then he kissed her.

But, when she sat alone as she rode back to Whitcombe Hall, she wondered who would be victorious in the end. Either way, she feared Eric might not be able to keep his promise to return to her.

# Sixteen

Bethany came down the stairs, looking at the list Mrs. Linders had given her earlier that afternoon. Some of the things must be ordered from London because the shops in Fair Cove did not have the fabrics that were necessary for new coats for her father and the boys. She sighed when she saw that Mrs. Linders and Nana had included enough fabric for a coat for Eric, too. She did not know if he would return here to wear it.

He had sent her a single message. Although she was not certain how he had managed to sneak it under her pillow without being seen, she was glad she had found it before Vella had. She doubted if her abigail would have been able to restrain her curiosity.

The note had been simple.

*My dearest Bethany,*

*I must be away longer than I had planned. I will be returning no later than a week from now. Please know that my thoughts will be with you as I wish I could be.*

It had been signed "With love, Eric." No clue to where he was bound or what he must do. As the days folded one into the next, she had become more anxious with each passing hour. She did not want to think of what she would do if the week passed and he still had not returned. Her tale that he had a final delivery to make before he could give up his life as a peddler had brought puzzled glances from her family, but she had not elaborated, fearful that her lies would tumble apart like a stack of child's blocks.

She glanced through a window on the landing, but could not see the stableyard from where she was. She needed to go into one of the rooms on the east side of the house if she wanted to check on whether Eric's wagon had returned to Whitcombe Hall.

As she came down the stairs, her spirits dragging, Titus stepped out of the parlor, his hands hidden behind him. She tried to smile at him, but her attempt was a miserable failure.

"You have chosen a rainy day for a ride," she said when she noted that he wore buckskin pantaloons beneath his dark coat.

"Will you go with me to the Gillettes' house?" He drew his hand from behind him and held out her favorite straw bonnet.

"If you want me to." She took the bonnet.

"Very much."

"Can I ask why you want me to come with you?"

"I would like you there when I speak today with Miss Gillette."

"About your affection for Tryphena?"

He looked away. "I thought this would be a good day to ask Miss Gillette to marry me."

"What?" She could not believe what she was hearing. "But you and Tryphena sat together through the whole of the blessing of the fishing fleet. You had nuncheon together. You even danced just about every dance with her. You two seemed so happy together. I saw that, and Mr. Gillette must have seen it as well. I thought—"

"Can we speak of this in the carriage?"

She wondered why he would not meet her eyes. Mayhap it was no more than guilt. Guilty he should be, for he had persuaded Tryphena to believe his affection for her was sincere. Then . . .

"Where are you going?" Jay bounced down the stairs as if he were still a child.

"To the Gillettes'."

"Great. Let me get my—"

Titus scowled. "No, we are not waiting for you. Come along, Bethany."

"Titus," she began, "if—"

"There is no time. We must leave now."

She saw her shock mirrored on Jay's face, but she did not want to bicker here in the foyer. Something was bothering Titus, and she would get no answer from him until they were in the carriage. She knew her brother too well to believe that either she or Jay or the two of them combined could wheedle anything from him before he was ready to speak.

Giving Mrs. Linders's list to Jay, she said, "Tell Father we must prepare to send an order to London for these items."

"I am not your maid," he mumbled.

"No, you are not." She tapped the list. "You will see that most of the items we need are for you."

"For me?" A boyish delight brightened his eyes. He bent to read the list, giving her a chance to leave with Titus.

When her older brother handed her into the closed carriage that was waiting by the front door in the steady rain, Bethany glanced along the drive, hoping to see Eric. She wondered where he had gone during the past few days. Was he with his French patrol still near to Fair Cove and Whitcombe Hall? If so, she hoped he would stay out of view of the road or any of the residents of the shire.

Her heart thumped in terror with every sound. She feared Titus had heard its frantic beat when he glanced at her as he sat across from her and said, "You are skittish today, Bethany."

"Mayhap because you are acting so strangely."

"These are strange times."

She wanted to agree with him fervently, but he gave her no chance as he slapped the side of the carriage to let the coachman know they were ready to go. As the carriage bounced out onto the road in front of the manor house, she clasped her hands in her lap. So many questions she wanted to ask. Some Titus could answer. Even more, he could not.

She grasped the handhold in the carriage as the road dipped sharply toward the sea. Glancing out, she saw the gentle rain tapping the leaves of the trees. She hoped this shower would blow past quickly. She did not like to think of Eric out in a storm, although she guessed he had weathered many before he came into her life.

"I know this is a shock to you," Titus said quietly.

"That you would offer for Miss Gillette when no one could mistake your attention to Tryphena?" She shook her head. "You are right. 'Tis a shock that you would be so unthinking and hard-hearted."

"It is not that simple, and you know it."

"Do I?"

"Not all of us can marry for love, Bethany."

"Why not?" She leaned forward. "You care deeply for Tryphena. I could see that. And she is in love with you. Why would you break her heart, which she wants only to give to you, to marry a woman who means so little to you?"

"You don't know what you are talking about."

"I don't?" She raised her chin. "Do you not recall the night of the beating-of-the-bounds ball?"

His mouth twisted. "When I interrupted you and Eric?"

"Yes, and, as you could tell that I longed to be with him, I could see that you did not want to be with Miss Gillette. You kept her distant. You did not look at her more than propriety required, and you heeded not a word she spoke."

"She speaks so many."

"Exactly." She reached for his hands, but he folded his arms in front of him. "Titus, you don't care a rap for Miss Gillette. So why are you offering for her when I know you care so much for Tryphena?"

"As I said, it is not that simple. Francis is strongly in favor of me marrying his sister."

"He should be. You will be the baron after Father, and marrying you would be an excellent match for his sister."

" 'Tis not quite that simple."

"So you've said over and over." She frowned at him. He was talking in circles, which was even more irritating than Eric's habit of doing so when he had first arrived at Whitcombe Hall. Eric had been hiding something then. Was Titus hiding something now? "It might be simple if you would explain what you mean."

"I am trying to do so."

"You are acting as if you are being forced into this match." She put a hand on his elbow, ignoring his scowl. "Titus, what is wrong? You were happy with Tryphena at the blessing of the fleet, and now you are as glum as a felon on his way to face the judge."

"I guess it is time to be completely honest with you."

"That might help, especially if I am to stand beside you when you propose marriage to Miss Gillette."

He winced at her words.

"Titus, what is amiss?"

"I—"

The carriage rocked to a stop so sharply that Bethany was almost thrown into her brother's lap. She nodded when he asked her if she was all right. That was not the truth, because she had banged her shoulder into the side of the carriage. It ached, and hot pulses jolted her arm like bolts of lightning.

Titus threw open the door beside him and called out, "Harris, why did you stop like that?"

Before the coachee could call back an answer, the other door was jerked open. Bethany gasped, fearing some highwayman was about to make his demands. Who else would ambush the carriage like this and be so discourteous? She put her hand over her wedding band. She did not want to surrender it to some brazen thief. When Eric left for what might be forever, this ring would be the only thing she would have other than her memories and a broken heart.

A man poked his head into the carriage. When he pushed back the floppy brim of his rain-soaked hat, she gasped, "Sir Asa!"

He smiled at her. Grasping her arm, he pulled her out of the carriage. She nearly tumbled at his feet into the mud.

Titus shouted, "Are you mad, Sir Asa? Do not treat Bethany so crassly. She is not our enemy."

"No, *she* is not," the baronet said with a laugh. "But the question is how much she knows about the man who is."

"I don't know what you are talking about," Bethany replied, wishing she had thought to bring a shawl. Rain coursed down her back, but she feared it was the least of her concerns when Sir Asa tightened his grip on her arm. She kept her voice calm and her expression vexed. No one must guess she was feeling anything but indignity at Sir Asa's churlish actions.

"No?" He whirled her to face him.

She could do no more than choke on a gasp when he gripped her cheeks in his big hand. He pushed her back against the carriage and smiled victoriously.

"You have always been a silly girl, Bethany Whitcombe."

"Bethany Pennington," she managed to squeeze out past his grip.

"And that was the silliest thing you have ever done."

"Sir Asa," Titus growled, "release my sister at once. If you don't, I—"

Hearing a grunt of pain, she tried to turn to see what had happened. Sir Asa refused to let her move. When Titus fell out of the carriage, clutching his stomach, she cried out in horror. She dug her nails into Sir Asa's wrist until he yelped. Then she kicked him, hard, in the shins.

His grip loosened, and she pulled away. She knelt beside her brother, who was groaning in pain. Water soaked through her gown, but she paid it no mind as she gasped, "Titus, we must get out of here."

Pulled to her feet, she started to snarl a curse. She froze when she saw guns pointed at both the coachman and her brother. For the first time, she realized Sir Asa had two other men with him. Had he been lying in wait for them? Why?

She realized she had spoken the last word aloud when Sir Asa smiled and said, "Because you are supposed to be mine."

"Yours? Are you deranged?"

"I was denied having your mother when she chose your father." He tipped her face back. "You are the image of her, mayhap even more lovely. I will not lose you, too."

"I am a married woman." Her façade of calm was splintering as he drew her even closer.

"Are you?"

"What do you mean?"

He smiled coldly. "A marriage made under false names cannot be legal."

"What are you talking about?" Titus asked as he pushed himself to his feet, his arms still wrapped around his middle.

"Bethany knows, don't you, my dear?"

Her brother's question had given her the moment she needed to hide her reaction. Somehow, Sir Asa had learned the truth about Eric. Or had he? Mayhap he was just guessing. She could not betray Eric now by conjecturing wrong.

"I have no idea what you are talking about. Eric and I are legally married. You heard Reverend Sullivan say so when you and Dunley burst into the wedding supper."

"You call him Eric or by his real name?"

"His real name is Eric." Or was it? She had simply assumed that Eric was his real first name, even though she had heard his men call him Captain Pellissier. He had not denied that his name was Eric, but she was no longer sure where the line now was between the truth and a myriad jumbles of lies. She must ask him to be honest with her about that when he returned. It should be the first thing she did, even though her lips ached for his upon them.

"Eric Pennington?" Sir Asa roared with laughter. "That is not a Froggish name."

This time, she could not conceal her reaction. When she drew in a frantic breath, she knew Titus had seen the truth on her face as well. She never had learned to think before she acted. She should have been prepared for this question, instead of lamenting about how far Eric was from her arms.

"You don't know what you are talking about," she whispered.

"Mayhap not, but I can tell that you do." Sir Asa ran a hand down her back.

Titus cursed viciously, but halted when a gun was poked at him.

As if her brother had remained silent, Sir Asa said, "I wanted your mother, but she refused me. I wanted you, but your father refused me. Dunley could have won you with the help of his friend." He looked at Titus and chuckled. "But he made a muddle of that by giving Pellissier the chance to play hero."

Bethany fought to keep her shoulders from sagging in defeat. Sir Asa knew Eric's real name. How could this have happened? Cold coursed through her. Sir Asa must be the leader of the smugglers. His cohorts could have brought him the truth, although she had thought Eric wise enough to seek out the smugglers' chief without revealing his own loyalties.

"Pellissier?" Titus stepped forward, ignoring the gun as he growled, "How do you know of Pellissier?"

Now she stared at her brother. What did he know of this? She did not want to believe he was somehow involved with the smugglers. Mayhap Tryphena's heart was not the only one he was determined to break, for Father would be disconsolate to discover his heir was aiding the smugglers in their ignoble work.

"Probably not as much as your sister," Sir Asa replied with a triumphant smile. "Why don't you ask her what you want to know about him?"

Bethany eased away from Sir Asa, amazed that he released her. Then she realized he knew she had no escape from what he had planned for her. She would prove him wrong. She spun about to flee. Her arm was grabbed, and she was turned around to see one of his men raise his gun and drive the butt against the coachee's head. She shrieked.

Running to where Harris was lying face down in the thickening mud, Bethany tried to push him onto his back. "Help me!" she cried. When no one moved, she stared Sir Asa directly in the eye. "If he suffocates in this mud, you will hang!"

"Turn him over," ordered the baronet as he grasped her arm and pulled her to her feet.

She looked to Titus for help. Why hadn't he come to her assistance? She recoiled from the fury in his gaze.

Elbowing away the other armed man, he stepped in front of her. "What do you know of this, Bethany?"

"Of what?" She did not want to lie to him, but if he intended to be Sir Asa's ally . . . That made no sense, for why would Sir Asa have stopped their carriage like this if they were allies? Nothing made sense now.

He snarled an oath. "Do not play coy with me. You know as well as I that Eric has not always been a peddler."

She bit her lip and brushed rain off her cheeks. Her bonnet was soaked now and could not keep the water from her face. "You are right. He has not always been a peddler." She must tell them something, and this they already had guessed.

"Then he is Pellissier!" Sir Asa snarled.

"I did not say that," she argued, trying to sound calm. "I said—"

"Enough to let us know you know much more." Sir Asa grabbed her arm again, twirling her toward him. When her feet slid in the mud, he laughed and pulled her up against him. His lips pounced on hers.

Bethany screamed again as she was ripped out of

his grip. Her gown was torn. She grasped Titus's arm as she heard a trigger being drawn back. She whispered Eric's name with what she feared would be her last breath.

A gun fired. She flinched, then stared when one of Sir Asa's men fell, his hands wrapped around his leg.

Titus leaped forward and scooped up the wounded man's gun. He aimed it at Sir Asa as more men stepped out onto the road.

When Titus smiled, Bethany stared at Francis Gillette, who was signaling to the other men. He no longer resembled her quiet, kindly neighbor who kept so much to himself, for he carried two pistols, both of them aimed at Sir Asa.

"Begone, Sir Asa," Mr. Gillette ordered. "You are no longer a part of this."

"Now see here," began Sir Asa.

"You have betrayed us for the final time." He glanced at Titus. "You are unhurt, my friend?"

"I am fine. Harris got hit pretty hard." He smiled as the coachee was lifted from the road and put in the carriage by some of the men who had arrived with Mr. Gillette. The man who had been shot was carried to a cart that was drawing up beside the carriage. Paying them no mind, Titus continued, "Bethany's feathers are ruffled, but that might not be all for the bad."

"Titus!" she gasped.

"Be silent, sister." He motioned with his head toward Sir Asa. "Bring him along. He apparently has information we can use."

"Use for what?" Bethany asked.

"I said be silent."

She backed away from his rage. When she bumped into a man, she whirled to flee. He took her arm, but with gentle respect.

"Stay where you are, Mrs. Pennington," he ordered.

In disbelief, she stared at Mr. Anderson. She knew all of the dozen or so men standing on the road. They were from Fair Cove. More than half of them were men her father had identified as possible smugglers.

Looking back at Titus, she saw he was nodding as Mr. Gillette gave orders. Francis Gillette must be the true leader of the smugglers. He was evidently the man Eric had been seeking to ask for help in arranging whatever he had planned for the French invasion.

Suddenly shouts resounded through the rain. Branches cracked as someone raced away into the underbrush.

"Let him go," Mr. Gillette ordered as some of the men turned to follow Sir Asa and his uninjured crony. "Good riddance. If we find we need him, we can get him." He walked through the mud to stand in front of Bethany. "But I don't think we'll be needing Sir Asa, for I believe, as I told you earlier, Titus, that your sister has much of the information we have been lacking. Mayhap we should thank Sir Asa for persuading *Miss Whitcombe* to own to the truth."

With the emphasis he put on her name, she knew Mr. Gillette shared Sir Asa's mistaken belief that her marriage was not valid. Or was it a mistaken belief? She had not checked the marriage license, but it could not have had Pellissier written on it. Mayhap that was why Eric had been so sure their marriage could be annulled. As she thought of the rapture of the kisses they had shared at the blessing of the fleet, she realized neither of them had mentioned anything about the annulment, wanting only to savor the few hours they had together.

"Thank you, Mr. Gillette," she said, hoping they would believe her feigned serenity. "I appreciate your arrival when Sir Asa was being so beastly. If you will excuse me, I think it would make good sense for me to sit down in the carriage for a few moments to regain my composure."

"Of course." When she reached for the carriage door, he took her arm and smiled. "My carriage is this way. My driver has not taken a blow to the skull, so he will be more sure-handed."

"You are very kind," she replied, unsure of how long she could act as if she swallowed the clankers he spoke. "However, Harris has served us well for many years. I want to be certain his head is tended to."

He did not allow her to turn back to her carriage. When he tugged her toward the other carriage that was a gray shadow in the dim afternoon light, she looked over her shoulder. "Titus!" she cried.

"Yes, Whitcombe, do come with us." Mr. Gillette's smile became as cold as sleet. "You will want to be a part of this."

"Of what?" she whispered, even though she feared she already knew.

"Of finding out the truth about the man who calls himself Eric Pennington," answered Mr. Gillette as he handed her up into a carriage which was not as fancy as her father's. When she was sitting on a patched cushion, he took a seat across from her.

Titus climbed in and sat beside her. "It now can go as we planned."

"Everything is set?" Mr. Gillette asked as the carriage began to move.

"Before we left Whitcombe Hall, I arranged for everything just as we spoke of yesterday."

Bethany intruded to ask, "What are you talking about?"

Instead of answering her question, her brother asked, "Do you expect Eric to return to Whitcombe Hall tonight?"

"Tonight or tomorrow, unless he has been delayed," she answered, although she had no idea. She could not tell them that he had not given her a specific day when he expected to return. That would lead to other questions she could not answer.

Titus frowned. "Father will be concerned if Bethany is not home this evening."

"Your father has been a problem before." Mr. Gillette wiped his wet hands on his breeches. "We can deal with him on this."

"Father will not be pleased that you are helping the smugglers, Titus!" Bethany snapped.

"Is that what you think we are doing?" Her brother laughed. "Little sister, you have always been sweetly naïve. We aren't helping the smugglers. We are trying to stop the smuggling."

"Why would they help you today if—?"

"Because they know we want to prevent an invasion of these shores and open trade again with France."

She stared in disbelief at her brother as she remembered Eric saying there were rumored to be people in this area who wanted to put an end to the war by negotiating a treaty with the French. They were willing to cede all of Europe to Napoleon in exchange for a promise that England was sacrosanct.

"You are insane!" she whispered.

"Are we?" Mr. Gillette smiled. "Only if you consider peace insane."

"But at what price?"

"Don't sound like Jay," Titus chided. "He doesn't want the war to end, for he wants to become a hero." He cupped her chin. "You asked for my help in keeping him from enlisting. An end to the war will solve that problem once and for all."

"Not if it ends like this. That disgusting Corsican will never keep any promise he makes."

Mr. Gillette leaned back and smiled. "That need

not concern you. What you should be concerned about is whether your husband will give you a look-in at my house shortly after he comes back from whatever mischief he has been creating."

"I don't understand why you want to compel Eric to come to your house. All you would need to do is extend him an invitation to call."

"We have." Mr. Gillette chuckled.

She stared at them. None of this made sense. If they wished to negotiate peace with the French, they should be acting as if Eric were their ally, not their enemy. She could not say that, because doing so would divulge the truth that must stay within her heart.

"If you are right, Bethany," Titus said, "nothing will happen, and we will return to Whitcombe Hall on the morrow."

"If I am right about what?"

He ignored her. "However, if we are right, your husband will betray himself and his scheme to stop us."

Mr. Gillette's lips pulled back in a sneer worthy of Sir Asa. "And then we will stop him."

# Seventeen

Eric heard shouts as he walked up the drive to Whitcombe Hall. He frowned. The voices sounded upset. *Dash it!* Young Jay had not done something foolish, had he?

"I should have gotten a promise from him to stay here until I got back," he mumbled to himself as he hurried toward the house. Dash it! This past week had been for nothing. Seven wasted days of tramping through the downs to no avail. Seven empty nights without the sound of Bethany breathing softly in the bed on the other side of the room. A week of realizing he had been a complete block. Now he was tired and chilled from walking through the rain and wanted to ease that fatigue in the warm arms of his wife.

The door was thrown open. Mrs. Linders rushed out to him. She looked as if she had seen a specter, for her face was as gray as her hair. He had never seen the housekeeper lose her aplomb, not even during the hurried preparations for the wedding.

"Thank goodness, you are here, Mr. Pennington!" she cried. "We have been hoping you would come home before dark. Lord Whitcombe needs your help right away."

"What is wrong? Has Jay—?"

" 'Tis not the lad. 'Tis Lady Whitcombe. She swooned in the foyer."

"Is she ill?"

"Heartsick, I fear. The family's carriage was attacked on the shore road."

"Attacked? Who was in it?"

"Mr. Titus and Mrs. Pennington."

He drew in his breath as if someone had struck him in the gut. "Bethany was in it when it was attacked? Where is she now?"

"I don't know, Mr. Pennington. I heard Lord Whitcombe say something about Sir Asa, but then he closed the door." She wrung her hands in her apron. "Sir, when you find out what has happened, will you let me know? The household is distraught with worry."

"I will inform you." He put a hand on her shoulder. "Where is Lord Whitcombe?"

"Gone to get Mr. Titus and Mrs. Pennington, but he asked that you go to Lady Whitcombe's rooms as soon as you arrived." She hesitated, then whispered, "Sir, do take care. I fear for her heart with this stress."

Eric did not wait to hear more. Taking the steps, both outside and in the house, three at a time, he raced to Lady Whitcombe's door. He pounded on it.

A maid responded. "Mr. Pennington, my lady," she called over her shoulder.

When Jay pushed her aside without apologizing, Eric scowled. He never had seen the lad treat anyone in the household with anything but courtesy.

"Thank heavens, you are back." Jay rocked from one foot to the other in anxiety. "We must—"

"Let me speak with your grandmother." Eric was not sure how much the lad, in his eagerness, would get right. Lady Whitcombe would provide every detail, even if she had given in to vapors in the foyer. "How are you, Lady Whitcombe?" he asked as he stepped into the room that was decorated with surprisingly calm shades of light blue. He had guessed Lady Whitcombe's bedchamber would be as extravagant as the outspoken lady herself.

"I am fine." As she sat, her trembling hands belied her words. Her face was nearly as pale as Mrs. Linders's. "Or I would be if everyone would pay less attention to me and do more to find my grandchildren."

"I thought Lord Whitcombe had gone to retrieve them."

"If he can find them."

"Find them? You don't *know* where they are?"

"Our coachman—"

"Harris?" Eric frowned. He had spoken with the man often while working on his wagon. "Where is he?"

"In his rooms, suffering from a nasty concussion." As Eric reached for the door, Lady Whitcombe shook her head and added, "Don't bother. He is still barely conscious. He won't be able to tell you anything. All he could provide was Sir Asa's name."

Jay clenched his hands. "Father is on his way with some of the stablemen to confront Morelock."

Eric cursed under his breath. Sir Asa had gone too far this time. He should have heeded Bethany's fear more at the blessing of the fleet and dealt with the baronet then. Instead, he had let anticipation of completing his mission lure him away from her.

Bowing his head toward Lady Whitcombe, he said, "If you will excuse me, my lady, I will endeavor to catch up with Lord Whitcombe."

Jay started to protest. "Eric—"

"You must watch over your grandmother," Eric said with a stern glance at the young man.

"Take care, my boy," Lady Whitcombe said.

"I shall."

"You are armed?"

He nodded, knowing this was no time for demurring. "I would be a widgeon to face Morelock without a way to make him see sense."

"Nothing may do that."

Again he reached for the door. It burst open nearly in his face. He stared at the footman, who was panting as he leaned against the doorjamb.

"This was delivered for you, Mr. Pennington." He held up the folded paper. "I was told it was for you, but . . ."

Eric took it. A single glance at the handwriting on the page explained the footman's disconcertion. In square letters was printed CAPTAIN PELLISSIER.

He ripped it open and scanned the few words within; then his knees threatened to buckle beneath him. They had been mistaken. Sir Asa was not Bethany's greatest enemy, because she was being held as bait to draw him into a trap set by a most unexpected enemy.

"Lady Whitcombe," he said as he folded the page and put it beneath his damp coat, "let Lord Whitcombe know that I borrowed one of his mounts to ride to the Gillettes' house."

"The Gillettes'?" Jay gasped. "Why there?"

"I believe they may know something about this."

Lady Whitcombe pushed herself to her feet. "Nonsense!" she exclaimed. Then her face became even more ashen. "Mayhap not, for Francis Gillette often invited young Dunley to join him and Titus in their evening conversations."

"Eric!" Jay grasped his sleeve. "Let me go with you. I know a way that—"

"Stay here, and watch out for your grandmother and the household."

Jay's eyes grew wide. "Are they in danger, too?"

"I honestly do not know." Eric went to the door, then paused as he looked back at Lady Whitcombe.

"You may be sure that I will do whatever is necessary to keep your granddaughter and grandson from harm, my lady."

"We do not doubt that," Lady Whitcombe said, her voice stronger with every word.

"Jay . . ." He would not be so distracted as to go without a vow from the lad.

"I will guard my family and household." His chin rose in a motion so like his sister's that Eric was nearly undone.

Eric rushed down the stairs, glancing at the clock in the foyer. He smiled when he saw the time. Mayhap his luck had taken a turn for the better, for he had planned to meet his men within the hour to discover what they had accomplished in the past week.

Mayhap before the next hour was past, they would have completed their mission. Then . . . No, he could not think past the next hour, for, if he failed now, he might have no future beyond that.

Bethany sat on the very edge of the chair and watched her brother and Mr. Gillette pace in opposite directions across the comfortable parlor. A cheerful fire danced on the hearth to hold the stormy day at bay, but there was nothing else cheerful about the lovely room with its red wall covering and dark furniture. The doors were closed. When Miss Gillette had knocked, she had been sent away with a tale that Mr. Gillette was busy with his work. Bethany's one thought of calling to Miss Gillette to bring help had vanished when she had seen her brother's scowl.

Chafing her hands, she said as she had before, "Titus, you must give up this mad course."

"No more of your mewling," he grumbled.

"Mewling?" She set herself on her feet and gave

him a scowl as venomous as his. "I am speaking good sense. You two alone cannot change the course of this war."

" 'Tis not the two of us alone. We are—"

Mr. Gillette snapped, "Watch your tongue! You are beginning to prattle as endlessly as my sister. I have worked hard to keep her from guessing the truth so she would not reveal the whole over tea."

"And what of me?" asked Bethany. She refused to let them daunt her with their grandiose plans that would bring doom on both families. "Do you expect that I shall remain silent about this when you learn that you have been betwattled by Sir Asa into believing that Eric is your foe when he is not?"

Titus gulped so loudly she could hear him from across the room. "Bethany, you must not bring ruin to all we have worked so hard for. Surely you do not want Fair Cove overrun by the French."

"Of course I do not, but I also do not want to bend my head and England's will in any way to that dictator who is using peace-loving folks like you to gain himself a moment of surcease on this front so that he may defeat Russia. When he has managed that, do you think he will be content with any treaty he made with our government?" She shook her head. "Then he will show he has no mercy for those who have trusted him. He has done that before. He shall again."

"I have no time to explain to you now."

"No time?" She glanced toward the window. "Is Eric here?"

Mr. Gillette spun about to point an accusing finger at her. "So you think he will come here?"

"If you told him I was here, he will come. That means nothing but that he cares for me."

Slowly Mr. Gillette's finger lowered. Dismay lined his face. "I had not considered that." He looked at

Titus. "You said the marriage was one only of appearances."

"It is!" her brother averred. "Bethany's abigail told me that—"

"You believed Vella over me?" Bethany demanded. Blast Vella, who clearly had been persuaded to spy on them by Titus. She should have guessed when he was so oddly silent after the wedding. He had wanted her to marry Dunley to complete the ties within their cabal, and it was not like Titus to give in easily when he was determined that something should go as he wished. Rounding on her brother, she said, "If you had asked me, I would have told you that I love Eric with all my heart."

"As he loves her!" came a shout from the doorway.

"Jay!" gasped Bethany as she saw her brother standing there, a servant behind him futilely trying to edge around him.

Jay frowned when he entered the room. It became more fierce when Mr. Gillette pushed Bethany into a chair by the hearth. With obvious reluctance, Jay sat when Mr. Gillette motioned toward the settee.

Mr. Gillette went to the door and called out, "Get the men here to guard this door."

"But, sir," said the anxious butler, "you sent them to the kitchen to have something to eat."

"Get them back here. I do not want to be interrupted without warning again."

Jay's hands fisted on the knees of his wet breeches. "Where is Eric?"

"He's not here," Bethany said, "and you should not be."

"I must have beat him by coming across the leas." His frown did not lessen. "But he left before me, because I had to sneak away from Nana."

"Nana knows you're here?" Titus asked.

Jay shook his head. "No, but she knows Bethany is."

"How?"

"Eric had a message delivered to him, and he told us he was coming here."

Mr. Gillette's face creased into a triumphant smile. "So he is Pellissier!"

"I don't know what you are talking about," Jay said.

Bethany leaned toward her brother. "Jay, they are talking about negotiating peace at any cost with Napoleon."

"Admit defeat?" He shook his head. "Eric wouldn't do that."

"Eric isn't a part of this," she said, glancing at Titus.

"Then why—?" Jay surged to his feet. "You think Eric will try to halt you in this? Is that why you brought Bethany here?" He looked from his brother to Mr. Gillette. "Let's go, Bethany. I shall not remain in this nest of traitors."

Mr. Gillette put a hand on her shoulder, keeping her from rising. "She is staying here until Captain Pellissier arrives."

"Who?"

"You know him as Eric Pennington, but he is a French captain, who is reconnoitering this area to plan the very invasion we are trying to halt. If we do not stop him, all hopes of peace are ruined."

Jay sniffed in derision. "You are dicked in the nob. Eric is not a French soldier. Tell them, Bethany."

Mr. Gillette smiled coldly at her. "Yes, tell us, Bethany. Or will you let your brother leave here and get caught in the web of deceit that you and Pellissier have spun? The attack is forthcoming. That we have learned from the smugglers Pellissier has been using to do his vile work. If Jay leaves now, will he walk into an attack?"

"I don't know," she whispered.

"Bethany," Titus said, "I am warning you that you will destroy all of us if you keep helping Pellissier with his masquerade."

She swallowed hard as she looked from Titus to Jay. She must think carefully before she spoke a single word. Too much depended on this. Through her mind ran memories of the first night Eric had been in Whitcombe Hall. She had been so sure of herself when she had told him she had done what she believed she must to halt the smugglers.

Eric had smiled as he had said, *I'm sure you always do what you must, no matter what you face.*

*I do.*

*I hope that's a vow you still will be able to keep, Miss Whitcombe.*

Had he sensed even then that it might come to this impasse where she must choose between risking one of her brothers or risking Eric? Had he suspected even then that she must put aside her love of honesty for her love for him?

She had not guessed her words would return to taunt her, but she knew what she must do now. With quiet dignity, she stood. She *would* do what she must, even if it meant shattering her heart.

"Mr. Gillette, you are right. Eric is not a peddler as he said."

"He is a French officer?"

She looked at Jay as she whispered, "Yes." His face went pale with shock, then reddened with fury. "I learned of it after we were married."

"And told no one?"

"I would not send my own husband to hang." She edged around the chair as she fought to keep tears from rolling down her cheeks. She must not think of how her words dashed any chance of her seeing Eric again before the war ended. If he survived it. "And I shall not stay here to betray my husband now."

Mr. Gillette grasped her arm as viciously as Sir Asa had. "You shall not go to warn him."

"Of what?" she fired back. "He must surely know why you brought me to your house. He has been seeking the leader of the smugglers, so he must have guessed that is you."

Jay peeled Mr. Gillette's fingers off her arm. "He does, for I saw his amazement at the note. I believe he thought Sir Asa was the man he sought." He muttered an oath, then added, "Francis Gillette, you have lied endlessly to my father when you offered your help to stop the smugglers."

"But this would help," Titus argued. "They could be honest men again."

"And willingly pay all of the king's taxes?" Jay shook his head. "You called me an idealistic fool. I would say you are, Titus. Let's go, Bethany."

"She's staying," Mr. Gillette retorted, "until Pellissier shows his Froggish face."

"You cannot hold my sister here against her will."

"Jay, be silent," Titus argued. "We do not want any harm to come to Bethany."

"From whom?" His eyes narrowed. "From you? Are you threatening your own sister?"

"Peace is—"

"For someone who keeps talking about peace, you seem far too ready to declare war on your own family." Jay took Bethany's hand. "If you wish to speak with Eric, you can speak with him at Whitcombe Hall. We—"

Shouts came from the foyer. A door slammed. *Open or closed?* Bethany could not tell. When a gun fired outside the house, she cried out in horror.

Mr. Gillette grabbed her hand. She tried to shake

him off. He opened a door and shoved her into the small, dark room that was adjacent to the parlor. When Jay tried to come to her rescue, he was pushed inside, too. The door was slammed shut.

Jay banged on it with his fists. "Let us out."

"Sweet heavens!" she moaned when she heard more gunshots.

"Look out!" Jay shoved her aside, knocking her to the floor when a ball pierced the door. It hit the wall behind them, lost in the shadows.

"Titus!" she cried, jumping to her feet.

"You can't go out there, Bethany. The door is locked." He pulled her down as another shot hit the door. Wood splintered over them. He pushed her aside and crawled to the door. "But it is not locked any longer. That ball destroyed the lock. Stay here while—"

She grasped his arm. "No, Jay, you can't."

"I have a gun. I can—"

"You can think cautiously for once." She squeezed each word past her chattering teeth. Could her brother guess how she longed to rush out there and assure herself that Eric was all right, that Titus had not been killed, that this all was a mistake? "Please, Jay."

She wished she could see his face, but only faint light came through the ruined door. When he said, "As you wish, Bethany," she squeezed his hand in gratitude. Her reply went unspoken when the door was shoved open.

Jay came to his feet and stepped in front of her, but she saw the unmistakable scarlet and gold coat of an English officer. Her first reaction of relief turned to horror. Had Eric been captured? If not, he might be riding into a worse trap than any set by her brother and his misguided friends.

"Are you Warren Whitcombe?" asked the officer.

Jay smiled. "Yes, Lieutenant. This is my sister, Bethany."

The lieutenant dipped his head in her direction. "Mr. Whitcombe, it would be greatly appreciated if you would escort your sister back to Whitcombe Hall. My colonel shall wish to speak with you later, but it would be more comfortable for you to wait in your own home."

"What of Titus?" Bethany asked as she stepped forward to see the parlor was filled with men in identical bright red coats and pristine white pantaloons. Their boots shone as if they were about to go on parade. She saw no sign of her brother or Mr. Gillette. She pressed her hand over her heart. Had they been shot?

"Titus?" The lieutenant's question pulled her out of her panic.

"Our brother. Titus Whitcombe." She hesitated, not wanting to condemn her brother, but fearful that he might be accused of treason out of hand if she remained silent. "He was with Mr. Gillette in the parlor when we were sent into the other room."

"They and the others are being questioned in the room on the other side of the foyer. The colonel—"

"I would like to speak with your colonel."

"You may, for he will be calling at Whitcombe Hall."

Bethany shook her head. Mayhap she was not thinking this through clearly, but she was certain she would risk the consequences to guarantee that the officer in charge learned her brother was not a traitor. "I will speak with him here."

"But—"

"Where is your colonel?"

He hesitated, then said, "Over there."

"Over where?" The room was filled with uniformed

men. Many had gold epaulets on their shoulders and white sashes across their chests, the mark of an officer.

The lieutenant eyed her up and down, a puzzled frown on his face. "By the door, I believe."

She ignored him as she crossed the room. Her steps faltered when she saw, past the other men, Eric's gold hair. Sweet heavens, she had thought he would have been far from here when the King's men were in the house. Elbowing aside the soldiers that seemed to be conspiring to keep her from passing, she pushed her way through them. Her bonnet was knocked forward, its brim cracking, but she did not care. She needed to help Eric. How, she did not know. There must be a way. There must be.

A man stepped aside, and she careened forward into the foyer. She winced when her shin struck the newel post. Dropping to sit on the stair, she pushed her bonnet back as she heard Eric say, "Ask your questions."

"And you will answer them?" That was Titus, she realized as she shoved hair out of her eyes. "And I should expect the truth from you, Colonel Pennington?"

She peered through her tangled hair and squeaked in astonishment, "*Colonel* Pennington?" She stared at the twisting of braid on his epaulets which denoted his high rank.

Eric turned toward her. She leaped to her feet and grasped his arms.

He smiled. "You are safe, Bethany!"

"Go!" she whispered. "They know the truth of who you are. You won't fool them in this uniform."

"No, I shall not." He pulled her to one side of the foyer, motioning to one of the soldiers to take Titus back into the parlor. "The only one who seems to be bemused by it is you, Bethany."

"But you are—"

"*This* is who I am. My masquerade is over."

She sat in a chair by the front door. When he knelt beside her, she put her hand out to him, but she drew her fingers back before she could touch the gold braid on his shoulders. "You are not a French spy?"

He smiled. "Actually, the French government thinks I am, but my loyalties have always been and always will be to the Regent and the Crown."

"The French think you are a spy for them? Why?"

"Because they sent me to England to help plan an invasion that I am determined will never happen."

She was growing only more confused. "But all you told me about being a prisoner of war . . ."

"Was true." His face hardened as it had before when he had spoken of being in prison. "Only instead of being on the prison hulks as you assumed, I was kept in a French prison near the Swiss border. When three of us attempted an escape, I was the only one to survive long enough to contact the owls to flee back into England."

Her eyes widened as she understood what he did not need to say. "By the time you reached the French shore, you had made enough contacts in France for the English government to send you back."

He smiled. "To own the truth, I offered to go back and take on the life of the man I have pretended to be for the past year. 'Tis fortunate that Boney's officers are not as clear-sighted as you, sweetheart. They swallowed my clanker of hating my superiors who had left me to rot in prison."

"I can understand that. You were very persuasive when you spoke of the horrors."

His mouth became straight. "It is something that you cannot erase from your memories. The French authorities believed I had decided, on my route back to England, that Napoleon and the English could exist peacefully." He chuckled. "They even convinced themselves, with a bit of help from me, that I was well acquainted with the groups here who were ready to negotiate peace. A few bribes in the right hands gained me a captain's commission and duty here, not far from Fair Cove. While I kept my French patrol busy on wild-goose chases, I did the work I had been sent here to do by the British government."

"Are you really Eric Pennington?"

"Yes. Pellissier was the name I took for my charade, to make my story seem more real."

She touched the braid on his shoulder, then met his eyes which glowed with longing at her caress. "What happens now, Eric? Titus—"

"Is guilty of nothing but being foolish. The same for Gillette, because there is scant proof that he has been deeply involved with the smugglers. As for Sir Asa, your father should be dressing him down right about now for his delusions of building his own fiefdom here along the shore to replace the power he thought he might gain in Parliament. If you wish, you can have him arrested for ambushing your carriage."

"That would only cause more trouble."

"I think he has learned his lesson." When she grimaced, he laughed. "For a few days, at any rate. I shall be in this area for some time, cleaning up the last of this mess, so, if he needs another reminder to recall his manners, I shall be glad to give it to him."

"What of your French soldiers?"

"They are on their way back to France, with enough misinformation to create all kinds of delusions in their superiors' minds. They will be reporting that Captain Pellissier has been captured and hanged for spying." He chuckled. "*Adieu*, Captain Pellissier."

She bit her lip, knowing she could no longer keep

from asking the question she had wanted to pose from the moment she had seen Eric among the other men. "And what about us?"

"I would ask you that same question." His fingers stroked her cheek. When the broken brim of her bonnet got in the way, he pushed it aside, catching the brim as it cracked and fell off.

"We are legally married if your name really is Eric Pennington."

"That is my real name, so we are married most legally."

She touched the gold buttons on the front of his chest. She wondered if any man had ever been more handsome or more tantalizing. As she ran her finger along the braid on his sleeve, she wished he would put his arms around her. "You spoke of an annulment when I was no longer in danger from Sir Asa."

He nodded. "Yes, I did. You should be safe from him now."

"But I am not out of danger."

"No?" His eyes grew wide. "Who else is a danger to you?"

"You." She put her fingers over the sash in the middle of his uniform jacket. Letting them slide down across his chest, she knew she was being brazen, for she could not be unaware of the other men milling about or of Miss Gillette calling down from the upper floors to find out what was happening. She did not care about anyone but this man beside her. Mayhap she had rushed headlong into things in the past, and mayhap she was rushing headlong into this, but she was sure of this as she had been of nothing else.

"Me?"

Taking his hand, she raised it to the valley between her breasts. Her voice quivered as yearning gleamed in his eyes. "If you insist on an annulment, you will break my heart. Can't you feel how it beats for you?"

"It beats more fiercely when I touch you," he murmured, his fingers straying along her breast.

"Because it longs to be yours." She bent to put her fingers under his chin as he had done to hers so often. Brushing her lips on his, she gasped as he stood and pulled her up against him.

His kiss contained every bit of his ravenous need for her. Her ruined bonnet fell back as his fingers tangled with her hair. When his tongue brushed hers, urging her to free every desire, tears flooded from her eyes. She clung to him, for only now, when he was safe and in her arms, could she own how much she had feared he would be lost to her forever. His lips smoothed the tears from her face before finding her mouth again.

A throat was cleared, and Eric raised his head. Bethany rested hers against his chest as she looked at the lieutenant whose face was almost the shade of his uniform. Behind him, Jay was grinning. Someone must have explained the truth to him.

"Colonel Pennington," the lieutenant said very correctly, "Lord Whitcombe wishes to speak with you."

"By all means, Thatcher, bring him to me. Jay?"

"Yes, Colonel Pennington?" His grin broadened.

"If you are still interested in a commission, I think I know the perfect assignment for you."

"With you?"

"Actually with another colonel I have known for several years."

As Eric grinned, Bethany gasped, "But Jay is too young to—"

"He is not too young to be named *aide-de-camp* to this colonel." He lowered his voice so that only she could hear him. "This colonel will never travel farther from Grosvenor Square than his favorite pub, so your brother can have a taste of military life and still stay safe until he is old enough to think it through."

"Which you clearly didn't."

"On the contrary, Bethany, I thought long and hard before I accepted this life. First, I thought only of glory as Jay does. Now I want this accursed war over so that no man again has to suffer what I did in that prison." He kept his arm around her as he stepped forward to greet her father. "Lord Whitcombe, we are grateful for your assistance in keeping Morelock from making this more complicated."

"Yes, yes," Whitcombe said, his gaze flickering again and again from the braid on Eric's shoulders to his smile. "Sir Asa understands how close he came to treason." Squaring his own shoulders, he chuckled. "You probably have guessed how astonished I was to hear that you were in charge of this mission, Lord Pennington."

"Lord Pennington?" Bethany repeated, arching her brows with a smile.

"You do not look surprised," Eric replied, smiling.

"Why should I be? Only a peer could afford the high price of a colonel's commission. Once you claimed the rank of colonel, I assumed you had another as well."

"You are, as you have been since we were wed, the wife of a marquess, sweetheart." He brushed her hair back as he whispered, "I have plied you with half-truths, but one thing I told you was undeniably true then and is undeniably true now: I love you."

"So you wish to remain my husband?"

"We are married legally and—" His rakish smile returned. "We are married most irrevocably. That is one thing I never want to change."

# AUTHOR'S NOTE

I hope you enjoyed *An Unexpected Husband.* I like writing stories where the characters are not necessarily what they seem at the beginning.

My next Kensington release will be the Zebra Splendor historical *Anything for You,* set in a logging camp. The heroine, Gypsy, is the camp cook; she was inspired by the mother of a friend who was a logging camp cook in northern New York. When a man comes to the logging camp and is put to work in her kitchen, Gypsy fears that her haven from her past will be breached and her heart touched by intriguing, sexy Adam Lassiter. It will be available in April 2000.

My next Regency will be the short story "Not His Bread-and-Butter" in *Sweet Temptations,* available in July 2000. This fun collection includes recipes that are used in the stories.

I enjoy hearing from my readers. You can contact me by E-mail at:

jaferg@erols.com

or by mail at:

Jo Ann Ferguson
PO Box 843
Attleboro, MA 02703

Happy reading!

"Nor do I. I love you, too, my lord."

"I shall never tire of hearing you say that, my lady." He put an arm under her knees and lifted her into his arms. When she gasped and put her arm around him, he called, "Thatcher, gather the rest of the information for our report; then release these men with a warning to think twice before they break the law again."

"Yes, sir." The lieutenant stared, mouth open, at his colonel. "Where shall I bring the information for the report?"

"To Whitcombe Hall." Eric smiled down at Bethany, so she could see the craving in his expression. "And don't be in a hurry to bring it to me."

Now she was sure *her* face was the color of his uniform, but she put her head against his shoulder, savoring his easy strength as he carried her out of the house. He continued to carry her as he stepped into a carriage. When he settled her on his lap as he sat, she said, "You can put me down. I won't run away."

He chuckled. "I'm not worried about that." His grin became the rakish one that stirred her blood to flame. "I missed the opportunity to carry you over the threshold the night we were married. I don't intend to miss that chance again."

Her laugh disappeared when he claimed lips that would be his for the rest of their days and for every night they were together. As he leaned her back on the seat, she knew that even though he had been a most unexpected husband, he was the one she had been waiting for.